Moonrakers and Mischief

Moonrakers and Mischief

———∿∿∿⦿∿∿∿———

G. J. FEAKES

IVES WASHBURN, INC.

New York

1962

Moonrakers and Mischief

First Published in the United States in 1962.

Library of Congress Catalog Card Number: 62-14656
Manufactured in the United States of America

I

"Bilton Parva! Change for Sede and Barnsby!"

Bilton Parva raised itself on to one reluctant elbow as the London train, fuming at what it felt was an unnecessary delay, fussed impatiently to a halt. Half the station staff moved towards the guard's van; the other half waited optimistically in his sentry-box to collect the ticket of any eccentric wishing to alight. It had happened before and, felt Bilton Parva, it could happen again.

Luggage bumped on to a barrow. A door slammed. A whistle shrilled. With a contemptuous "Pshaw!" the train eased itself out of the station. Bilton turned over to resume its siesta, little recking that its teeming dozens had been temporarily augmented by one.

George Loder sauntered across the platform and looked over the rose-tangled fence to where the road shimmered in the afternoon sun. Miniature etnas of tar bubbled and popped on its surface; the glare smote his eyes fiercely after the shade of a first-class carriage. July, spitting on its hands, had produced the kind of weather they used to have way back when.

To George's right, about half a mile up the road, stood a squat grey church steeple, gathering red roofs about itself as a hen does chicks. Bilton Parva, he supposed, as he lit a meditative cigarette. To his left lay the station yard, empty save for a passé-looking hound stretched out by a hoarding. A poster, with the air of an unbiased adviser, suggested the return of a Milton Threep ("He Knows You – You Know

Him") in a long-past General Election. In all other directions marched mile after mile of seemingly undiluted Wiltshire.

"No car," murmured George, "and I'll bet The Leas isn't an inch under seven leagues away. Let's see what Helen says, again."

He frowned as he re-read the letter which he took from the pocket of a nattily-cut sports jacket:

"George Darling,

"I'm so glad you can manage to come down for a few days to meet Mother. She hasn't really forgiven me, you know, for becoming engaged before she'd met you. She says we should have waited until she'd returned from Nice. She's right, I suppose. Never mind – I know everything will be all right when she sees you.

"Only two trains stop at Bilton. One arrives at 11.50 a.m. and the other at 4.30 p.m. I'll send the car to meet the 4.30 one, unless I hear otherwise from you. As you know, I shan't return from Devizes until early evening.

"Until Tuesday, Darling, "Love, Helen."

Well, here he was. Bilton, Tuesday, and three-ten. Not four-thirty, or eleven-fifty. Trust Helen to get the trains wrong, bless her! There'd be a taxi, of course.

The active half of the station staff touched down with his barrow. About George's own age, he was the longest, thinnest porter George had ever seen. His blue uniform gave a first impression of disconnected ankles and wrists. Paid by the foot, he'd have made the higher income bracket easily. Even as he drooped over the barrow-handles, he seemed to top George's five-foot-eleven with several feet to spare.

"Two cabin-trunks, a golf-bag, an' a 'tashy-case. Thine, Oi think, sir," he announced with the quiet certainty of a man who's worked the thing out for himself.

"That's right. I'm going to The Leas, at Winthringham. Will you get me a taxi?"

"That Oi can't do, today. There's only the one, old Amos Flower's, and 'e've gone to Sede."

This struck George as both apt and reasonable.

"When's he likely to be back?"

"Well, Amos 'ad a peg to take, and the Sede pubs don't shut 'til ten."

"A peg?"

"Ar. A peg. A porker, d'ye see? 'E took 'n in in 'is taxi. Amos took the peg," the porter added, patiently, in case George lost the gist.

"Well, peg – er, pig or no pig, I've got to get to Winthringham. How'm I going to do it?"

The porter thought a moment. This chap asked a load of questions. 'Mazed a body, it did. An idea struck him, beautiful in its simplicity.

"You could walk," he volunteered. "'Tain't more'n 'arf a moile as the crow flies."

"I see. And supposing the crow has to walk, with a golf-bag, two cabin-trunks and a 'tashy – that is, an attaché-case? How far then?" inquired George, who wasn't afraid to face up to the truth, bitter though it might be.

The porter thought again. He wasn't going to make any statement he'd regret later, when he'd had time to consider. His forefinger explored his right ear, questing for information. Finally, words came.

"Oi won't say 'twere more'n two moile."

"Very well: don't."

"No, call it nearer two an' a narf. Though it could be a bit less," he amended, for he was a man who dearly loved an argument. "You goes down the 'ill, turns roight at Mercer's pond, an' up the Sede road. The Leas is about 'arf a moile past the Angry 'En. Oi lives up that way meself," he added, giving Winthringham a cachet of respectability, "Farrer's me name."

"Mine's Loder. How d'ye do? How about my luggage?"

"Oi'll bring 'n up on me barry, w'en Oi comes 'ome at foive-fifteen, if that'll suit?"

"Fine. Do that, please. I'll walk up, then. No point in phoning at this time of the day."

George stepped out on to the road. It was pleasant to be walking in the open air, after the train journey. Curious, he mused, how all railway carriages had the same smell; like the inside of a disused crypt. Somebody's job to keep them that way, George supposed.

Meanwhile, the drowsy peace of the station was shattered by the persistent summons of the telephone bell. Farrer gave the instrument a distasteful glance. He didn't like answering the telephone, an invention he distrusted. He hated having to raise his voice; and of course you had to shout to get it through them thin wires. Stood to reason. He lifted the receiver.

"Bilton station 'ere," he bawled, lips caressing the microphone.

There was a startled exclamation from the other end. Then,

"I'm speaking from Mrs Bollanger's, at Winthringham. What time does the London train arrive, please?"

"Jer mean the one wot 'aven't come yet, or the one wot's just left?" roared the Oracle.

"Please don't shout. I can't make out what you're saying. Did you say that it's just left?"

"Naw." Farrer lowered his voice to a shrill shriek. "The next 'un 'aven't come yet. Stands to reason," he added, driving the point home.

"Look, my man; has the train come in or not?" The voice,

mild enough, hardened a little. "Mrs Bollanger is expecting a guest to arrive on it. Try and answer a simple question." The inquirer seemed to be labouring under some stress. The porter wasn't destined to relieve it.

"Oi ain't your man, an' the next train 'aven't arroived. The last un's arroived, though ..."

"Don't quibble. This is Milton Threep, here ..."

"Quibble, ay? An' don't *thee* quibble. Memmer o' Parlyment, ain't yer? *You* orter know all about quibblin'."

"You're being impertinent. I shall report you to your employers. I asked ..."

"Report wot 'ee loikes. Do 'ee good. Me name's Farrer," said the porter, scorning anonymity's protection. "We'll 'ave thy lot out, nex' Elexshun. Jus' wait," he added, darkly.

He heard the receiver click down, and slowly replaced his own.

"Quibble! Oi'll gi' 'n quibble," he muttered. "'As the next train arroived?' Must think Oi'm daft." He brightened up. "Oi told 'n off, though. 'E got no change outer me. S'pose it was the young gent 'e were askin' about," he mused.

The young gent, little knowing that he'd become a *cause célèbre*, was stepping smartly along the road, almost wishing he'd waited a day and brought the car down. They'd have that crown-wheel fixed by tomorrow. But who'd wait a day longer in London, with Helen in Wiltshire? Not George! He'd have come by three-legged camel, if necessary.

Helen's mother sounded the only discordant note. A tough cookie, by all accounts. Helen'd said little about her, but George had gained the impression that Mrs Bollanger went through life reorganizing anything that seemed to be working smoothly. A snapshot, in Helen's handbag, had strengthened this belief; unless the camera lied, Mrs Bollanger could claim to be the closest living likeness to Oliver Cromwell.

George's friends, too, had dropped dark hints. Nobody dared argue with her, they said. It was rumoured that the late Mr Bollanger had once dug his toes in, buttressed by a pint of vodka. Just once. And he'd never smiled again, until the day he died. On his death-bed, though, he'd seemed to cheer up, and had made the Great Change with an eager anticipatory chuckle. So said the cynics.

Maybe she wasn't as bad as all that. With a daughter like Helen, how could . . .

"Please, Mister, could yer gives a nand wiv ar Ron?"

The familiar Cockney accent came like music, here in the wilds of Wilts. George paused in his stride and looked down at the little mud- and sweat-stained face gazing, full of appeal up into his own.

The face topped a short gingham frock, efficiently plastered with mud. What appeared to be black socks proved, on closer inspection, to be more mud. Mud, moreover, with a distinctive hue and odour. George took a pace upwind.

"Nothing could give me greater pleasure. Where is ar Ron, and how may I best serve him?"

"Well, 'e's fallen in Mercer's pond, see, an' 'e's startin' to bubble a bit. I can't get at 'im."

"Pond? Good Lord! Where—? Oh, I see."

The pond ran almost to the edge of the road, separated from it by a thin strand of wire. More mud than water, it stank to high heaven. Mercer was no doubt proud of it, his own bit of moist England; as George saw it, it was just a smelly pond and he could have struggled along without it. He leaped lightly over the wire.

Judging by Ron's howls, the worst had yet to happen. He was thrashing around in about six inches of water and a foot of mud. What was normally a blond head was black with ooze, and artistically weed-hung. Ron's lot was plainly mud, sweat and tears. As Neptune's sorrowing grandson, he'd have romped home at any Fancy Dress ball.

A few quick strides, and George had pulled him from the mud like a cork. Ron's death cries changed to surprised hiccups. Events were moving too fast for him.

"There you are, young Ron. No need to cry any more." George stepped gingerly on to terra firma and deposited his burden on to the grass verge. "Let me see, haven't I got a shilling somewhere? Here; now buzz off home and get changed. You're all right."

The girl took Ron's hand, clasped oyster-like on the hush-money, and gazed wide-eyed at George. She pointed a horrified finger at his legs.

"Coo! You'll cop it when you gets 'ome! Look at vem muddy trahsis!"

He glanced at her sharply. The child had a neat sense of description. 'Muddy,' or some similar-sounding word had sprung to his own lips. He surveyed the trahsis.

What had once been dove-grey perfection in gents' flannel trousering now looked like a camouflage-artist's dream; and his feet were feet of clay. George, who'd stroll down Saville Row with the best of them, felt his spirits sink as the children ran off.

What a ghastly mess! What on earth would Mrs Bollanger think when he turned up like this? What sort of impression was he going to make? Nobody is really at the top of his form in a strange house, being interviewed by a prospective mother-in-law: a mother-in-law, moreover, who was probably at this moment whetting her teeth on a rough file. And when, in addition, the interviewee, as it were, knows that his shoes and flannels are oozing foul-smelling mud and weed, he may be forgiven a certain lack of *savoir-faire*.

Still, one couldn't have let ar Ron just disappear down into

11

the mud like a lugworm. Was it a lugworm that he was thinking of? Or was it . . . ?

"Good afternoon. Water warm?"

George turned to meet the friendly gaze of a pair of unbe-
lievably blue eyes, twinkling with amusement. Their owner,
a nicely-proportioned collection of curves and curls, looked
down at the muddy trousers.

"Polly! What on earth . . . ?"

She looked at him again, surprise giving way to pleased
recognition.

"George Loder! How lovely to see you again! And just as
handsome as ever. You're about the last person I'd have
expected to meet here!"

George looked at her affectionately. Polly Fenner was the
type of girl men call a "good sort". Twenty years on the
stage had broadened her outlook almost to bursting-point.
Many a man, George included, had fed her at the Berkeley
and other fashionable spots, but never for more than three
consecutive days. Polly sought safety in numbers. Now,
barely on the complacent side of forty, she still retained her
charm and held grimly on to her figure.

"This is a little off your beaten track, isn't it?" she continued.
"Are you searching for a lost missionary, or something?"

"I've just come down to stay with my fiancée for a week or
so."

"Nice work, if you can get it," she remarked.

"We're being adequately chaperoned by her mother, if
that satisfies your low mind."

"But of course. Who'd think otherwise? Do I know the
lucky girl?"

"Helen Bollanger? I don't think . . ."

"George! You've not gone and got yourself engaged into
that family, have you?"

"What do you mean, 'that family'? Helen's one of the sweetest girls on earth! We've only . . ."

"Oh, Helen's all right, I suppose, if you like them tall and clinging. It's her dragon of a mother I object to. Needs brain-washing. Don't tell me that you're fond of *her*!"

"Well, we haven't actually met, yet," he said, picking his words carefully. He was suddenly reminded of the ruined trousers. "She'll probably tear long wide strips off me when she sees me in this state."

Polly wagged a knowing finger.

"Aha! So you *do* know what she's like! You've probably heard a few tales, eh? Well, my boy, no matter what you've heard, it wasn't the least bit exaggerated. Believe me, she'd make Boadicea look like a first-term schoolgirl."

"How do you come to know so much about her? And why this excess of blind admiration?" George was intrigued. Polly wasn't the sort to form unreasonable dislikes.

"Come along to my cottage and we'll see if my daily can do something to make those trousers more liveable with. I'll tell you about la Bollanger on the way. I feel I owe you something, anyway. I was just going to Ron's rescue when you did it for me. Saved my nylons and shoes." She gave an affectionate glance down at sheer stockings and diminutive white buckskin footwear.

"I've left the theatre," she continued, as George squelched along by her side. "I'd saved a little, and a small legacy made me independent, though not rich. I'd always hankered after a little place in the country, so I rented a cottage here in Winthringham."

"You didn't marry, then?"

"No. Apparently I'm good company for lunch or dinner, but not for breakfast. Not that I haven't had a few near misses, mind," she added, complacently. "You should've seen some of the ones that got away."

"I can well imagine it."

"Well, having got the cottage and spent some of my capital on furnishing it, I found I needed a little more money for luxuries – you know, toilet soap, three meals a day, and other extravagances. Anyway, I keep the wolf at snarling distance by giving dancing lessons to the village children."

"My word! How the other half lives!"

"Oh, it isn't so bad. Most of 'em dance as if they'd one foot in a bear-trap, but I enjoy it. In fact, I'm putting on a dancing act with my pupils at next week's Church fête."

"I'm very pleased to hear it. Local girl makes good. But what's all this to do with Mrs Bollanger?"

"The cottage, young George, belongs to your Helen, left to her, among other things, by her grandfather. Mrs Bollanger manages Helen's estate, the same as she manages everything else belonging to her."

"I still don't see how . . ."

"Since she's found out that I've been on the stage, Mrs B. believes the worst about me, and her worst is a good deal worse than most people's. Walks past the cottage at all hours, hoping to see something she wouldn't look at. Lascivious-looking men, and things. I also happen to know that she wants the cottage for one Threep, some sort of relative."

"Threep? Threep? Where've I heard that name?"

"He's the local M.P. Minister for something or other. Probably connected with the Government experimental station here. All very hush-hush; everyone knows about it. He's staying at The Leas. Yes," she continued, "if it weren't for my year's agreement, Mrs Bollanger'd have me out of the place tomorrow. When it expires, in about three months' time, I'll be out on my neck, at the mercy of the crool 'ard world."

14

George digested this. The Bollanger certainly added up to something. Well, he could put up with her for a short yearly visit, once he and Helen were married. Or maybe they could just invite her for their silver wedding anniversary? One had to take the rough with the smooth, after all. The point was, just how rough could Mrs Bollanger get? There must be some upper limit.

"Here we are." Polly stopped at a low-roofed thatched cottage, dazzlingly white in the afternoon sun. "Liberty 'All. My little place in the sun."

"Good – ha – afternoon, Miss Fenner."

The voice, delicately modulated as a peevish hen's made them turn to see an elderly woman hurrying a few paces behind them. Her face, long, sharp and inquisitive, shone with the exertion of trying to catch up with Polly and George.

George had never seen anyone who looked more like a horse, though some horses have a more contented expression and smaller front teeth. It depends, of course, upon the horse under examination. Years of minding other people's business had given Myrtle Kettle the look of a horse who is constantly listening out for a Stewards' objection.

She wore a long grey costume, made of a kind of superfine sackcloth, partnered by a modest high-necked blouse. Her sole concession to the thermometer was a black straw hat, bought during the crazy excesses of VE day. Grey hair was drawn back under this period-piece with a tightness that made George's scalp tingle. She eyed him myopically, as he murmured something vaguely polite.

Polly returned her greeting perfunctorily, shepherding George up the flagged path. Myrtle Kettle whickered and trotted off up the road. George couldn't feel that she'd contributed anything really significant to Polly's day.

"That," said Polly, "was Miss Kettle. Should've been boiled long ago. Known locally as the Bilton and District Advertiser. If anyone's not sure about what they're going to do tomorrow, she tells them. In the past tense. She was anxious to get a good look at you, of course."

"Really?" said George, flattered. "Perhaps my autograph would have cheered her a little?"

"I doubt it. She just likes to know things. Anyway, I'm glad, for my reputation's sake, that Mrs Watt's in. Come in and remove the pants." She laughed. "Wouldn't Mrs Bollanger love to hear that?"

George followed her through a low doorway into a large cream-distempered room. Copper utensils gleamed on a cold old-fashioned range, and nosegays of flowers peeped haphazard from the darker corners. Two or three prints of ballet scenes took the bareness off the walls, and a solitary armchair sat squatly by the window. Here, no doubt, was where the aspiring Pavlovas did their stuff to the music of the radiogram opposite the door.

"I'll just see what Mrs Watt can do with those pants of yours," said Polly. "Mrs Watt! Mrs W-a-a-tt!" she called, on a rising note. There was no answer.

"She's probably gone around to the post office for something," ventured Polly. "Our post office sells most things, with the possible exception of submarine spare parts. Her sister runs it, and Mrs W. usually manages to pop in for a spot of gossip at least once a day."

She opened a door leading off the living-room.

"Go in there and hand me out your unmentionables. You'll find blankets in the linen-chest; wrap one around you if you want to come out and talk."

"Right-ho." George stepped into the tiny bedroom. His first impression was of lavender, chintz, and sunlight. His second was of the Eiffel Tower falling on him, as his head struck one of the low beams. He yelped.

"Anything wrong?" called Polly.

"No. Well, not really wrong. Nothing a good surgeon couldn't put right. Just sliced the top off my head, that's all."

"Oh, the beams. I'm sorry; I should have warned you. My head doesn't reach them, of course."

"Convenient," remarked George.

He took off the offending trousers and shoes. A gaily-coloured bedspread caught his eye, and he knotted it around his waist, sarong-fashion. The effect, reflected in the wardrobe mirror, pleased him. He'd always had an eye for colour.

With a careless hitch of the knot, he sauntered jauntily from the room. Or would have done, if another beam hadn't leaped out at him.

"?!!!?"** howled George, adding, to drive the point well home, " !???**!"

He staggered from the room, trousers in one hand, nursing his tortured head with the other. As the door closed behind him—

"For goodness' sake go back!" hissed Polly, frantically. "Mrs Bollanger's coming up the path! She *must* have heard you! I'll bet she won't rest until she's searched the house. If she sees you, I'm a dead duck!"

2

Clara Watt leaned comfortably against the post office counter, weight thrown over on to one adequate hip.

"And if you asks me, Norah," she said, impressively, "I think they'm usin' Stony Lane as one o' they aatom plants. Why else'd they 'ave sojers guardin' it day an' night, jumpin' out an' shoutin' ''Alt!' all over the place? Someone oughter write up about it!"

Norah Long paused in the weighing of half a pound of "best back".

"I don't think . . ."

She broke off as two diminutive mud-caked figures insinuated themselves into the shop, ranging themselves just inside the door to safeguard their line of retreat. Ron knew, from bitter experience, that you couldn't be too careful. Auntie might guess, somehow, that he and Julie'd been to the pond.

Mrs Long showed no surprise. Having had the care of Ron and his sister for a week (A week? Was that all it was?) she considered she'd seen it all. She jerked her head resignedly in the direction of the living-room door.

"Go on; get theeselves washed. And you see that 'is ears are clean, Julie." Turning to Mrs Watt,

"Mercer's pond again, I'll be bound. Attrax them two like glue to a magnet. What was we sayin', now?"

"About this Stony Lane carry-on. I was readin' in me Sunday paper about that there chain recreation, as they calls it, and the radio fall-out. Jew know that Amos Flower's ackshully seen the fall-out?"

"'Ave 'e, then? When was this?"

"Last Thursday. 'E left the Angry 'En at 'is normal time – just after the police'd give 'im 'is usual warning – and started off fer 'ome.

"Well, what with one thing an' another, 'e'd clean forgot about Stony Lane bein' closed, an' began to walk up 'n. To this day 'e can't tell 'ow 'e got through the wire. Then guess what 'appened?" Mrs Watt knew the value of the pre-climactic pause.

"Well, what *did* 'appen?"

"A yuge mushroom o' smoke, like they 'as in the Pacific, come up out o' the ground near what used to be old Parfitt's cottage. Amos distinkly saw thishyer fall-out. Like a lot of pansy petals, 'e says it was, only it smelt of 'ops."

"'Ops?"

"That's what 'e *said*. Anyway, a sojer come up be'ind 'n, and nearly stuck a baynit in 'is – nearly stuck a baynit in 'n, and sent 'n off 'ome. Real nasty, 'e was."

"You say Amos'd just left the Angry 'En?" Trust Mrs Long to put her finger on the weak point.

"An' what if 'e 'ad? 'E've got witnesses to prove that 'e'd 'ad no more than usual that evenin'."

"Amos *couldn't* 'ave any more than usual. You can't get any fuller than full. If you remember, it was Amos as tried to rescue 'is reflexshun from the pond, last New Yurr's Eve. Three weeks in bed, 'e 'ad, after that little affair."

"Well, seein's believin', Norah, and Amos believes 'e see it. We'll 'ear more of this, mark my words!"

"Are thy ears clean?"

The question, judged by some to border on the personal, wasn't addressed to Mrs Watt, but to ar Ron, passing furtively through the shop, out to High Adventure.

"'S. An' me neck. *She* washed 'um."

There was no bitterness in Ron's tone; just resignation. He'd suffered indignities, true, but his was a soul that could rise above them. His escutcheon, like his ears, was clean.

"Well, you keep outer Mercer's pond, now. An' off the road," Mrs Long called after the fast-disappearing figure. She turned to Mrs Watt.

"Ever since the new shofer come to The Leas I goes in fear an' tremlin' for they children. 'E drives too fast, an' I don't care 'oo 'ears me say it. Mrs Bollanger aids and abets 'n too."

"Stefan, that is." Mrs Watt was *au courant*. "A refugee, I've 'eard. They say 'e was 'ounded out of 'is own country by they Secret Police – you know, like our Specials – for talkin' out o' turn."

"Refugee 'e may be, but there's no need to drive as if they'd still be aafter 'n. I'll warrant . . ."

A long drawn-out wail came from the kitchen. Mrs Long wiped her hands on her apron.

"Ah, that'll be me whistlin' kettle Julie've put on to boil. Could 'ee do wi' a cup, Clara?"

Clara could.

Milton Threep gazed moodily out of the window to where a smooth spread of grass sloped gently away to a yew hedge bordering the road. A noble chestnut tree cast welcome shade at one end of the lawn; gregarious sunflowers shouted defiantly back at the sun from the other. A few wispy clouds, with nothing better to do, hung around idly, emphasizing the blueness above.

Somewhere near at hand a thrush was telling the world, and telling it good. It sang of thrushly pleasures; of slimy worms, unwary slugs, and maggots in rotting wood. It sounded heavenly.

In the distance, far enough away not to be annoying,

Threep could hear that gloriously soporific sound of someone else mowing a lawn. All was peace and orderliness. Indeed, at The Leas it wouldn't dare be anything else.

And yet – and he'd be the first to admit it – all this beauty and tranquility was lost on Threep. If he noticed anything at all, it was that damn' bird's infernal racket. If only he could – eeh! – another twinge!

His tongue cautiously prowled around his teeth for the thousandth time during the last twenty-four hours. Hup! That was it! A searing pain shot from his lower jaw, tried to burst out of the top of his head, then danced back to its lair beneath a neglected grinder.

The sensible thing to do, of course, would be to see a dentist. Attack the trouble at its root, as he'd so often said in The House. But then, nobody was expected to mean what they said there; this thing was personal. It was Hell. It was tooth-ache.

There was a good dentist in Sede, and as far as Threep was concerned, that was near enough. His horror of dentists – a will-sapping phobia – often made him suspect that he'd been bitten by one, as a child. That is, when he, Threep, was a child. His whole body, from his thinning grey hair down to his slightly splayed feet, cringed at the mere thought of the surgery. Butterflies fluttered around his ample stomach whenever dentists were mentioned.

He daren't tell Hester. Because she was his cousin, Mrs Bollanger took it for granted that she should do all the things for Milton Threep that a doting mother had neglected to do. Like making him take long walks, or go to see dentists. One hint of his present condition and she'd insist on accompanying him to the Sede charnel house. Not if he knew it! If he went, he'd go kicking and screaming, or under chloroform.

Continue to bear the pain silently and bravely, that was the thing. After all, it took a lot of real courage not to go to a dentist. If you looked at it the right way.

"Milton, did you find out whether Mr Loder had arrived at the station?"

The voice was high and metallic. Though not really loud (compared with, say, a Town Crier) it had a penetrating quality which made Threep's tooth start up in protest. Outside, the thrush stopped singing, listened a moment, then slipped quietly away. You never knew. . . .

Mrs Bollanger followed her question into the room, like a Dictator come to quell a rising. Threep was thankful to see that she was dressed for outdoors – white hat, coat, and gloves. Her figure, shapely as an unconditioned walrus, conspired with the white outfit to give her the appearance of a melting snowman. Hard, coal-black eyes enhanced the illusion.

She repeated her question, not in irritation, but rather as one asks a pet Labrador why he bit the nice postman. Threep's soul wriggled uncomfortably.

"I – er – that is, I spoke to Farrer . . ."

"Farrer!" Mrs Bollanger guillotined Farrer with one word. "You might just as well have spoken to the station clock. Did he say anything, beside talking?"

"Well, not exactly. He didn't quite grasp whether the London train that was expected hadn't been, or was gone before the one ..." Threep felt that all this had been said before, somewhere. He sneaked up on it, quietly. "Wouldn't Loder have phoned, if he'd arrived?" That was better. Less involved. He tapped a cigarette nonchalantly on a silver case. Mrs Bollanger looked at the cigarette. He replaced it.

"Do you really expect this modern generation to do the rational thing?" she asked. "From what I've gathered from Helen, Mr Loder is no better than the rest of them. Cars, cocktails and idleness. I shouldn't be at all surprised if it were not just her money he wants. Why didn't he see me before he asked Helen to marry him?"

Threep wondered what the chap would have done if he *had* seen Hester first. Probably panicked and run straight for the nearest monastery – preferably Trappist. Helen'd much to be thankful for. She'd never realize it, of course.

"Oh, I don't know. Isn't he a consulting engineer, or something? Earns his living, anyway. Money of his own, too, hasn't he?"

"So had Bluebeard. I might as well be frank – I don't trust that young man. I shall watch him very carefully."

Threep sympathized with the absent George. If Hester had taken a dislike to him, his goose was already cooked. Nothing would change Hester's mind, much as it might be improved thereby. She swam to the door.

"I'm going to see that Miss – ah – Fenner. I'm not too sure that her pupils' dancing act will be suitable for the fête. These people have no sense of the fitness of things. We don't want a recurrence of anything like the Farrer episode of last year."

"Oh? What was that?" This promised well.

"Quite disgraceful. Farrer came on to the stage to sing a song. You know how the Vicar likes to encourage the villagers. The song was entitled "Salome", which seemed just the right thing."

Threep started. Surely they hadn't . . . ?

"Imagine our surprise," Mrs Bollanger continued, indignantly, "when we found that the words were nothing like anyone had expected. Pure vulgarity, as far as he was allowed to go. Those fools from the public-house only encouraged him. He'd been drinking, of course. The Vicar was quite distressed, but I . . . I see nothing to laugh at, Milton." Her voice hardened, and the room temperature dropped several degrees.

"I wasn't laughing. I was thinking." He tried to look like a man who is thinking of something pleasant, despite the immediate outlook.

"If thinking makes you look like that, it's fortunate that you chose a career that requires only a minimum of it," iced Mrs Bollanger.

Threep tried diversionary tactics.

"Has Miss Fenner said anything more about vacating Rose Cottage?"

"No; but I can safely say that it will be free within the next few months. You're not in a hurry to move, are you?"

"No. Certainly not. No. I like it here." The Recording Angel wearily picked up a black pencil. "Seems curious that anyone should want to leave the cottage, though. Enchanting little place. Too quiet for Miss Fenner, I suppose."

"Perhaps." Mrs Bollanger preferred that Threep should believe that Polly wanted to leave. Men were such fools over these things. No realism. "You know what actresses are. Not really happy unless they're surrounded by men, lights and noise."

Threep, to whom Polly was just a name, felt vaguely resentful. Why should she have all the pleasure while others who'd worked hard, eschewing Life's champagne and oysters, had nothing to show for it except toothache? It was unfair. If he ever met . . .

Mrs Bollanger broke in. "Please make sure that Stefan leaves in adequate time to meet the four-thirty train. He's had his instructions. I intend to be home before Mr Loder arrives." It wasn't a threat; it just sounded that way.

Left to himself, Threep lit a cigarette, and pressed the bell-push, over by the huge stone fireplace. Why must *he* remind the damn chauffeur about his duties? It wouldn't be so bad,

24

but the chap's English would have disgraced a cleft-palated aborigine.

Threep suspected that Stefan deliberately misunderstood, sometimes. He had bitter memories of the day he'd sent the chauffeur down to the post office for some blood-purifier. He could still hear Mrs Long's outraged voice over the telephone. Never again!

"Did 'oo ring, sir?"

The parlourmaid's lilting Celtic accent interrupted his thoughts. Gwyneth had interrupted many a man's thoughts, setting up new and exciting ideas in their place. Whether it was her figure – full of dangerous curves as the Mille Miglia – or the large liquid eyes like melting brown sugar, is not important. Power was vested somewhere. Threep approved the tiny white cap, perched high on the black masses of hair. Worn by some as a badge of servitude, on Gwyneth it became a battle-flag.

"Ah, Gwyneth; would you bring my tea, and send Stefan along? I want to make sure that he knows which train he's to meet. A-a-rrch!" The tooth twisted around in his jaw.

"Arroo in pain, sir?" Gwyneth's motherly soul was touched by the sight of suffering. Besides, she liked Mr Threep. There's quiet he was, and always being put on by Madam. Poor gentleman 'oodn't hurt a fly.

"Between us – and only between us, Gwyneth – I've rather a nasty toothache. Very painful. I don't want Mrs Bollanger worried about it, though," he added, unselfishly.

Gwyneth understood.

"I see, sir. You'm scared of dentists, innit? Some people are. I remember Morgan Coal, back in Aberbeeg, couldn't stand 'um. 'E'd black the dentist's eye every time 'e went to see 'im. A big fella, was Morgan."

Threep's thoughts dwelt admiringly on this saga of the

redoubtable Morgan, champion of the dentally oppressed. There was an Old Testament ring about Morgan Coal. An eye for a tooth, as it were.

"Shall I get you some oil of cloves, now? Cook's got some, in the kitchen."

"No thank you. I'll be all right." Maryrdom shone like an aura around his head. "You know that Mr Loder will be here for tea, don't you?"

"That's right. Stefan's going to meet 'im, the poor young man."

"Who, Stefan?"

"No, Mr Loder. 'E'll be a bag o' nerves by the time Stefan've drove 'im from the station. I 'oodn't trust meself in that moto' with Stefan. Nor anywhere else," she added, sagely.

Threep gave a paternal smile.

"You don't like foreigners?"

"Oh, foreigners is all right, sir. Live and let live, I always say. If there wasn't no foreigners in the world, where'd we all be, isn't it?" The point was well taken. "No; what I don't like is the way 'e looks at me when I'm not lookin' at 'im."

"When you're not . . .?" This was a trifle above Threep's head. He'd little experience of woman.

"Yes. Kind of cal-cul-atin', like. Bob Farrer says 'e'll break every bone in 'is bl – every bone in 'is body if 'e tries any of 'is Continental tricks by yere. There's jealous Bob is," she added with quiet pride.

"Farrer the porter? What's he got to do with it?"

"'E's me Friend, sir. One of the best, Bob is. Gentle as a cow."

"Reassuring for Stefan, I'm sure. And are you going to marry Farrer?"

26

"Yes, sir. I think I will. 'E 'aven't ast me, yet. Bit shy, like. 'E will, soon."

Threep looked at her admiringly. If only he could push a Bill through, with that calm certainty! Women knew, of course. But it was rather frightening, all the same. Just suppose that he . . .

Gwyneth gave a squeak.

"Five to four! There's dull I am, standing by yere, and no teas ready! I'll send Stefan in now just, sir."

Threep smiled as she paraded out of the room. She and Farrer, eh? Tokay and bitter beer. How on earth had Farrer managed to attract . . .? Yet there'd been no mistaking the look in her eyes as she'd mentioned his name. And her voice had gone all soft and gooey, like treacle running down a spiral staircase. Well, one could hardly report Farrer, now, for that interchange on the telephone. Mistakes on both sides, perhaps.

Mention of his own name, Threep knew, had never brought that look to any woman's eyes. He'd put career before love and hadn't done so badly, after all. Lonely, perhaps, sometimes; and that feeling of – of – unfulfilment? – could be a little depressing.

Anyway, who'd want to raise a family, these days? We were rapidly becoming a nation of button-pushers, knob-twisters, and cathode-ray tube watchers. If people knew a quarter of what was going on behind the Peace Conferences, there'd be mass suicides. Even that was better than having it all arranged for them.

Look at that frightful experiment going on in Stony Lane, within a stone's-throw of this very house! "The Colonel", it was called. So secret that only he and one or two V.I.P.s knew of its existence. Mass destruction in its most convenient form. Why did . . .?

"You coll, sair?"

A blue-uniformed figure stood at his side. He hadn't been aware of anyone entering the room, yet here was Stefan, eager and inquiring. Threep put on a benevolent face. After all, if there wasn't no foreigners in the world . . .

"Yes, Stefan. You know, don't you, that you're to meet Mr Loder off the London train?"

" ? "

"Mr Loder. London train. Sh-sh, sh-sh. Train. Dammit, you know what a train is?"

"I to meet gellerman off four-thirty train, nit?" Stefan was trying to help.

"Ah! That's right. Four-thirty. Better go now, and be in time."

" ? "

"I say go now. *Allez, toute de suite. Gehen Sie.*" He pointed to the clock. "Start now."

"Not unnerstan'. But, pliz, I must go now." Stefan had no time to waste in idle chatter. "Not to be late for gellerman. I go?"

"Yes, for Go—. Yes; go now."

Stefan was deep in thought as he accelerated the powerful Mottram down the drive and aimed it at the road outside. Another guest at the house, eh? Who this time?

He couldn't afford to take too many chances. So far, things had gone well – far better than he'd dared hope for. But luck mustn't be pushed too far.

It'd been a wonderful break, finding someone as important as Milton Threep at The Leas, too. There'd be information there, surely? The English always discussed State secrets in public. Not in front of spies, of course. But then, everyone knew that spies wore dark glasses, red beards, and carried globular, smoking bombs.

Who was this new man, though? Mightn't this Loder be from M.I.5, to keep an eye on things? The English weren't complete fools, though they kept trying. Perhaps he, Stefan, was already suspect?

It was unlikely. He'd been here three weeks, now, an unknown refugee who just happened to be working near a Government experimental station. Everyone sympathized with him, but his terrible English accent had discouraged too much conversation. Stefan, who'd once taught English in Warsaw, smiled to himself.

He glanced to his left. Stony Lane, with its usual disinterested sentry strolling around. It didn't seem possible that just a hundred or so metres down there lay "The Colonel", whose secret he must crack. Must. The SNABU accepted no alternative. To them, one micro-film was worth a ton of excuses.

Anyway, he'd keep an eye on this Loder man, just to be on the safe side. Might even be another SNABU man, sent to watch himself. *Quis custodiet....*

As he turned into the station yard, he noticed a young man standing on the station platform. Had the four-thirty arrived, then? No; it needed a minute or so, yet. Probably an intending passenger. The man had disappeared, now, anyway.

A question which had been worrying Stefan returned to nag. Where did Threep keep the brief-case he'd brought to The Leas? Stefan had searched Threep's room thoroughly, but had failed to find it. There must be a safe, somewhere.

One thing: if Threep was so careful about it, then the case must contain something worth seeing. Anyway, there'd be time for another look, during dinner this evening. You could be certain of everyone being downstairs at that time.

The London train snorted in, and Stefan watched for his passenger. Tall, young . . .

What was this? Surely not this one? This was the man who'd been standing on the platform *before* the train arrived. And had quickly disappeared! Yes, here he was, heading for the car, all right.

So Mr Loder wasn't Mr Innocent, after all. Stefan began to feel that someone had played a dirty trick on him. If this was the kind of treatment a foreigner could expect in England . . . He stepped down from the car, smiling ingratiatingly.

"Meester Lodder, sair? I aff kom to meet."

3

Nobody could call George Loder slow on the uptake, but there comes a time in everyone's life when reactions are liable to be a trifle sluggish. As George stood outside Polly's bedroom, trousers flung carelessly over one arm, his reactions underwent complete paralysis at the news of Mrs Bollanger's approach. Bemused, perhaps, by the battering his head had taken, he became the planner rather than the man of action.

Given the option – which he hadn't been – he'd have much preferred to be wearing muddy flannels for this meeting with his mother-in-law elect, rather than shirt, socks and sarong. His choice of venue, too, would have been different. Anywhere outside a ten-mile radius of Polly.

The knocking on the cottage door redoubled in vigour and frequency. George's panic increased proportionally. He gave a helpless look to left and right, like an exhausted rabbit; then he tried to climb up the door-frame.

Miraculously, it seemed, the door reopened and he found himself hurled back into the bedroom. Polly was no weakling. She felt a pang of pity as she saw his head hit the beam yet again, and heard the hollow thud like a dropped marrow. She shut the door behind him as the knocking ceased and Mrs Bollanger's face appeared at the open window. Polly hummed loudly, to drown George's muffled groans.

The face framed in the window wouldn't have launched a thousand ships, but it would certainly have given the riveters hell. Black, close-set eyes darted inquisitive glances around the room. Fingers drummed impatiently upon the window-sill.

"Miss Fenner! Am I to be kept waiting out here all day? Is someone in there with you?"

The mouth, almost devoid of lips, chopped the words out like bullets from a repeating-rifle.

"Why, good afternoon, Mrs Bollanger." Polly tried to create the impression that, now she'd seen Mrs Bollanger, her day was complete. "Do you want a hand over the window-sill," she asked, pointedly, "or shall you use the door?"

"I was merely looking through the window because my knock wasn't answered," retorted the framed face. "I thought I heard voices," she added, suspiciously.

"Voices?" Polly threw open the door with the air of one who has nothing to hide. "What sort of voices?"

"Voices! Voices! Just voices." Mrs Bollanger swept into the room, which immediately became crowded. "What sort of voices did you expect me to hear?"

"I don't know. Might be something in your system. You know, like Joan of Arc."

"Well, I'm not Joan of Arc."

"No." Polly tried to keep the wistful note out of her voice. "They burned her, didn't they?"

The breath whistled through the elder woman's nostrils, nostrils which wouldn't have disgraced a Roman matron from whom gladiators fled to the comparative peace of the arena. She sat stiffly, sweeping searching glances, like a lighthouse-beam, around the room.

Polly strained her ears for sounds from the bedroom. None came. George was either unconscious or lying very low.

"I came to talk to you about the fête," began Mrs Bollanger. "Your pupils are giving some kind of ballet exhibition, I believe. We can give you just ten minutes, between the home-made wine competition and the puppet show. Now," she continued, severely, "we hope your programme will be – ah

– suitable, if you understand me. The Vicar will be there, you know."

"Suitable?"

"Yes, suitable. We want your act to be in keeping, if you see what I mean."

Polly saw.

"Mrs Bollanger, my eldest pupil is eleven years old; the youngest is five. I'll warn them to be on their best behaviour. Black suspenders and white frills will be definitely out. Nor will they lend their slippers for champagne drinking orgies."

Mrs Bollanger's left nostril quivered.

"There's no need to be sarcastic. You actresses. . . What was that?"

"What?"

"That. Sh."

"I can't hear anything." There was a suspicion of hysteria in Polly's voice.

"Gracious, girl, you must be deaf! There's either a horse in that bedroom or the roof has fallen in!"

"How absurd, Mrs Bollanger!" Polly gave a light, carefree laugh. "Mrs Watt is out. Who could be in there?"

"Anyone," retorted Mrs Bollanger, libellously. She rose and walked towards the door. "Come out! Come out, whoever you are!" It sounded like a musical-comedy song. "I know you," she added, illogically.

"Just a moment," Polly pleaded, desperately. "I'm sure you're imagining things. There's no . . ."

"Open that door and see. Here, I'll open it."

Before Polly could operate any further delaying action, Mrs Bollanger had turned the handle and thrown open the door. Polly followed her over the threshold, like a lamb to the sauce-boat, and peered over the plump shoulder in front of her.

She saw the bed, its cover neatly laid. The dressing-table, smugly tidy. She saw the wardrobe, too small to hide an under-nourished squirrel; the linen-chest, blandly innocent. And the open window, near which, quite unembarrassed, stood ar Ron. Of George there was no sign.

Mrs Bollanger recovered gallantly.

"What are you doing here, boy?" There was a tinge of disappointment in her tone.

"Goin' aht," answered Ron, equably.

"Yes, yes. But why are you here?"

"Me ball come in frew ve window. I clumb in after it."

Ron's was the simple direct mind. If a ball come in frew a window, then it must obviously be clumb in after. No problem there, surely?

A great wave of gratitude swept over Polly. This could only be a miracle, of course, but why question it? Everyone is entitled to a small miracle, at least once in a lifetime. Here was hers. What had happened to George she neither knew nor cared. Something *had* happened to him, and she was happy to accept it. *Sauve qui peut*, as the miser said.

"And did you get your ball?" she asked ar Ron, sweetly. Dear little boy, she thought; how nice – how sensible of him to be here just at this moment! Infinitely preferable to George, banging his head all over the room.

"'S. It rolled under ve bed. Kin I go nah?" Not for Ron the boudoir. The Great Outdoors called.

Polly ushered him from the room, noting that some capable hand had cleaned the mud from his blond hair, and clothed him with clean raiment. He scampered off down the road, in the direction of Mercer's pond.

"Curious behaviour, I must say," sniffed Mrs Bollanger. "Undisciplined, the children of today." They went out into the sitting-room. "I should inform his aunt, if I were you.

Mrs Long, at the post office. He and his sister are staying there for the holidays. I don't like their London ways." Mrs Bollanger knew everything; who was living with whom, and who shouldn't have been.

"Oh, it's not important." Polly was eager to forget the whole matter. "As long as he only clumb – climbed in for his ball, I don't mind."

Mrs Bollanger walked to the door, shimmering with disapproval. She felt that there was something wrong, but couldn't put her finger on anything definite. Still, she'd get to the bottom of it. Nobody ever got the better of Hester Bollanger! She marched out of the gate, colours flying and drums beating.

And, in Polly's bedroom, a head peeped coyly from under the bed. Like a bear checking up on the spring world after hibernation, George crawled from his lair.

Much has been made of the merits which are said to accrue from the simple – yet seemingly wasteful – act of casting one's bread on the waters. Little did George realize that, by pulling ar Ron from Mercer's pond, his bread, figuratively speaking, was going to be returned so quickly.

When, propelled by Polly's shapely but efficient arm, George's forehead struck the beam for the third time, he realized that this cottage was the one place where he should be anywhere else but. Physical pain, within reason, he could stand; but the mental torture of Mrs Bollanger's cat-and-mouse tactics was more than he could bear. But what could he do?

No good going out into the sitting-room and trying to pass off the whole thing with a good-humoured chuckle. He could well imagine how the conversation would go:

"Oh, good afternoon, Mrs Bollanger. Fancy meeting you here. I'm your future son-in-law."

"I doubt it. What are you doing in Miss Fenner's bedroom?"

"She had my trousers. Er – that is, she was doing me a favour . . ."

"I can quite believe it. But why did she have your trousers?"

"They were muddy. You see . . ."

"Muddy? Mr Loder, we've had no rain here for over three weeks!"

No, the tale was too involved. The most credulous Marine would laugh the thing to scorn. There must be some other way. He looked through the tiny latticed window, out on to the road. No hope there. Nice mess he'd be in if he got stuck half-way. Like a French farce act. And – he felt it in his bones – Mrs Bollanger would soon be in here.

"'Allo, Mister."

A vaguely familiar voice from the roadside cut in on his thoughts. A clean and shining face gazed up at him through the open window. George's heart leaped like the high hills as he recognized ar Ron. A Ron now unadorned with weeds and mud, but still recognizably Ron. This, then, was the guise in which Guardian Angels appeared.

The sight acted as a stimulus to George. Within ten seconds he had formulated a plan, perfect in its simple psychology. He whispered urgently to the cherub below, clinking certain coin to reinforce his sales-talk. Finally, Ron nodded, and wriggled over the window-sill.

"Yes," said George complacently, as he sipped tea in Polly's sitting-room. "I *do* get a good idea, now and then." He blew out a luxurious cloud of cigarette smoke. "Hiding under the bed was too obvious – I'd have been spotted in a minute. All women look under beds, either fearfully or hopefully, depending on their age-group."

"Go on," encouraged Polly. "Cut out the comic inter-polations."

"Well, I just reasoned that if I could produce some kind of diversion, under the bed would be as safe a hiding-place as any. Young Ron created that diversion as if born to it. That boy'll end up as a master-criminal or an M.P."

Polly sighed contentedly, like one who's emerged unscathed from the Inquisition.

"Anyway, we made it. As soon as those pants are dry, just get along and don't come near here again. I've aged ten years in as many minutes."

George considered a moment.

"Look, they're sending the car to meet me off the four-thirty train. If I get back to the station before the train arrives, they'll think I came by that one, after all. Save a lot of unpleasant questions, don't you think?"

Polly gave him an admiring glance, much as one would give to a hen that has just laid a negotiable bond.

"Clever boy! This *is* your afternoon, isn't it? The trousers'll be dry in ten minutes, which will give you nice time to get to the station before the train arrives. Pity Stony Lane is closed to the public; it'd save you half a mile. The place is stiff with troops, though; you'd need a tank to get through."

"Troops? What is it – manœuvres or something?"

"No, it's that experimental station I told you about. Something to do with radar, I believe. You can see the masts rise out of the ground, sometimes. Queer things happen in Stony Lane, George. Devil's work."

"Such as what?"

"Such as old Harry Bryant losing Sheilagh, for instance."

"Who's Sheilagh? His daughter?"

"No, a cow with a touch of wanderlust. She'd strayed from the herd, one evening, and Harry swore he saw her

walking along the road into Stony Lane. To do that, the
wire must have been opened for her. Then she vanished.
Pouf! Just like that. She's not been seen since. Of course,
everyone laughed at Harry's story; his yarns run sweeter with
lubrication. But what do you think happened?"

"The herd demanded a recount?"

"No, idiot. This is serious. Harry put in a claim for Sheilagh, and the War Department paid up without a moo. You
can't get near the place for straying cows, now."

"Curious, the Government paying up like that. Still, I suppose Sheilagh fell down a hole or something."

"A rabbit hole, perhaps? There's not the sign of a hole
around there."

"Well, I'll go back the same way as I came. Thank you for
the tea and valeting. I'll be seeing you around, I suppose?"

"Of course. Mind you turn up at the fête, next week. It'll be
worth the money just to hear Farrer recite."

"The porter? That I must hear. I'd better get along and
square him. He was going to bring my luggage up on his
barry, but there'll be no need, now. Chuck over the trouser-
ings, there's a good lass."

Twenty minutes later, George waited unobtrusively on
Bilton station platform. A small bribe had made Farrer co-
operative, though he couldn't understand why the gent
wanted people to think he'd arrived later than he had. Queer,
these toffs.

A few minutes before the train arrived a large Mottram
saloon, driven by a uniformed chauffeur, swept into the
station yard. George guessed that this was for himself and
moved behind the ticket-collector's shelter. The chauffeur
remained at the wheel, for which George was thankful. It
would make his little deception easier.

The train drew in, disgorged one small parcel, and left

irritably. After a short interval, George went out to the waiting car. The driver came forward.

"Meester Lodder, sair? I aff kom to meet."

The man touched his cap and opened the car door. As George climbed in:

"Some lugs, sair?"

"Lugs?" George was nonplussed. Something he should have brought?

"Yais. Luggages, nit?"

"Oh, bags. The porter's bringing them now."

While Farrer stowed the lugs, George eyed the driver with interest. He was small, and almost perfectly square, his uniform emphasizing the equilateral effect. His face, flat with high cheek-bones, proclaimed Slav blood. A refugee of some kind, surmised George; the Continent must be nearly empty by now. As the man took his seat, George had a view of a neck almost as wide as the head it supported, and ears which protruded like banners on a gala day.

Whether the man could drive, or whether he was just lucky, George couldn't decide. The car was hurled along the narrow way as if it carried some life-saving serum. A farm-worker, somnambulating along the Sede road, made as fine a leap as George had ever seen outside White City, thereby prolonging his, the farm-worker's, life. Some village Hampden, no doubt . . . . The car rocketed on.

George leaned forward.

"I say, do you always drive like this? What's your name?"

Without slackening speed, the chauffeur turned almost fully around in his seat for a nice chat.

"Przlcz; my mistress call me Stefan."

"I'm not interested in your personal – oh, I see. You mean Mrs Bollanger?"

"Yais, my mistress. She laike fast mans, so I drive laike shtinko. You laike?"

"No. And please turn around. The pedestrians are getting thicker on the ground, now."

The chauffeur glanced around.

"Zut! Zese pipple just cabbages! Not mens. What you call serbs, no?"

"Serbs?"

"Yais. Serbs. Under-dogs. Serbing-mans."

"Oh, serfs. Probably; but you can't decimate them just for that. Take it a little steadier."

The car swung into a wide drive, tree-lined, with neatly-kept flowered borders. A serb, weeding a flower-bed, leaped for his life as the car dropped to a crawling fifty miles an hour. Amid the rattle of gravel and the urrch of tortured tyres, Stefan pulled up at a flight of wide steps, surmounted by a Doric-pillared porch.

George had arrived.

4

George stepped from the car feeling like the new boy at St Dominic's. With the exception of St Paul's, The Leas was the largest building he'd seen at such close range. The majestically-pillared entrance drew itself up, contemptuously, to its full height at his approach. He felt as significant as a carelessly-written comma.

The flight of steps leading up to the huge doors, he considered, could no doubt be scaled by an experienced climber without ropes and crampons. Mellowed grey stone walls wandered off to left and right on some business of their own. George caught a glimpse of french windows giving on to a balcony shaded by a gaily-striped awning.

"Mr Loder?" The voice had the pleasant lilt of a badly-fitted coffin-lid being forced open. George had heard the tone before. His thoughts flew back over the years to the day he'd been caught removing certain vital screws from his Formmaster's chair; an experiment for which, in George's view, humanity had cried out.

Mrs Bollanger stood just inside the open doorway, eyeing him up and down. George fingered his tie nervously, and with what he hoped was a frank, open smile, commenced the ascent.

The smile was definitely a mistake. He saw that, afterwards. A smile, to be worthy of the name, should at least be spontaneous, but the spontaneity had died from George's long before he'd climbed half-way. It became a leer – the mirthless grin of one seeing off a casual acquaintance when the train refuses to leave.

To add to his misery, he'd half-outstretched his right hand in readiness for the warm, welcoming handclasp. As the steps rose ever upward, he began to feel like a walking pump. Mrs Bollanger's eyes spotlighted him, step by step, until he stood in the hall.

"Mrs Bollanger? How do you do? It's very good . . ."

"How do you do? You're Helen's guest, of course. Come in, please." Mrs Bollanger gave the impression that her daughter might have invited some shady customers in the past, but in her mother's opinion she'd just hit an all-time low.

Her voice softened noticeably as she spoke to the chauffeur. "Take Mr Loder's luggage to the Balcony Room, Stefan." She seemed to be regretting that the dungeons had been filled in.

She led George into the lounge, where the unaccustomed shade sent him staggering over a footstool, and watched with silent interest as he tried to support himself by an inadequate coffee-table. Milton Threep, sitting like a depression over the Atlantic, looked up in mild surprise. George longed for death.

"Milton, this is Mr Loder. Mr Loder, Mr Threep. A more mutton-headed pair of nitwits I've yet to meet." The last sentence wasn't uttered, but both men sensed the implication. A bond, a kind of defensive union, sprang up between them.

"You'd like some tea, Mr Loder?" Mrs Bollanger was out of hemlock.

"I've had . . ." began George, thoughtlessly, then saw his mistake, ". . . a very thirsty afternoon. I'd love a cup, please." Near thing, that. He'd certainly have got off to a flying start if he'd said he'd just had a cup with Polly! He pulled out his cigarette-case.

"Do you mind if I smoke?" he asked.

"You may," replied Mrs Bollanger, grimly, adding, as an afterthought, "Nobody else ever smokes in this room." George returned the case to his pocket.

"Did you have a good journey, Mr Loder?" Threep didn't really care what kind of journey George had had, but a fellow-human needed succour. Threep wasn't the man to withhold the conversational life-belt.

"Quite pleasant, on the whole. I'd have preferred to have come by road, but my car's laid up."

"Oh? What's the trouble?" asked Threep. The next moment he wished he hadn't.

"New crown wheel, I'm afraid. The teeth of the old one were completely chewed up." Threep winced. "Never seen anything like it. Just as if someone had gone over each tooth with a rasp. Is anything wrong?"

A look of intense suffering had passed over Threep's face. George's small-talk could have been better chosen, addressed to a man who feels that open-cast mining is being clumsily carried out in his lower jaw.

"No. Nothing. Just a touch of indigestion. I . . ."

"Not enough exercise, Milton." Mrs Bollanger loved prescribing exercise. "You need a three-mile walk each day, or a couple of hours in the garden. You can walk over to the Vicar's with the fête records, tomorrow. I've chosen some suitable ones."

"Good Lord, Hester!" The worm half-turned. "It's nearly six miles to the Vicarage and back. Why can't Stefan take them?"

"Don't be absurd, Milton. It's barely four miles, and you need the exercise. Besides, it's Stefan's day off, tomorrow. Perhaps Mr Loder will walk over with you?" Her look dared George to refuse. He didn't.

Later, as he unpacked in his room, he reviewed the situation to date. Not an auspicious start, and the characters at The Leas weren't wildly exciting. The chap Threep seemed decent enough, except for some secret sorrow. Probably a surfeit of Bollanger. But more important was the adverse impression he'd made on his future mother-in-law.

He looked at himself in the mirror. Not a handsome face, perhaps, but pleasant, surely? Not the face to give a strong-minded woman the screaming hab-dabs, yet Mrs Bollanger had taken instant dislike to it. He felt that. Of course, lurching all over the lounge like an intoxicated ostrich hadn't helped things along much.

How did one gain her goodwill? Throw her a couple of Christians every day? One thing, the minute he and Helen were married, Mrs Bollanger could cut her goodwill into five-inch lengths and curl her hair with it.

He lit a cigarette and strolled on to the balcony overlooking the rich, undulating landscape. From this height on the third floor, the chestnut tree on the lawn looked like a giant cauliflower. Away in the distance, to his right, he caught a gleam of silver. Mercer's pond. Was it really less than three hours ago . . . ?

That must be Stony Lane, disappearing mysteriously into the trees, at a tangent to the Sede road. What *did* go on, up there? One or two straddling black Nissen huts gave the place a sinister air. One could well imagine cows disappearing within its sphere of influence. Horns and all. . . .

Six faint chimes came from the stumpy spire of Bilton church, peering over the hill at the far side of the valley. Helen should be back from Devizes any minute now. Surely, between them, they'd be able to sweeten up the old lady? Of course, if Helen was as much under her mother's thumb as Polly'd hinted, there wasn't much point in unpacking.

A two-seater car, looking like a black beetle, came demurely up the drive. George's heart did a couple of hand-springs as he recognized the head, a golden sovereign, behind the wheel. Helen! He dived back into the room and down the stairs. After touching one or two stairs in the top flight, his feet gave up the unequal struggle and just tagged along obediently after the flying body. Helen and he reached the hall together.

"Darling!"

"Darling!"

As a speech of welcome, it probably had its limitations, but George and Helen weren't critical. After a satisfactory silence, Helen disentangled herself and they seated themselves on an old oak chest by the door.

"George, do be careful of my hair. I've had it set especially for you. Like it?"

"Adore it, dearest. It looks like golden rain. And you've had your eyes dyed a deeper blue. How d'ye manage it?"

"Idiot! It's probably the blue dress. That's new, too."

"It's a lovely shape, I must say. You improve with age, though I don't suppose it's a day over ten years since you left me in London."

"It's eight and a half days, and you know it. I had to prepare Mother before you came down. How did you get on with her?"

"Well, she didn't run around uttering little clucks of approval when I arrived. On the other hand, she didn't open up with chain-shot. A good omen, that, I feel. Not quite sure of me yet, perhaps, but she'll come round. To know George is to love him. Sheer personality, I'm told."

"Be nice to her, dear. It'll mean so much to us. Her bark's worse than her bite, you know."

"That I can well believe. Anyway, she hasn't bitten me yet. When she does, I'll let you know, just for the record."

"George! You mustn't talk like that! She's doing what she thinks is best for me, after all."

"Of course she is, darling. She and I will get on like David and Jonathan, or Dan and Beersheba, whichever it was. Inseparable. You'll see."

Helen went upstairs with a lighter heart. It only needed a little patience – a little tact. A little?

Dinner, that evening, didn't sparkle. Threep, quietly suffering, brought little wit and humour to the table, and Mrs Bollanger lay in ambush along the conversational paths. A thick grey silence hung over the salt-cellar. As Gwyneth cleared away the soup-plates, Helen tried again:

"And what do you think of The Leas, George?"

"Perfect. The view from my window is superb, and I've never seen a more beautifully-proportioned hall."

"There's damp-rot in the writing-room," observed Mrs Bollanger.

George contemplated a piece of dead duck on his plate. It was under conditions like these, no doubt, that Cato had taken his course in public speaking. He returned to the attack.

"You grow your own vegetables, I suppose? These peas are excellent."

He was rewarded by a grateful look from Helen.

"They are, aren't they? I'll show you around the gardens, after dinner. We're rather proud of our roses, too, though some of the best are at Rose Cottage."

"Rose Cottage?"

"Yes, a small thatched cottage on the Sede road. I've let it to a Miss Fenner. You passed it, coming from the station."

"I do remember passing a rather pretty cottage." George tried to look like a man who remembers passing a rather

46

pretty cottage. "They were certainly beautiful roses, the largest . . ."

"The rose-garden's at the back." Mrs Bollanger pointed out. "You can't see the roses from the road."

Silence swirled around the room again.

"Helen," Mrs Bollanger put down her coffee-cup, some twenty minutes later, "I'm not satisfied with the state of things at Rose Cottage. Miss Fenner acted very suspiciously when I saw her this afternoon."

"Suspiciously? What has she to be suspicious of?"

"Not she. Me. I."

"How?"

"What?"

George wondered how they'd disentangle that lot.

"Oh, I see. You mean that you were suspicious of Miss Fenner." Helen caught up. "What did she do?"

"She was most reluctant to let me search her bedroom . . ."

"Mother! Search her bedroom? Whatever for?"

"I heard noises. When we eventually did get in there, we found a small boy who'd clumb – climbed through the window to get his ball."

"Nothing very terrible in that, surely?"

"No, but I was watching Miss Fenner's face, and I'm sure she expected to find someone else in there."

"Well, who'd have expected to find a small boy, however enterprising?" put in Threep, logically. Political training tells.

"Be quiet, Milton. This is a serious matter. I didn't want to mention it, Helen – you know how I dislike repeating gossip – but I spoke to Miss Kettle on my way home. It might interest you to know that she saw a man going into the cottage with Miss Fenner." Mrs Bollanger paused with the air of a Q.C. who has just produced an archbishop as his principal witness.

George felt as if someone was sawing away the boards from around his feet. Miss Kettle! The old acid-vat they'd met outside Polly's cottage!

"There's nothing wrong in that, surely?" defended Helen. "Mrs Watt . . ."

"Mrs Watt was in the post office most of the afternoon," Mrs Bollanger observed, grimly. "Miss Kettle happened to see her there."

George groaned. The Kettle Information Bureau was devilishly efficient. He might just as well go and pack.

"Mightn't the man have been a salesman or something?" asked Threep. "What did he look like?"

"Does it matter what he looked like? We are not interested in Miss Fenner's taste. Anyway, I had no time to ask Miss Kettle. She kept talking of the fête, as usual. She's as determined to sing that awful song of hers as I am she'll not. She's coming here tomorrow to discuss it." George gave another wriggle on the hook.

"Well, what do you want me to do about her?" Helen wanted to know.

"Miss Kettle?"

"No, Miss Fenner."

"Tell her to leave. Tell her . . ."

"I can't very well turn her out, Mother. Her lease has a few more months to run. Besides, she's probably nowhere to go."

"Very well. Don't say that I didn't warn you. I hope you won't have a scandal to deal with," said Mrs Bollanger, who obviously did.

"If I have proof of anything wrong, she'll go at once. We'll hear what Miss Kettle has to say. But I don't think there'll be anything. After all, you can't give a woman notice to quit because of her profession."

Mrs Bollanger's "Oh?" made Helen wish she'd phrased it differently.

"Anyway," persisted her mother, "she was most impertinent when I offered her advice on her pupils' performance at the fête. If the Vicar had only listened to me, he'd have had the Sede Pipe Band, instead."

A low rumble emanated from Threep's throat.

"He's probably thinking of what happened three years ago." He turned to George with the air of a man who is going to let you in on something good. "There was the Pipe Band, all bonnetted and kilted, and the platform gave way. All you could see was . . ."

"Milton!" Mrs Bollanger's lash reached across the table. "This is no place for your coarse reminiscences. Save them for the smoke-room!"

"Coarse?" Threep registered hurt surprise. "I was only saying that all you could see was planks and bagpipes." He retired behind his coffee-cup with the peevish look of a salmon caught out of season.

"I see that the Vicar is allowing Farrer to recite," continued Mrs Bollanger. "I only hope the poem has been thoroughly censored. I've a feeling the Vicar is going to regret this," she added.

Dinner oozed to an end.

George leaned against the sundial in the sunken garden, the smoke from his cigarette rising unwaveringly in the still air. The dusk was warm and heavy with the scents of roses and lavender. From the ornamental pond, near by, came the occasional plop of a surfacing fish, venturing into Outer Space. A late bee, hoping, no doubt, to catch the queen's eye, made busy noises in the dahlias.

Flame-and-pearl skies, melting into grey, promised

another scorcher for tomorrow. Helen's hair tickled George's nose as she rolled and unrolled his tie. All was peace and un-Bollangered content.

"George darling," Helen murmured, "have you ever been in love before?"

"No, dearest," answered George, who thought he hadn't. "What put that into your head?"

"I don't know. I don't think I could bear it if I thought you'd ever loved anyone else."

"Silly girl." George kissed the top of her head. A sparrow, fooling about on a near-by twig, leaned nearer. This was going to be good.

"When are you going to speak to Mother about the wedding, George?" asked Helen dreamily.

George's ears quivered like aspens.

"Good Lord! Do I have to speak to her? I thought 'speaking to' died out with the gavotte. Surely everything's settled?"

"Of course it is, darling, but I think you should do Mother the courtesy of letting her confirm it. She deserves that much, don't you think?"

"If she got all she deser . . . Oh, well, just for you. But supposing – just supposing for a moment – she ridicules the whole set-up? Supposing she calls the able-bodied male staff to heave your George out on his ear? What then?"

"Don't be absurd, George. Of course she won't." But he saw her eyes cloud. Doubt lurked there. "She wouldn't stand in the way of my happiness. I'm sure she wouldn't," she added, firmly. George hoped she'd convinced herself; she certainly hadn't convinced him. Unless Mrs Bollanger wished, he and Helen would never brush the confetti from each other's clothes. And the odds were heavily against Mrs Bollanger wishing.

"Very well; I'll go now." George decided to put it to the test. "She can't eat me." He considered a moment. "Can she?"

"Oh, George dear, will you really?" Helen turned a hopeful face up to his. "Mother's in the writing-room. I'll be in the lounge, if you want me. Please be as quick as you can. I'll be dying to hear what she has to say."

George looked at the eager face, and the courage coursed through his veins like the sap through spring plants. Just let anyone try and stop their marriage! He put the other arm around her. The sparrow gave an embarrassed chirp and flew off for a night with the boys.

Threep looked up glumly as Helen came into the lounge. The tooth had settled down to a steady dull ache, like a Budget speech.. Not even the open Hansard on his knees could conjure a smile to his lips.

"Hallo, Uncle Milton."

The honorary title had been bestowed upon him years before, when he used to draw impressionist pictures for an eager, uncritical Helen. He still didn't understand how she'd changed from a plate-faced, pig-tailed child into something straight out of a beauty competition. Must have happened that week he was away.

"Hullo, m'dear. On your own? Where's young Loder?"

"He's gone to see Mother about the wedding. I . . ."

"Gone to see your mother? Man must be mad! If Hester has any say in the matter, he's as much chance of marrying you as I have of becoming Prime Minister. Which isn't much," he added, for he was a man who knew his limitations.

"Why does Mother dislike him? George is one of the sweetest men breathing!"

"I can't imagine. She can hardly object to his doing that – breathing, I mean. And mightn't you be just the tiniest bit biased? Look at it from your mother's point of view: if you two live here after your marriage, she loses control of the estate. If you go away, she'll lose control over you. No, my dear, whoever marries you will have to carry you off like that chap Samovar."

"Samovar?"

"Yes, you know: in all the wild border his steed was the best."

"Oh, Lochinvar. But I'm over twenty-one, Uncle; I can marry whom I please."

"Can you? Try it. It'll be an interesting experiment, anyway. You're like your poor father, my dear – do anything for a quiet life. And I'm the same, dammit. One word from your mother and we all roll over on our backs to have our tummies tickled. I only hope your George has more will-power than we have."

At that moment, her George's will-power was fluttering against the walls of the writing-room, trying to get the hell out of there. As he stood beside Mrs Bollanger's desk, George had an almost unconquerable urge to put his hands behind his back and shuffle his feet.

So far, Helen's mother had done little to put him at ease. He'd started the ball rolling by saying that he and Helen wished to get married. Mrs Bollanger's "To whom?" had rather taken him aback.

"How long an engagement had you in mind, Mr Loder?" Helen's mother read through the letter she'd just finished.

"About five months. We'd thought Christmas . . ."

"Christmas? Do you really think you'll know anything about each other by then?"

"We were going to leave that until after the wedding."

"Mr Loder." Mrs Bollanger's eyes stabbed through him. "Helen is over twenty-one, so legally I have no say in this matter. On the other hand, I'm sure my daughter wouldn't go against my wishes. You became engaged – and without telling me – so let that suffice . . ."

"Suffice? Won't our children expect . . .?"

". . . for the present. Get to know one another for a year or so and then we'll talk the matter over again. After all, you may be a fortune-hunter for all we know."

"I've enough to keep us both. I'm not worried about Helen's money."

"I'm glad to hear it. Perhaps it was pure coincidence that I happened to be abroad when you became engaged." She turned to her writing. "Don't shut the door as you go out, Mr Loder. There's hardly a breath of air tonight."

George slouched dejectedly from the room. So that was that. Two years! Twenty years. Two hundred years. What was the difference?

He found Helen alone in the lounge, Threep having taken his tooth to bed.

"What did she say, George, dear?" Helen's face turned anxiously to his, trying to find some gleam of cheer.

"Two years, darling!" He almost added, "Without the option."

"She wants us to wait two whole years?"

Helen moved silently into his arms. George knew by her silence, by the very droop of her head, that she'd accepted her mother's dictum. He tried to raise her morale.

"We're not going to stand for that, are we, dearest? She can't stop us, you know."

A half-sobbed "Oh, George!" confirmed his fears. They were and she could. Helen's habit of saying "Yes" to her mother had become too ingrained.

So, decided George, the habit must be broken. And, some-how, he must find a way to do it.

53

5

The moon, impaled like a huge Wiltshire cheese on Bilton church spire, softened the outlines of the sleeping countryside. Bilton station, quartered with black and silver, was taking a recuperative half-hour off before the 3.10 Up, when it would resound to the clang of three milk-churns and a crate of chickens. London had to be fed, and Bilton faced up to its responsibilities.

Mercer's pond, like cooling molten lead, slept but fitfully. Now and then, its surface, disturbed by some gadabout amphibian, danced into a million fish-scales of light.

Rose Cottage posed and preened itself in the soft radiance. It knew when it looked its best. In the bedroom which had seen such stirring events a few hours before, Polly slept the sleep of one whose day has yielded much. The bedclothes, on the floor, were inadequately but more picturesquely replaced by a pillow balanced across a silk-covered rounded hip.

The post office, too, came in for its share of glory, but wore it more sedately, as befits a Civil Servant. The moon's rays rested gently on ar Ron, curled up on a bed-settee in Mrs Long's parlour. His face had the beatific expression of a favoured cherub. He was dreaming he'd found a machine-gun with real bullets. . . .

Stony Lane became a place of shades and shadows, causing sentries to peer nervously into patches normally unnoticed in the frank light of day. In a clearing surrounded by three sets of safety-fences, a short mast backed by a parabolic reflector became silver-plated by the moon's favour. A hare, lolloping unconcernedly in front of the mast, suddenly disappeared without fuss or trace. The moon shuddered and passed on.

It shuddered again as it peeped into Farrer's window and saw him, flat on his back, dreaming noisily. Two chalk-white feet stuck far out of the southern end of the bed, like petrified cacti. The moon grimaced; surely Wiltshire had more to offer than this?

It couldn't get past the modestly-drawn curtains at The Elms, where Miss Kettle slept serenely, a loaded 12-bore double-barrelled gun at her bedside. Since The Elms had been broken into, twenty-three years previously, Myrtle Kettle had religiously loaded the gun each night, unloading it every morning with a sigh of relief. Not that she was in any personal danger from marauders; in fact, it was rumoured that the man who'd broken in – mistakenly, as it had turned out – had himself phoned the police upon seeing Miss Kettle. This she hotly denied. As far as she was concerned, she'd been desired, notwithstanding Amos Flower's slander that she kept the gun there to stop the poor devil getting away next time. Miss Kettle and Amos Flower were not really simpatico.

Farther down the road, the moon shed its lustre over the whitened gables of The Leas, giving that imposing façade the two-dimensional appearance of a Ruritanian musical-comedy stage-set. Peering brazenly into Helen's room, the moon gave a long low whistle. This was something! Golden hair, peach-bloom cheeks (did raindrops glisten there?) and a care-lessly-flung arm, grouped just so, were enough to make any full-blooded moon pause.

It tried the same game at Mrs Bollanger's window, but excused itself and hastily backed out. No percentage there; Mrs Bollanger slept strictly to rule.

Gwyneth's room, though, paid off handsomely. The moon nodded approvingly, being more in favour of brunettes, given the choice. It wondered what Farrer would say if he were here. Probably "Cor!"

Milton Threep, who'd been dreaming that Mrs Bollanger, dressed in kilt and bonnet, had been clumsily excavating his jaw with a blunt harpoon, sat up in bed. How could anyone be expected to stand this? Sheer torture, that's what it was. Spartans, he supposed, could take it in their stride. As far as he was concerned, they could take it now.

He wouldn't have wished this hell on any human being, or even the Opposition leader. His jaw throbbed like a pre-war car. If his face swelled any more, they'd have to throw out another wing to accommodate it. He rocked gently.

What was it Gwyneth had said about – what was it? – oil of cloves? Maybe there'd be some in the kitchen? How did one use it, though? Drink it? Rub it into the cheek? Probably, being a Welsh prescription, special words had to be said over it, like "Sosspan fach" or whatever it was. He got out of bed and fumbled for his torch.

In his room above the garage, Stefan, puffing at a brown cigarette which smelt like a burning arm-chair, knotted the cord of his dressing-gown around him. During dinner he'd gone through the upstairs rooms like a matron at the Autumn Sales and had found nothing. Then an idea had struck him. What about the lounge, where Threep spent so much of his time? Mightn't the brief-case be there, locked in some little-used drawer or cupboard?

It had been easy to undo one of the spring catches on the french windows after Gwyneth had locked up for the night. Now, all he had to do was cross the lawn, enter through the window, and make a thorough search at his leisure. Snap the window shut after he left, and there you were. Money for caviare. He took a small pencil-torch and went downstairs.

For the twentieth time since he'd gone to bed, George tried

to empty his mind and let Sleep have her way. It was a hard process. Every time he managed to stop thinking, he'd wonder what it was he wasn't thinking about and his mind would start buzzing again. Helen, Polly, Helen, Mrs Bollanger, Helen, Threep – all kept prodding him awake as they waltzed past. He felt about as sleepy as a hermit who's wandered into the *Folies Bergère*.

At last he began to feel the first welcome drowsiness of sleep. His mind floated about seventeen inches above his body, deliciously detached.

Even that creaking on the stairs sounded somehow soothing. Like the sound of leather-bound oars in row locks, on the upper reaches of the Thames. In, out. In, out, Creak, creak....

Stairs? His mind whipped back into his body, ready for business on the old stand. Who'd be on the stairs at this time of night? The luminous hands of his travelling-block pointed to twenty past two. He slid out of bed, reaching for his dressing-gown....

Stefan's torch cut the velvety blackness in the lounge. Side table? Notepaper, envelopes and *Punch* – nothing else. Music-stool? Ah, locked. A quick operation with a steel rod, and the lid was open. *Il Trovatore, Madame Butterfly*, and a petrified rock-cake. Nothing to ... Hallo, a cupboard under the bureau ... Empty.

Milton Threep made his cautious way along the serving-passage from the dining-room to the kitchen. The toothache was a little easier, now, probably due to the threat of the oil of cloves. Still, he might as well try the stuff, having come so far.

What was that? His heart crowded his tonsils. Sounded like someone in the hall, or on the stairs. He switched off his torch, replaced his stomach, and listened for a moment.

Stefan, in the lounge, switched of his torch and listened too.

As the door opened stealthily, he realized that whoever came in would be between him and his line of retreat. He edged his way across to the window.

George's hand fumbled for the light-switch which some individualistic electrician had placed on the wrong side of the door. Suddenly, he was blinded by a torch flashing in his eyes; then a rocket hit him on the side of the jaw, bursting into a million stars. Stefan's timing was perfect, as sweet a hook as anyone could wish for, outside Madison Square Gardens. He stepped out of the window and let it click shut after him.

Threep, heroic as a hyper-sensitive mouse, tried to sidle past the room just as George reeled round the door-post. He grabbed Threep, heaved him into the lounge, and went into action. George's plan, simple yet satisfying, was to dismember this prowling perisher and pile him in three neat heaps on the floor. Having done that, he could consider further operations.

"Help!" shouted Threep, valiantly, right arm lashing out with the force and precision of a chaffinch's leg. "Gragh!" he ended, as George gave him the old one-two.

The light snapped on.

"May I ask what you two are doing?" Mrs Bollanger, in purple dressing-gown and white head-scarf, appeared like an Olympian time-keeper in their midst.

The two principals broke cleanly and stood back. On each face, initial surprise gave way to looks of suspicion. What the blazes was *he* doing down here at this time of night?

"Milton! What are you doing here at this hour? And you, Mr Loder? Isn't your bed comfortable?"

Threep had nothing to hide. "I heard a noise, and came downstairs to see what it was. I came in here and Mr Loder attacked me like a wild tiger," he said, indignantly. There'd been few wild tigers in Threep's life, but he was a man of imagination.

"And you, Mr Loder?" The Truth Machine swung around to George.

"Well, stop me if you've heard this before, but *I* heard a noise and came downstairs to see what it was. I came in here and Mr Threep attacked *me* like a wild tiger." The law of the jungle had come to Winthringham.

"It all sounds most peculiar. We keep Christian hours in this house, Mr Loder. I think you'd both better go back to bed. We'll talk about this in the morning." She looked at Threep. "Milton, your face is badly swollen. Is there something . . . ?"

"Yes, I had a bit of a bang on the jaw," said her cousin, quickly. "I'll put a cold towel on it."

Mrs Bollanger gave George an accusing glance.

"Helen and I dislike violence in any form. You must try to suppress these primitive instincts as long as you remain here, Mr Loder. Good night." She swept out of the room.

George turned to Threep.

"Look here, you *did* attack me just now, didn't you?" The more he thought of it, the less likelihood there seemed to be of such a thing. The only way Threep could have landed the blow he'd felt would be by a system of springs and levers. The man's muscles hardly made him self-supporting.

The other looked indignant.

"I certainly did not! I thought there were two of you in there. . . ."

"That's it!" Light dawned on George. "There *was* someone else in here, and he got away after handing me that pile-driver. Did anyone pass you?"

"No, but he could have left by the window, as I came in. That's probably what happened."

"You're right. Of course you're right." George felt a pang

59

of contrition. "I say, I'm sorry about that welt on the jaw.
You *do* understand that I . . ."

"Oh, you didn't do that. It's toothache, but I daren't tell
Hester or she'd have me off to the dentist."

"You don't like dentists?" George had no positive feelings
about dentists. There had to be such things, just the same as
there had to be furniture-removers, or caraway-seeds. Still, he
always liked to hear the other man's point of view.

"Like dentists?" Fire flashed from Threep's eye. "I'd rather
have my liver out, or my lungs, or an arm . . ."

"Yes, yes. I see." George arrested the rapid disintegration.
"We'll take it that you're not keen on dentists. But have you
ever tried gas?"

"It wouldn't do any good. I'd still feel it, I know I would.
I suppose I'm a coward," said the sufferer, fully determined to
remain one.

"Look," persuaded George, "why not come in to Devizes
with me tomorrow – that is, today, and give this gas a try-out?
We could make the appointment by phone. I've had gas
twice, see," he opened his mouth and hooked a finger into his
cheek, "urr ah urr. Ee?" The mouth sprung back to the
status quo. "I never felt a thing, I swear."

Threep considered. The chap seemed genuine enough.
After all, he wasn't a politician. Another pang, like a white-
hot drill, decided him.

"Very well. I'll do it. Thank you. We'll take my car and
deliver the Vicar's records at the same time. No point in telling Hester," he added, off-handedly.

George sensed that here was an ally. Not, perhaps, the best
choice, but an ally all the same. Anyway, he felt he must
confide in someone.

"Do you know what happened this evening? Mrs Bollanger calmly told me that I must wait until I'm nearer

retiring age before I can marry Helen. What would you have done?"

Threep knew too damn' well what he'd have done, but felt that George sought encouragement rather than truth.

"Done? I – don't – know," he answered slowly, giving the impression of quiet strength. "But don't you be bullied, my boy. If you once give in to Hester, you'll have no more freedom of thought than a Helot."

"What *is* a Helot?" George had often wondered.

"Does it matter?" Threep didn't know, either. "If they've no freedom of thought, why worry about them?"

"You've a point there. I'll try and stop."

"Anyway, what ever they are, don't be one. Sweep her off her feet."

"Who? Mrs Bollanger?"

"No, Helen. She'll thank you for it, in the end."

George's opinion of Threep soared skywards. He wished he'd got the chap's easy confidence. Weak on dentists, maybe, but way out in front when it came to women.

"I suppose you had no bother at all about proposing?" said George, enviously.

"Me? Good Lord, I'm not married! I wouldn't dream of asking a woman such an intimate question." Threep shuddered at the idea of it.

"Oh," said George.

"You might as well go on up to bed," advised Threep. "I'll report this little matter to the police, by phone. I don't suppose they'll do anything until morning."

As George went upstairs, he heard Threep trying to explain matters as simply as possible to a sleepy policeman who was apparently holding the phone the wrong way around. Who said that the country was restful. . . ?

In his room over the garage, Stefan smoked a meditative

cigarette. So Loder *was* after him, it seemed. It might have been coincidence, of course, but . . . No! He couldn't afford the risk of uncertainty; there was too much at stake. Loder must be eliminated. Either by 'accident' or the direct method, it didn't matter which. Just a matter of choice or opportunity.

But, decidedly, Loder must go.

Across the fields came the melancholy wooing of a love-sick owl in the yews of Bilton church. From somewhere in the distance, a badly-regulated cock crowed a false dawn.

The moon yawned and swung lazily across the heavens, another routine night nearly completed.

6

"Mr. Loder," Mrs Bollanger firmly spread marmalade on to a piece of toast, "to what do you attribute your exceptionally keen sense of hearing?"

Across George's face spread the agonized expression of a man who'd like to answer but has just taken a man-sized bite of sausage. He gulped, and an indignant stomach wondered what that sausage-happy mouth would send down next.

"Hearing?" George was never at his best at the breakfast-table, he knew, but the question had struck him as pretty much *a propos de pas*.

"Yes. You are on the third floor, presumably asleep, yet you hear sounds down in the lounge. What was your burglar doing – a clog dance?"

"Oh, the burglar? Well, I heard the noise on the stairs, first, then I went . . ."

"That would be me you heard," Threep interposed, "I was going down to the kitchen . . ."

"At two in the morning, Milton? Had I known you were hungry I'd have had a tray sent up to your room."

"It wasn't that." George could have sworn he heard a whirring noise from Threep's head as the brain raced desperately. "I was going down for some – some – some liniment," he ended, triumphantly.

"Liniment?"

"Yes." Threep was well into his stride, now. "I have a touch of rheumatism in my right knee, just below the knee-cap," he explained, putting in the master-touch of detail.

"The pain woke me up. I thought I'd rub a little liniment on and save worrying anyone."

"Oh." Mrs Bollanger was still uncertain. "And are you better now?"

"No." Threep was determined to wring the utmost out of this heaven-sent inspiration. "The knee's rather painful when I walk." A cunning look came into his eye. "I'm afraid I won't be able to walk over to the Vicarage, today. Never mind," he added, with the cheerful courage of a man who's willing to make the best of a bad situation, "I'll pop over in the car."

George gave him an admiring glance. Here, he felt, was the real Threep in action. The true Threep; the verbal strategist; the politician; the accomplished liar.

Helen came into the room looking like a prima donna with laryngitis. She kissed her mother's proffered cheek and floated gently down on to a chair.

"Good morning, Mother. Good morning, Uncle Milton. Good morning, George." She seemed aloof, preoccupied, as George rose and helped her to coffee and grape-fruit. Last night's news was still rankling, obviously.

"Helen, have you managed to get the revised fête programme typed? We are showing it to the Vicar this evening, remember."

"Yes, Mother," Helen answered, languidly. "We have definitely decided against Miss Kettle's song, then?"

"Quite definitely. I'll tell her this evening. She'll be here about half past eight, after we return from the Vicarage."

George nibbled a thoughtful crust while Helen was regaled with Mrs Bollanger's version of what had happened during the night. Miss Kettle was bound to recognize him, this evening, as The Man With Miss Fenner. She'd had plenty of time to study him, outside Rose Cottage. What to do? Feign sickness? Not worth it; Threep's fortuitous rheumatism had only just been accepted. Besides, it would do no more than delay the inevitable. The only thing left to do was to brazen things out.

Why on earth hadn't he confided in Helen, last night? He'd intended to, but somehow, after their conversation in the garden, he didn't think the story would have been well received. There'd certainly have been raised eyebrows, if nothing worse.

Gwyneth came in, pores oozing importance.

"P.C. Ammidge've come, 'M. Says 'e'd like to see Mr Threep about 'is burglar." A burglar! Their very own! Might've all been murdered in their beds, look you!

"Show him into the lounge, please, Gwyneth."

Threep rose, wiped his lips, and limped pathetically from the table. He paused at the door. "I suppose you'd better come, too, Loder. After all, you had more to do with it than I."

"I'll see Ammidge myself," announced Mrs Bollanger. She wasn't going to have the thing half-done. "He'll no doubt want facts. I can put the matter quite clearly to him." They left the room, an aircraft-carrier and attendant destroyers.

Police-constable Ammidge stood up as they entered the lounge. Since he'd been transferred to the Bilton district from Devizes, nothing had happened to relieve the routine except for a case of a lost dog, and a warning to Amos Flower about the Gaming and Lottery regulations. Last night's affair at least held promise.

"Good morning, madam. Good morning, gentlemen. I won't keep you long. P'raps one of you would give me a rough outline of what 'appened, last night?"

"It was . . ." answered Mrs Bollanger, Threep and George. They stopped.

"I came . . ." they all re-commenced, and stopped again.

P.C. Ammidge looked up from his notebook. "Just one of you, please," he appealed, not unreasonably.

Mrs Bollanger gagged the two men with a glance.

"I heard a scuffle, at about two o'clock, and came down here to find Mr Loder attacking Mr Threep."

George looked at her aghast, and wondered whether Ammidge had handcuffs with him, or would have to send back for them.

"The case is one of assault, then?" queried Ammidge.

"Attempted robbery. So far, we've found nothing missing."

"You mean that this gen – Mr Loder here was trying to commit robbery with violence?" Ammidge pounded hopefully after the elusive facts.

"Did I say that? Apparently Mr Loder found a thief in the lounge, dragged Mr Threep in, and punched him on the jaw."

Ammidge had stopped writing. This wasn't a report, it was a fantasy. The man Loder's actions seemed strangely unco-ordinated. Just felt he had to hit someone, presumably.

Threep stepped into the breach.

"Perhaps I can make it a little clearer, Constable. I happened to be passing the lounge, at about two-fifteen" – Ammidge's eyes widened; The Leas sounded as peaceful as St Pancras – "when Mr Loder, under the impression that I'd just assaulted him, started to struggle with me. Mrs Bollanger came in just at that time."

"And why should Mr Loder think you'd assaulted him?" Ammidge studied George for signs of persecution mania.

"He'd just been struck by the thief, and was completely in the dark."

And he's not the only one, thought Ammidge. He turned to George.

"And what were you doing in the lounge at two a.hem, sir?"

George took a deep breath. At last he could get a word in, straighten things out, and step from under the shadow of the gallows.

"You see, officer," he began, pleasantly, with the air of a man whose movements are an open book, "I heard Mr Threep come downstairs, and came down to see who he was." Ammidge groaned inwardly. Another of 'em! "That is, not knowing that it was Mr Threep, I came down. I went into the lounge, not knowing that it wasn't Mr Threep who wasn't . . . Er, then he flashed a light in my face and gave me a bang on the jaw."

"Who? Mr Threep?"

"No. The burglar."

"Where'd 'e been all this time?"

"Who? The burglar?"

"No. Mr Threep."

"In the hall, I suppose. Anyway, I caught hold of him and . . ."

"Who? The burglar?"

"No. Mr Threep. He hadn't been in the room, you see, and the burglar got away. That just about sums it up, I think," he ended, with the quiet pride of one who has just simplified a complex explanation.

"I see," said Ammidge, who didn't. "Well, I'll go back to the station and sort out this load of – er, transcribe these statements. I'll let you know if there are any further developments. Good morning." He left the room, after a searching look at George, like a man who has just come through Hampton Court maze, blindfolded. A policeman's lot, one gathered, wasn't all honey and handcuffs.

Mrs Bollanger turned to George and Threep.

"If Ammidge is satisfied with that, I strongly doubt that crime doesn't pay. Now," she continued, "we've delayed long enough. You'll find the records for the Vicar all ready on the hall table. Please remind him that Helen and I will be seeing him this evening."

Threep brought the car to rest outside the sober, brooding door of L. Mewell, Dental Surgeon. As he applied the handbrake, he felt his new-found courage draining away like stoneginger at a choir outing. He turned to George.

"You're sure he confirmed that the appointment *was* for this morning? Telephone line isn't always as good as it should be, you know. I wouldn't like to inconvenience him. Besides, there doesn't seem to be any pain, now."

"Don't let it fool you, Threep. It's just waiting for you to drive away from here and – Bingo! – in will go the old red-hot spear again."

Threep climbed out of the tumbril with the alacrity of a rheumatic tortoise.

"By the way, please keep an eye on that brief-case. I don't like to let it out of my sight, especially as the locks don't lock properly. Not that there's anything in it of particular importance," he tried to sound off-hand, "but I wouldn't like its contents to be discussed." He lingered at the car door.

George applied the goad.

"Look, L. Mewell is in there waiting for you with a record of years of painless extracting, just anxious to carry on being painless. You're not afraid, are you?"

"Yes," said Threep.

He mounted the three shallow steps and pressed the bell-push. There was time for one helpless look over his shoulder as the door opened. George could have sworn that other muscles than Threep's sent him to The Chair.

The brief-case lay on the back seat of the car and George wondered idly what it might contain. Rough drafts of a new law or so? A White Paper? A Blue Paper? Or maybe even the complete seidleitz. Looked innocent enough, anyway. Brown pigskin, two large locks – shams, these – and the letters "M.T." in gold script, on the flap.

George had smoked scarcely half a cigarette when Threep appeared at the window. A new, confident Threep, this, almost overpowering in his relief at losing the tooth, added to the uplifting after-effects of the gas.

"Well, Loder, my boy," he exclaimed, and people three streets away paused, interestedly, "everything's fine! Never felt a thing. Zing! Just like that. Child's play. Feel a bit light-headed, though. You'd better drive."

George headed the car for Winthringham as Threep chattered on. The dentist had certainly done a smooth job. Now and then, Threep broke into little snatches of song. His gloom had been left, like an old coat, with L. Mewell.

"We'll celebrate this, tonight," he promised George. "While they're at the Vicar's . . . That reminds me, we must deliver those records. Go straight on past The Leas for a mile or so down the Sede road, then turn up a lane to the left. We'll be back in nice time for lunch if the Vicar doesn't keep us talking about his vegetable garden."

George drove on, past hedge and fence, determined dog-rose and prim hawthorn. The car's movement created enough breeze for comfort as the sun's rays splashed off the polished radiator. Flies committed suicide against the windscreen for the sheer joy of having known a morning like this. Horses stood rubbing their chins on gates, and cows just stood. George would have wallowed in it all, if it hadn't been for the ever-present shadow of Mrs Bollanger and the looming threat of Miss Kettle.

As they sped by Rose Cottage, he caught a glimpse of red and white in the garden. Polly lay back in a deck-chair, idling with a book. George begrudged her her peace of mind. Pity he couldn't stop; mention of the Kettle would soon wipe that complacent look from Polly's face.

The Vicar, busy with a hoe, came to the gate as the car pulled up at the Vicarage. His voice rang out joyfully, like a victory carrillon.

"Good morning. Good morning. Another glorious day, what?"

He was short and stout, and little beads of perspiration oozed from his red skin. Long strands of silver hair escaped from the sides of the straw hat which his housekeeper was constantly sending to the jumble sales, and which regularly returned to its place in the potting-shed. He breathed enthusiasm and goodwill as he wiped his hands on a huge red-and-white spotted handkerchief.

"Good morning, Vicar. This is Mr Loder, staying at The Leas. Loder, this is the Reverend Honeydew."

George grasped the hard, earthy palm.

"How do you do, sir?" asked the Vicar. It wasn't just a salutation. George felt that he really wished to know how George did. The large grey eyes peered anxiously into his own, searching for some lurking illness.

As they chatted, Threep handed over the records.

"Mrs Bollanger asked me to give you these, Vicar. The records for the fête, you know. Perhaps you could play them over, and let her know whether they're suitable. She'll be seeing you this evening, she says."

"Ah, capital. Thank you, indeed. I'm sure they'll do perfectly. Do thank her for me, won't you, and tell her that I'm looking forward to her visit? She and Helen have promised to check the final arrangements for me, you know.

A tower of strength, sir, Mrs Bollanger," he added, turning to George. "I don't know what we'd do without her." George wondered whether he'd ever given it a try-out.

Declining an offer of sherry, they set off for The Leas, the Vicar leaning over the gate like an interested cow, watching them down the lane.

"Nice old boy," commented Threep, as the hedges sped by. "Completely under Hester's thumb, of course. We did well to refuse his sherry. Adds bulk to it with permanganate of potash, or something. He's got some fine brandy, though," he added, reminiscently.

Mrs Bollanger carefully pulled on her gloves. She frowned as she saw her daughter staring listlessly out of the open windows.

"Do pull yourself together, Helen. It's gone six, and you're not ready yet. I don't know what the Vicar will think. Aren't you well?"

"I'm all right, Mother."

No point in telling her mother that the world was crumbling away. Helen could see the years stretching on and on into the dim future, when she and George would become known as the longest-engaged couple in England.

Other girls would marry, raise families, and disappear into that mysterious private heaven where one's married friends always seemed to go. But not she and George. People would say, "Oh, yes. They're just celebrating their Silver Engagement anniversary. Such a devoted old couple. It's a wonder they don't marry."

She looked gloomily at her mother, swathed in white. Had she any feelings at all, beside the desire to manage everyone and everything? Had she loved Daddy? Must have done, in her own inexplicable way, one supposed.

George, moodily doodling at the writing-table, felt a sense of impatience as he watched Mrs Bollanger preparing to go to the Vicarage. Somewhere in his mind, the lines kept recurring;

> "Why do you walk thro' the fields in gloves?
> Oh fat white woman whom nobody loves."

He didn't know who'd said that, but he was willing to bet that the chap had a mother-in-law like Mrs Bollanger. Even Helen must find filial affection fraying around the edges. Why didn't she stand up to her mother? Hard to do, of course, after years of complacent obedience. If only something would happen to jerk her out of the rut!

Mrs Bollanger was briefing Threep:

"We'll be back before Miss Kettle arrives at eight-thirty, Milton. You and Mr Loder should be able to look after yourselves until then." She had her doubts. "And if you wish to indulge in wrestling or football, please go outside." She forged out of the room, Helen in tow.

Threep, still rejoicing in the knowledge of a tooth well drawn, turned to George.

"Gwyneth's off, this evening, Loder. Cook will bring sandwiches later. How about a walk down to the Angry Hen? Quite an interesting little pub. Seventeenth century," he added, as if it mattered.

George assented, indifferently. It would pass one more evening towards the day when he and Helen, ageing bodies supported by strong men, went to the altar. A drink might brighten things up, anyway.

The Angry Hen (Prop. Jno. Murk) was beginning to fill as they entered the low-ceilinged bar-parlour. Jno. welcomed them as a prop. will do when he sees potential spirit-sales among the many "arfs o' mixed".

"Lovely evenin', gennlemen. What can I get you?"

They seated themselves at a corner table, ordering, to Jno.'s disgust, bitter beer. Threep carefully placed his brief-case on the chair behind him before he sat down. The hum of conversation, interrupted by their entry, rose again. To George's surprise, it followed the same pattern as that of the London pubs. Except that there seemed to be more meaning to it, here.

Time floated gently along the flowing bitter. George began to feel that life might be tolerable, after all. Several glasses later, Threep became confidential.

"Do you know, young Loder, you're going to marry the sweetest little girl in the world? I've as good as dangled – or is it 'dandled'? – Helen on my knee as a child. When *she* was a child, I mean," he added, wishing there to be no mistake. "She's lovely and kind and good and . . ."

"Are you telling *me*, Threep?" George didn't have to have a good thing pointed out. "She's the quincence of all that's perfect."

"Quincence?"

"What do you mean, 'quincence'?"

"You said it."

"What?"

"Quincence."

"I didn't. I said quintent – quintessence of something or other." George knew what he'd said. After all, he'd said it.

"Oh. Have another?"

"Last one, then. It's gone eight. Miss Kettle's coming, don't forget." Gloom settled over George as he reminded himself of his impending doom.

The glasses were replenished, and Threep looked thought-fully into the amber depths.

"You know, Loder, I once loved a woman. A Good

73

Woman," he said, in capitals. "I saw her for two hours, one evening; then she went out of my life. And I still lov'er: deeply. Never spoke to her, of course. Nobry to intruce – introduce us. Gloria, her name was," he added, filling in the details.

"Couldn't you wangle a meeting? Phone? There *were* phones, weren't there?"

"There were phones. And steam-engines. And radio. I'm not a damn' centuri – centen – I'm not a hundred years old, young Loder. I *did* try to see her, but she'd gone off to Wigan or somewhere. You've got your Helen, Farrer has his Gwyneth . . ."

"Yes, but poor old Bollanger had Mrs Bollanger. It cuts both ways, you know."

"True. But Gloria wouldn't have turned out like that." Threep drained his glass. "If anyone here likes to say that Gloria would have turned into another Hester, I'll break his neck. Anyone." Threep had no favourites.

"People don't turn out like Mrs B. They're hewn that way."

"Hewn. That's good." Threep chuckled hugely.

He was still chuckling as they went up to the house. The walk was pleasant, Threep filling in the fleeting moments by giving George a description of the more interesting Parliamentary sessions. Twice, only George's agility saved him from a clout with the brief-case as Threep waved his arms to illustrate a point.

Mrs Bollanger and Helen were waiting for them in the lounge, much as the Argonauts' wives used to wait, wondering whether that idiot Ulysses would call it a day at last. Mrs Bollanger's foot tapped impatiently as they came in with the defiant look of men who are sober and can prove it.

"Milton! I suppose it was necessary for you both to stay

74

out until the last moment, then come in reeking of beer? What do you suppose Miss Kettle will think?"

Threep's views on what Miss Kettle might think, full of gripping interest as they no doubt would have been, were never uttered. Helen's mother rose from the chair.

"Ah, there she is coming up the drive, now. Let her in, please, Helen. Gwyneth is out for the evening."

As Helen left, George's beer-begotten bonhomie disappeared. Well, this was it. What was the word? Denouement. That was it. Or Nemesis. Whatever it was, the curse had come upon him.

Then he remembered. Salvation – temporary, it was true – lay in the hall. He walked out, unnoticed, behind Helen.

7

"Good evening, Miss Kettle." Helen tried to look pleased as Miss Kettle paused in the porch. "Do come in." They walked through the hall together, and into the lounge. Helen wondered, idly, where George had gone.

"Ah, good evening, Miss Kettle." Mrs Bollanger had the expression of the title-holder as the contender climbs into the ring.

"Good evening, Mrs Bollanger. I've only a few minutes I'm afraid. I must do my watering before dark. I just wanted to make certain about the fête arrangements. Oh, good evening Mr Threep," she added, as Threep sidled past her into the hall.

He closed the door as the two women sparred up to one another. Where the dickens had Loder gone? Damn' quick, wasn't he? Smart, though, the way . . .

"I say," said George's voice, coming from slightly to the bottom-left of nowhere.

Threep spun round.

"What? Where the blazes . . . ?"

"I'm here," said George, hoarsely. "In the chest. Is it all clear?"

"I suppose so. What were you expecting, dive-bombers?"

The lid of the oak chest lifted, and George peered around. Reassured, he stepped out.

"Look," said Threep, reasonably, "I know it's no business of mine, but what on earth . . . ?"

"It's Miss Kettle. I didn't want to see her," George explained.

"Well, I admire your taste, but do you always dive into chests when you don't want to meet people?"

"No; you see . . . Oh, it's hard to explain, but . . ."

"I'll bet it is. But don't bother. Come into the library and have a drink."

"Thanks. And listen, Threep," George laid a hand on the other's arm, "it's nice of you to take it like this. I'll tell you all about it soon, I promise."

"Don't give it a thought," said Threep, largely. He led the way into the library and made heartening noises with whisky decanter and siphon.

"Bung-ho," said George.

"Cheers," answered Threep, chummily.

George looked out of the window. He'd only just realized what a glorious evening it was. The sun was dragging the day down over the hills by its tail-end, and there was a welcome coolness in the air. A bat, either through sheer exhibitionism, or possibly for experimental purposes, was doing low-level swoops and turns, educating and entertaining a rook who applauded hoarsely from a fauteuil in the chestnut tree.

If this was country life, it was all right with George. Here a man could breathe; a man could have his roots; a man could . . .

"Have a drink?" invited Threep.

More splashing, then:

"Bung-ho!" said Threep.

"Cheers," answered George.

Twenty minutes later, they saw Miss Kettle leave. From the tilt of her head, and the faint heat-haze over her ears, it was fairly obvious that she'd lost her point with Mrs Bollanger.

Even worse, she'd been talked into running the refreshment-stall. And, if that were not enough, Helen had as good as told her to prove her story about the man at Rose Cottage. It hadn't been Miss Kettle's evening.

"There goes a woman who's not going to sing at the fête," observed Threep, wisely. "Care to bet on it, young Loder?"

George didn't. They strolled out into the grounds, full of camaraderie, whisky, and sandwiches. Twilight was fading into darkness as Threep took George to see the new automatic door-opener which he'd persuaded Mrs Bollanger to fit on the garage.

"Magic-eye principle," he explained, learnedly. "You just drive up, and the car interrupts a ray of light. That operates a mechanism which slides the door up and over. Look."

He approached the closed door like a man stalking an antelope. Nothing happened. He walked back and tried again. The door remained immobile.

"Burglar-proof, anyway," commented George.

Threep looked up at an unobtrusive switch-box, about a foot above the garage door, just below Stefan's window.

"Ah! There's the master-switch. Stefan's probably closed it." He rooted around by the side of the garage and came back with a short ladder which he propped against the wall.

"Just pop up and throw the switch, will you? My shape's not quite right for mountaineering, these days."

George did as he was bid, and Threep spent many happy minutes demonstrating the automatic door. He walked at it; ran at it; crept up on it. However he approached it, the door would give a slight shudder, then slide smoothly up and over. They strolled back to the house.

"I wonder whether anything's been heard of our last night's visitor?" mused George.

"I don't suppose so. Some tramp, probably, who imagined

78

he was on an easy thing. Didn't expect to find half the household wandering around in the dark."

George stopped. "That reminds me: I've left that ladder standing up against the garage wall. Asking for trouble. I'll just nip back and replace it."

And that was why Stefan, returning from an evening stroll, saw George removing a ladder from below the bedroom window. The chauffeur stepped into the shadows until George had gone. Then he walked thoughtfully to his room.

So. Loder certainly let no grass grow under his feet. The sooner he was out of the way, the better.

Gwyneth sat contentedly on the stile, watching Bob Farrer moodily kicking the turf below it. The evening had been perfect. They'd just walked from the Angry Hen, where she'd had a small port and lemon, while Farrer had had a mild. She looked her best, she knew, in a black skirt and red jumper. In fact, there was nothing to cause Bob a moment's gloom. Unless . . . Feminine intuition (woman's term for the blind guess that comes off now and then) told her – nay, shouted at her – that Bob was Going To Say It. Well, as far as she was concerned, it was just a matter of putting him out of his misery.

"Gwyn," he looked over her right shoulder to the breathtaking vista of the mangold field beyond, "s'posin' Oi ast 'ee to wed. Wot'd 'ee say?"

Gwyneth looked at him. She'd intended to tease him a little – oh! just a little – before saying "Yes", but the pathetic anxiety on his face touched her. Besides, her heart had started to thump in such a stupid way that she didn't think she'd be able to carry off the "hard to get" act. Her vision blurred for no sensible reason.

"Why don't you ask me, Bob, and find out?" she said,

softly. "You've 'eard what they say about faint 'eart, 'aven't you, boyo?"

The next moment, she was off the stile, her feet dangling six inches from the ground, caught in a hug that would have caused a bear to shamble away in hopeless despair. Hollywood spends many hours and dollars trying hard to teach its stars to kiss with half Farrer's technique. Unsuccessfully. But then, Farrer was in love.

Several thousand years later, he let her gently down to the ground. Then he fumbled in four of his pockets before he found the ring.

"R-foop," he said, as he thrust it awkwardly on to her finger. "You always said you'd loike a r-foop o' di-monds." They stood looking at the finger as though it was a treasure they'd just unearthed.

"Oi dunno wot we'm goin' to do fer a 'ome, Gwyn." Farrer sounded troubled. "Oi got two 'undred saved. That'll put the deposit down on one o' they new 'ouses by Sede; or it'd buy us the furnicher. Not both. An' a foine zany Oi'd look wi' one an' not t'other. Wot'll us do?" He waited humbly, knowing that her Celtic brain worked nine times as fast and ten times as effectively as his own.

"Can't we rent a house?"

"Oi on'y know of one, an' that's Amos Flower's. Oi want no truck wi 'e if Oi can 'elp it."

Gwyneth nodded agreement. Whilst nobody could state categorically that Amos Flower was a swindler, it was generally felt that he didn't leave much to chance. The old station-wagon he'd sold to Harry Bryant, for instance, was still cited as a typical Flower transaction. Fifteen pounds, Harry'd given him for it, and it hadn't run since Amos had driven it up to Harry's barn. After many threats and much bad language he'd no doubt regret in calmer moods, Harry had made Amos take it back for seven pounds. Amos had promptly sold the engine for a fiver, and the chassis for four pounds. That left the body, which he advertised for two pounds as a hen-house. Harry Bryant bought it.

As it was pointed out, nobody could say that there was anything dishonest about Amos's business deals. He just didn't lose, that was all. Shorn of its colourful adjectives, Harry Bryant's opinion was precisely that.

Gwyneth stooped and picked up an object from the long grass by the stile.

"Look, boyo. Someone's left 'is moosic-case." She gave a start of recognition. "Why, it's Mr Threep's! See? There's 'is 'nitials. I'll take it up to 'im. There's worried 'e'll be." She looked at her wrist-watch. "Ten o'clock, Bob. I'll be getting in. No need to come up to the 'ouse; we'll say good night at the post office."

They ambled slowly up the road, arms around each other's waists, Farrer carrying the case for Gwyneth. They said "Good night" outside the post office. . . .

At eleven-fifteen, as Gwyneth let herself in at the back door of The Leas, she realized that she hadn't got the case. "Never mind. Bob'll bring it up tomorrow morning," she contented herself.

Farrer paused as he turned the key of his mother's cottage door. "Did Gwyn take thic case?" he mused. "Must o' done. I ain't got 'n now, anyways."

And, in the pale moonlight outside the post office, Threep's brief-case lay forlornly in the road.

A shaft of sunlight climbed over the window-sill of Mrs Long's parlour, and started a slow tour of inspection around the walls. It picked out the television, dead and uninteresting as a glass eye. It caressed a picture of Balaclava, wherein fierce cavalrymen charged, hopelessly out of formation, on sur-prised-looking horses. It rested on a minnow-net, as yet unbaptized, in a corner of the room. And, finally, it rested on ar Ron, or rather, on his eyes and nose appearing over the top of the sheet on the bed-settee.

Ron awoke and blinked. Then he lay for a moment savour-ing the delicious feeling of a comfortable bed, and the prospect of a long sunny day in which to do as he pleased. Trees to climb; fields to explore – why, anything could happen on a day like this! Mercer's pond, and the . . .

Mercer's pond! He sat up with a jerk. Coo! He'd almost forgotten! He'd resolved to get up really early and try out the new newt-net at the pond. He scrambled out of bed wishing he knew what time it was. He looked at the clock; small hand on five, big hand on six. What'd Julie told him that meant? Never mind; it *felt* early. He dressed, quickly and inefficiently. No need to disturb Auntie Norah; she needed her sleep. And she'd only stop him, if she knew. . . .

After an anxious moment with the shop-door bolt, he stood out on the road, net grasped in one small fist, an old jam-jar in the other. The morning felt fresh and unused. The faintest breeze stirred the grass in the hedgerows, while from Mrs Long's apple tree a blackbird tried out a few arpeggios. With the arrogance of childhood, Ron accepted it all.

Then his eyes fell on the brief-case, standing below the post-box let into the wall. Coo! A bag! He swooped on the treasure, and raced off to Mercer's pond.

"Oh, there you are, Loder. Good morning." Threep came hastily into the lounge where George, after an early and solitary breakfast, sat reading yesterday's *Times*. "You didn't happen to see that brief-case of mine when we came in last night, did you?"

George looked up at the anxious face gazing down at his own. One didn't have to look at the odd shoes that Threep was wearing to tell that the man was preoccupied.

"I can't say that I did." George cast his mind back. 'You definitely had it when we left the pub, because you nearly hit me with it when you were describing your idea for a helicopter park in London. But I can't remember seeing you with it, here. Surely you haven't left it somewhere between here and the pub?"

"I'm beginning to think . . . ." Threep was interrupted by Gwyneth, bringing in the mail.

"Oh, I almost forgot, sir," she said, handing Threep a much-embossed letter, "I found ewer case, last night, down by the stile. Bob Farrer'll be bringing it up for 'oo, later."

Relief and puzzlement chased each other across Threep's face.

"Why Farrer? It wasn't all that heavy, was it?"

"No, but 'e carried it for me, see, and what with this and that I forgot to take it off 'im when we said good night." Gwyneth blushed.

George grinned. "This and that" described it beautifully. He, too, had said "Good night".

"Oh, I see." Threep didn't, really, but felt it might be indelicate to pursue the matter further. "Well, I'll ring up the station . . ." He paused. Lord knew what kind of tangle he'd get into if he tried to ring Farrer about it. Compared with a train's arrival, this matter was pretty complicated. "Perhaps you'll phone him? If he has the case with him, I'll go and fetch it."

"As 'oo please, sir." Gwyneth's disinterested compliance was ill-assumed. She hadn't expected a few minutes' talk with Bob, at this time in the morning. She went out to the phone in the hall.

"Lucky thing, that," commented George. "Anything

might have happened to the case if Gwyneth hadn't happened to pass by." Threep shuddered, and George continued, 'We weren't really in the mood to look after brief-cases, were we? I mean to say, your impersonation of the Speaker selling fruit was good, but not, shall we say, indicative of the watch and ward spirit."

"I wouldn't like to lose that case, Loder. There are several papers in it that I'm working on; between you and me, they're not the kind of thing one likes to have noised abroad."

George was a hundred per cent for this kind of thing. M.P.s with secret documents all over the place. Urgent B.B.C. appeals for lost brief-cases. If only there were a spy or so, as well! Still, you can't have everything. If they were in Brazil, now . . .

Gwyneth hurried into the room, eyes clouded.

"Oh, sir," she wailed, "Bob 'aven't got ewer case! 'E said 'e thought I 'ad it, but I 'aven't!"

"Then where the – then where is it?" Threep tried to pitch his voice in a normal key.

"I can't say for sure, sir, but I think we must've left it outside the post office, last night!"

There was a rush of wind, and George and Gwyneth found themselves alone in the lounge as Threep stood in the hall frantically phoning the post office.

"Mrs Long? This is Mr Threep speaking. Good morning. Have you seen anything of a brief-case on the road outside your shop? No, a BRIEF-CASE. On the road. You'll look now? Yes, I'll hold on." Pause. "Yes?" Pause. "Yes? No? Brown pigskin, two locks, and my initials on the flap. Never mind what it looks like. If there are *any* brief-cases at all on the road outside, they are mine." Threep was rapidly approaching hysteria. "Oh. Well, if you hear of anyone finding one, please let me know. Thank you. Good-bye."

Threep slowly replaced the receiver and turned around to encounter Stefan's blank stare.

"Yes?" Threep couldn't give Stefan his full measure of attention.

"Pliz. Orders for day. You say. No?"

"No. Come back later. See Madam. Understand?"

Stefan nodded and went out, much to Threep's relief. His cup was full enough without having to indulge in a crazy cross-talk act with the chauffeur.

Outside, Stefan thought quickly. The brief-case, eh? How had it got outside the post office? And where was it now? Not a bad idea to go down to the post office and have a look around; there'd be time before Mrs Bollanger came downstairs. He couldn't let this Heaven-sent opportunity go by.

A few minutes later, he stopped the car outside the post office, whose half-open door showed a shop full of customers. (Three average-sized people were enough to give Winthringham Post Office the appearance of a trade boom.) He stood outside a moment, and lighted a cigarette.

Now what? He didn't want to go in there and ask his questions in front of a lot of gossiping women. And he hadn't much time.

"Wanna buy some newts, Mister?" Ar Ron paused hopefully in front of him, a revolting-looking jar of water, slime, spawn and newts held temptingly aloft. His other hand grasped a cane, a cane which had once proudly born a net, now – alas! – sunk without a trace.

Stefan looked down at Ron, interest and disgust vying with each other. The boy had obviously caught his newts by the unorthodox method of going down after them one by one. He couldn't have got into that mess by legitimate means. Ron pressed his wares.

"Gottum first fing vis morning, before anyone wiz up. You kin 'ave um fer frippence," he said, naming his top price. Ron felt that it was pointless to deal in chicken-feed. Think big, was his motto.

"'Aven't 'ad me breckfuss, yet," he volunteered, to put this prospective buyer at his ease. Then came the real object of the transaction. "Don't suppose Auntie Norah'll give me any, if she sees these."

Stefan thought. Out early? How early? He spoke slowly and carefully, with an accent which would have opened the locals' eyes.

"Did you see a case – a brown case – out here this morning? I might buy your newts if you tell me the truth."

Ron nodded. "'S. It wiz down vere." He pointed to the bottom of the wall, by the post-box. "I took it."

Stefan started. Was this his lucky day, or was the lad lying?

"And where is it now? Speak the truth. You know what happens to boys who tell lies?"

Ron nodded his head vigorously. "'S. Vey don't get no pudden." The transgressor's punishment could be terrible. No pudden.

"So you will speak the truth? You will tell me where zis – this case is?"

Ron thought. He hadn't a high opinion of this man, but it was Thursday, caramel-pudden day. Yes, the truth was called for.

"I've left it in Mercer's pond," he said, simply.

"Mercer's pond?"

"'S. I stood on it to keep me feet dry, but it sunk down in ve mud. Broke me net, too," he added ruefully.

"Broke your neck?" If this were truth . . .

"Me net. See?" The cane was exhibited as proof.

86

"I see. Now, if you'll come in the car with me and show me just where the case went down in the mud, you can have a new net, I'll buy your newts, and you can have an extra sixpence. Will you come?"

Ron gasped. This was fortune! This man must be a million-aire – probably spent frippence a day on toys alone! He started to climb into the car.

"Ron!" Authority reached out from the shop counter. "Come in 'ere at once. What d'ye mean be goin' out without no breakfast?"

Ron rebounded from the car like a golf-ball. "I gotter go," he explained, unnecessarily. Before Stefan could stop him, Ron was in the post office, trying to convince Mrs Long that he'd been the victim of circumstance. Cursing his luck, Stefan drove back to The Leas.

Mrs Bollanger waited for him, dressed for going out. She looked like a woman who has been waiting some time.

"Stefan," she enunciated, coldly and distinctly, "WHERE HAVE YOU BEEN?"

Stefan did his perplexed foreigner act. Mrs Bollanger started to repeat her question, then thought better of it. Life was short. "I want to go in to Sede," she said, "and stop at the Vicarage on the way."

Stefan nodded brightly and held open the door.

It was hard to shake Mrs Bollanger out of her normal sang-froid, but she gaped into the car like a drunk at a two-headed calf. Stefan's eyes followed her startled gaze.

On the floor, nestling comfortably in the deep pile of the purple mat, was a jar of newts. Water had slopped out of it, creating a small pool in which strange fauna cavorted without improving the interior of the car. And Stefan, whose silver tongue had once saved him from a firing-squad in Ecuador, was speechless.

Tight-lipped, Mrs Bollanger watched him remove the offending aquarium.

"I don't mind you fishing, Stefan, but you must NOT use the car. Do you understand? *Not use car for fish.* Car not place for fish!"

Stefan nodded glumly as his thoughts wandered longingly to Ron. Just two minutes with him, that was all Stefan asked. He dabbed at the mess with a car-sponge.

As they drove off, Mrs Bollanger said, "Mr Loder will want the car for an hour or so, this afternoon; he'll drive himself. Bring it around at two-thirty."

Stefan cheered up. So Mr Loder was going to drive himself eh? At last things were beginning to go his way. A few minutes' work on the steering, and it was doubtful if Mr Loder would return! All he hoped was that Mr Loder liked a bit of speed. A week or so in hospital was just what friend Loder needed, if nothing worse!

8

The Mottram saloon, purring like a contented tiger, drew up at the steps of The Leas. George called from the hall as Stefan got out.

"Just leave it, Stefan. I'll be out in a moment or so."

The chauffeur saluted and turned away. So. Nothing had gone wrong. According to Gwyneth, Loder was going to the Sede library; far enough, surely, for the loosened bolt to vibrate off? After that – well, they'd see. Loder might even break his interfering neck. With which charitable thought, Stefan went back to the garage.

Of course, after the accident, some mechanically-minded busybody might notice that the steering had been tampered with, but that risk had to be taken. As Stefan saw it, the man who plays safe usually has little to show for it, except a clean record. He jacked up Threep's car, which was to have a new tyre fitted, and was soon involved in tyre levers and *sotto voce* bad language. He heard the Mottram leave, and the afternoon trickled slowly by.

The road from Sede to Winthringham is fairly straight, as Wiltshire roads go. It is a pretty highway, with enough gradients to take away the tedium of driving, and its low hedges are picturesque without hiding the sweeps of poppy-strewn ripening corn beyond. Now and then a flock of jumbling absent-minded sheep will test driving ability and patience; or a cow will amble nonchalantly in front of the car, hips and undercarriage swinging in unhurried rhythm. There are few dull moments.

There is one curve – a kind of half-straightened hairpin – not far from Rose Cottage, but nobody takes it seriously.

The Mottram, gleaming in the afternoon sun, sped along towards Winthringham. It had done the six miles from Sede in something under nine minutes, and felt a certain quiet satisfaction. A further pressure on the accelerator sent it smoothly up the rise past the lane leading to the Vicarage. At the summit, it leaped forward, the road flowing beneath it like a mill-stream. Its speed slackened just perceptibly as Rose Cottage whisked into view and it was aimed confidently straight at the bend. Straight, and still straight, as the steering-wheel swung uselessly between frantically-moving hands. Straight up the bank, to crash half-way through the hedge with a noise like a marquee being torn up by an infuriated giant. It halted, one wing crumpled, and a slightly self-conscious look on its radiator, pointing skywards.

"Point-and-Point-and-Point-and-Point," sang Polly appealingly to a disinterested dancing class. Seven small feet swung out, toes pointing, with the grace of lame turtles and the uniformity of falling leaves.

"Four o'clock." Polly tried not to sound relieved. After all, this was jam for her bread-and-butter. "That's all for today, then. Don't forget, we've only one more rehearsal before the actual fête." Seven small stomachs thrilled as they contemplated the imminence of their first public engagement. An appearance before All The Crowned Heads of Europe could hardly have been more awe-inspiring.

The class straggled away, exchanging slips and slippers for outdoor wear. Polly shepherded them down the path as the Mottram swung into view; it flashed past as she waved good-bye to the last little seeker after terpsichorean perfection. She heard the crash and turned around to see the car half-way through the hedge, looking strangely still after its seemingly irresistible passage up the road.

Polly ran to the car, calling for Mrs Watt as she went. Her legs felt like sticks of gelatine as she saw the figure slumped over the wheel. She tugged at the door, snagging dress and stockings in the briars and twigs; she gently eased the head back into the driving-seat. Eyes flickered open and gazed at her for what seemed minutes. Then the bloodless lips moved.

"Hallo, Gloria," said Threep, slowly and distinctly. A contented look passed over his face as his eyes re-closed. He began to snore gently.

Helen looked up from her book as George put an inquiring head around the lounge door.

"Ah, there you are," he remarked, unnecessarily.

Helen admitted it. "I thought you were going to the Sede library," she added.

"No, Threep wanted to go in on business, so he's getting my book. Besides, I wanted to speak to you. Alone," he continued, with a suspicious glance around the room for concealed Bollangers.

Helen laid down her book.

"I know what you're going to say, George dear, but there's nothing we can do about it. I've thought of everything I can . . ."

He seated himself at her side, separated, perhaps, by the thickness of a razor-blade.

"Have you thought of telling your mother that we're going to be married whether she likes it or not?"

Helen's imagination reared up on its haunches at this loose talk. People, she gave George to understand, just didn't do things without her mother's consent. Royal commands were faltering requests, compared with Mrs Bollanger's edicts. "No," she concluded, "Mother's made up her mind and . . . What is it, Gwyneth?"

Gwyneth stood at the door, gloomily important.

"Miss Fenner've just rang up from the post office, Miss Helen. Mr Threep've 'ad a naccident in the moto'. They've took the bod – they've took 'im to Rose Cottage, and sent for the doctor. Miss Fenner says will someone come down, please? Madam's over at Bilton."

George and Helen hurried to the garage, where Stefan was light-heartedly playing a hose over Threep's car. The chauffeur looked at George like someone who's been followed home by a cat he'd thought he'd drowned.

"Stefan," Helen climbed into her two-seater, "come with us to Rose Cottage. Mr Threep has had an accident; there might be something you can do. Get in, please."

Stefan shrugged himself into his jacket and put on his cap. What had happened? Threep must have taken the car at the last minute. How could one do one's job efficiently, thwarted at every turn by bungling politicians? He took one or two bolts from a shelf and climbed into the dickey of Helen's car.

A few minutes later, Polly opened the door of Rose Cottage to George and Helen.

"It's not quite so bad as it appeared at first," she said, in response to Helen's anxious inquiry. "Doctor is with him now." She led the way into the bedroom, Helen introducing a poker-faced George as they went in. He ducked instinctively in the presence of the murderous beams. The doctor pinned a bandage into place, and stood up.

"Well, he doesn't want too many cracks like that, but I think he'll do. There's a slight concussion, but nothing appears to be broken. Miss Fenner's kindly said that he can stay here for a while, and I'd advise that. Twenty-four hours without moving will make all the difference. I'll see him again, tomorrow, and we'll probably send him back to you then. Shall you need any help?" he asked Polly. "I'll send Nurse Adams, if you like."

"No, thank you. Mrs Watt and I can manage quite well. It isn't as if we'll have to sit up all night. Perhaps Miss Bollanger will send some things down for him, though?" She looked at Helen, who nodded thoughtfully.

Threep opened his eyes and gave a tentative glance around the room.

"Hallo, Helen," he quavered. "What happened?"

"Don't bother, Uncle. You've had a bit of a spill. Everything's all right, now. How do you feel?"

"Rotten," he answered, politely. He saw George, trying to look necessary, at the other side of the bed and tried to struggle up. "The case. Try and find the case. Don't report it, but . . ." Someone started hammering on his skull from the inside, and he sank back on to the pillow. The doctor stepped forward.

"That'll do. Try and sleep, now, unless you want to cause a by-election. There's no business all that important." He shooed George and Helen from the room, and remained to give Polly her instructions.

"What did he mean about the case?" asked Helen.

"He's mislaid his brief-case and wants me to help find it." George tried to make it sound unimportant. "I'll have a look around for it as soon as we get back."

They went out to the Mottram, where Stefan was doing technical things with the steering.

"Much damage, Stefan?" asked George.

"Littles. Maybe drive too fast for bend, sair?"

George wondered idly why Stefan was using a spanner, but

didn't pursue the matter, as Helen walked over to the two-seater.

"You stay here, please, Stefan," she ordered. "I'll phone the Bilton garage to come and tow the car in. They won't be long. Perhaps you'll come back with Uncle's things, George?"

As they drove off, Stefan busied himself removing the evidence of the faulty steering. The plan had miscarried, but he was lucky to be able to get at the car before the Bilton mechanic saw it. He looked up as a shadow fell across his work.

"'Allo, Mister."

Ron stooped interestedly beside him, intending to miss nothing of this heaven-sent diversion. Stefan paused. His hands itched to avenge the newt episode, but better judgement stayed the stinging swipe. Tact was called for.

"Ah, the fish boy. Tell me, where did you leave the case we were talking about?"

"In ve pond."

"Yes, but where?"

"In ve wa'er."

Control. Self-control, thought Stefan. Much as he'd have liked to tear this lad apart, he must string along with him until he'd got the vital information.

"WHAT PART OF THE POND IS IT IN?"

"Just by where ve 'oller tree is."

Stefan remembered. Yes, there was an 'oller tree, stunted and twisted, between the pond and the road. It shouldn't be hard to probe around there.

"Very well. If you are telling the truth I'll give you a shilling. If not, the police will come for you."

Ron shuddered. Ever since a small error of judgement involving a cricket-ball, a window, and an aspidistra, in

94

Camden Town, he'd had a healthy respect for the police. Anyway, a bob was a bob; more than pay for the newts this bloke had pinched from him.

His mind switched back to the car. Didn't seem quite right for it to be here. He mentioned this. Then he started to question Stefan. He was still questioning when, to Stefan's relief, the breakdown truck pulled up.

In Rose Cottage, Polly sipped a thoughtful cup of tea. Gloria. He'd called her by a name she'd almost forgotten. Fancy his remembering, and she hardly knew him from Adam; except by name, of course. As far as she could remember, this was her first meeting with Milton Threep, though she'd seen him once or twice. She wondered which show he'd seen her in. 'Lucky Boy'? 'Lads and Lasses'? There were so many. Well, it was nice to know that Gloria Dean was still remembered.

She opened the door and peeped in. Sleeping. Good. He looked so helpless, lying there. Like an elderly Puck. Not *really* old, of course; just at what Polly would call the sensible age. And he'd recognized her immediately, even after the shock of the accident. Her eyes became moist as she stepped softly from the room.

George stepped over the stile on to the Sede Road. Six o'clock. Might as well go and report the loss of the case to the police. No need to mention the importance of its contents – Threep didn't want a hue-and-cry if there was a possibility of finding it without. There'd be a police station of sorts somewhere about. This chap would know.

Homing on the newly-opened doors of the Angry Hen came one eager of pace and parched of throat. His eyes were fixed on the doorway with the purposeful gaze of one who sees Heaven within his reach. George waylaid him.

"Could you tell me where I can find the police station?"

The man paused. If ever Wiltshire needed an advertisement, he was it. His face reminded George of three tomatoes, two large ones for the cheeks, and a slightly smaller one for the nose. Thick white hair stuck up stiffly from a brown forehead. Shrewd blue eyes, mobile as mercury, seemed to be assessing George's wealth within about two per cent.

"You'm a stranger, then?"

George admitted it, with due humility. An oversight on his parents' part, of course, but there it was. He hadn't been born in Wiltshire.

"Well, you'm quite a ways from the p'lice station. Oi could run 'ee there in me taxi, if 'ee loikes."

George rapidly put two and two together.

"Amos Flower, I presume? I hope you did well with your peg, at Sede."

Amos stepped back. This chap knew a lot, for someone who'd never seen him before. A detective, maybe? No; if he was he'd surely be able to detect his way to the police station. Perhaps one of them thought-readers? What did they call 'em?

"Be you one o' they telepathetic blokes?"

"No, but it sounds good."

"'Ow d'ye know about Oi, then?"

"Elementary, my dear Flower. I'd heard that Amos Flower ran a taxi, and that you'd gone to market on Tuesday. Now, if you'll just direct me to . . ."

"Oi s'pose you'm from London." All strangers came from London. "Well, our p'lice bain't so many as they Scotland Yard crew. P.C. Ammidge d' deal wi' all our crime in these parts; much good it dooz 'n," he added with a certain bitterness.

George had a brief but entertaining vision of P.C. Ammidge, complete with forensic lab., criminal dossiers, and police-dogs, grimly hounding down the vice-rings of Bilton Parva.

"Well, assuming he's not out after his man now, where am I likely to find him?"

"Yurr."

"Wurr – I mean, where?"

"Yurr. Thic cottage, near th' Angry 'En. See 'n?"

George saw 'n, a small cottage, almost hidden by privet and creeper, lying back from the road.

"But I thought you said it was a long way from here?" he said, not unreasonably. Even a Texas oil-magnate would think twice about taking a taxi that distance.

"No, Oi didn't. Oi said the p'lice station were. P.C. Ammidge comes down of an evenin' to give a 'and to 'is Ma's garden." There seemed to be no prospect of an immediate fare and good licencing hours were fleeting unmoistened. "Oi'll leave 'ee, now, Mister. Don't forget, if you d' want a taxi in a 'urry, leave a message at the 'En, or in the post office. Oi'll get 'n, sooner or later. S'long." He disappeared into the welcoming portals like a rabbit into its burrow.

George turned towards the cottage, then paused as a familiar figure trudged up the road towards the post office.

"Hallo, Ron," he called.

Ron acknowledged the greeting, somewhat dispiritedly.

"What's the trouble?" asked George.

"I can't find ve case."

"Case? What case?" Not Threep's, surely? Or was ar Ron really Fate, in an earthly form? If so, the disguise was perfect.

"Ve brown case wiv ve shiny locks, wot I put in ve pond." The questions some people asked! "Ge'man wants it, but it's sunk down into ve mud."

"Which gentleman?" George was sure about the case, but the gentleman raised a complication. Threep certainly hadn't seen Ron today.

"Ge'man in a blue suit. 'E's very rich. Gotter big car."

It was beyond George. Still, the point was that the case might be rescued without any publicity. "Where is it now?" he asked.

"In ve gerridge, I s'pose."

"Not the car; the case."

Ron told him, and described the spot. "An' it's gorn right down in ve mud – right down to Orstrilia," he concluded.

George could well believe this. Mercer's pond was no aqua incognita to him. Still, it was worth a search. Surely if one probed about with a stick, or, better still, a rake . . . ?

"All right, Ron. I'll try and find it. If I do, I'll give you five shillings. Better run off home, now.'

Ron ran off contentedly. It had been a good day, after all. Except for that bloke pinching his newts.

George hurried back to the house. Dinner first, then a rake and a good pair of rubber boots, and back to the pond. Or should he send Stefan down? Better not, perhaps; the fewer people who knew about it, the better. Besides, he remembered, Mrs Bollanger had sent Stefan to Salisbury with a vegetable contribution to the Woman's Institute rally. Well, finding the case would do Threep more good than a gallon of medicine.

The moon was just disentangling itself from the 'oller tree when George returned to Mercer's pond. One thing after another had conspired to delay him. Mrs Bollanger had kept him talking – or, rather, listening – after dinner on the subject of letting Threep go out to have an accident that had been clearly meant for George. Then he'd had to take her and Helen to see the invalid, carrying various necessaries. Now, it was nearly quarter past ten.

Here was the pond, still as a half-crown on a billiard-table. It looked vaguely mysterious, and very deep. George waded in to the spot indicated by ar Ron, and started to probe about with a rake borrowed from the garden shed.

Nothing. His sleeves became clammy, and he suspected that his left boot was leaking. Had the damn' case gone down to Orstrilia? The moon looked up at him, its brow furrowed with the pond's ripples.

A sound, half-cough, half-burp, made him look around. Amos Flower stood by the single-strand wire fence, swaying gently like a poppy in the breeze. Amos, one gathered, had had no more than usual.

"You'll never get 'n that way," he informed George, gravely.

"Get what?"

"Wot you be arter, o' course." A hand waved vaguely towards the pond, a risky gesture for one who needed both hands and a firm lamp-post for the efficient maintenance of balance. He swayed dangerously, at impossible angles.

"And what, precisely, am I after?" George wasn't in the mood to humour drunks. There was water up his sleeve, and some zoological freak with forty-three legs was crawling down his back. Water, lapping quietly around his calf, confirmed his suspicions regarding the left boot's unseaworthiness.

"The moon. You be moonraking, bisn't?"

"Moonraking?"

"Ar. 'Tis said that Wilshermen d' try to rake the moon outer ponds. Thass woi we be called Moonrakers. But that rake's no good, that's sartin."

99

"Oh? And why not?" George felt that he had to know why this particular rake wasn't up to the perfectly ordinary job of raking a moon out of a pond.

"'Tis a 'ay-rake, you needs."

George fought off the feeling of unreality.

"Don't be absurd. I'm trying to find something."

"Danged good place to look for 'n, too," commented Amos. "Woi don' 'ee go an' look for 'n outside the 'En? They got more light there."

"You go along home," advised George.

Amos drew himself up. Nobody was going to tell him to go home. Free country, wasn't it?

"Oi'll bide wurr Oi'm to," he stated, categorically.

"All right; bide where you're to. See if I care. But isn't anyone waiting for you at home?" asked George.

This drew a sentimental burst of music from Amos:

"There's a queen waiting there," he informed George, wheezily,

"With 'er silvery 'air,
'N a shanty in o-o-ole Shanty Town."

He struck the classic busking pose, one hand cupping the ear, the other outstretched in supplication, but the effort proved too much for his already overworked stabilizing mechanism. He swayed, fell to his hands and knees, and looked up at George reproachfully.

"Fancy pushin' a man old enough to be thy vaather," he chided, more in sorrow than anger.

"Pushed you? I didn't push you! Why, you old stinker, you're pie-eyed! You need buttressing. Don't you know when you've had enough?"

The remark hit Amos on the raw.

"Oi knows w'en Oi've 'ad enough," he said, with all the

dignity of a man on his hands and knees, "w'en Oi've 'ad enough Oi falls over backuds," he explained.

George accepted the implied rebuke.

"Here," he offered, "give me your hand."

Amos took the proffered hand, waited until George heaved, then let go suddenly. George sat back in the pond, up to his waist in ooze. He remained a moment, thinking uncomplicated, vengeful thoughts. Amos cackled gleefully.

"Sarves 'ee roight! That'll teach 'ee! There's a nold sayin' 'bout 'e'oo laffs last laffs laffs laffs . . ." He tailed off, uncertainly. The sentence was too ambitious, and he realized that he should never have started it.

George, meanwhile, rose slowly to his feet, his hands slipping in the clayey mud. A sudden thrill shot through him as his groping fingers encountered a leather handle. He drew it out, slimy and weed-decked.

"There you are! See? Eureka!" he shouted, waving his treasure at Amos. Neither of them noticed a third face, ears akimbo, peering at them over a near-by blackberry bush.

Stefan thought furiously. Again, this Loder had thwarted him at the last minute! Even so, one had to admire Loder's information service. He'd beaten Stefan to it by a short head. Right! Somewhere between here and The Leas, the case must change hands. No mistakes this time!

George splodged out of the pond and away towards a hot bath and a drink. Amos, who wasn't quite abreast of events, turned and sinusoided off up the road, the strains of "Buttercup Joe" floating beerily in his wake.

Arrived at The Leas, George stopped warily outside the garden-shed. He wasn't particularly anxious for anyone to see or smell him in his present condition. He'd just return the rake and rubber boots, put on the shoes he'd left there, and nip away for a bath and a whisky-and-soda. He laid the case down by the door, turned the key, and went in.

He stepped carefully inside the door, mindful of the para-phenalia the place contained. One doesn't attempt a *pas seul* in a dark garden-shed. Lawn-mowers, scythes, and garden-rollers all wait in ambush to dissect, or remove the rough edges from the unwary. George trod delicately.

To no purpose. A sudden shove from behind sent him staggering into the shed. A garden-roller, never missing a trick, got in some fine shin work *en route*, causing him to measure his length with his head resting in a potted plant. The plant, had George known it, was a simple *Rhus cotinus atropurpurea*.

Even as he scrambled to his feet, he heard the key turn in the lock outside. He was alone with his thoughts, the garden tools, and the *Rhus cotinus atropurpurea*.

And no brief-case.

9

The dying sun's red-gold rays slanted in through Polly's window, setting her hair aflame as she bent over some sewing. The evening was deliciously cool and loud with the silence of the country. Birds which had whistled happily during the day now twittered snappishly at each other, overtired, no doubt, by the extra hours of sunshine. Gnats whined up and down in that incessant, irritating way that gnats have. A wasp, trapped in a window-corner just above Polly's head, zoomed repeatedly against the glass, wondering what the hell.

Polly looked up from her work as she heard vague waking noises from the bedroom. Her patient – she liked that phrase – could take his medicine now, if he were awake. She peeped in through the half-open door.

Threep smiled at her palely as she stole into the room. It was the smile of a man who's found that running a Mottram into a hedge has its compensations. Polly smiled back, and his spine twanged like Top E.

"How are you feeling now?"

"Bit of a headache, otherwise reasonably sound, thank you," he answered, hoping she'd realize how ill – how uncomplainingly ill – he was.

"You had a nasty knock, you know. I was quite frightened until you spoke to me. Do you remember what you said?" asked Polly.

"No. A critical remark or so about the car, perhaps? If so, I'll apologize now."

"No. You said 'Hallo, Gloria'. Why did you call me that?"

"Only because your name happens to be Gloria; I suppose I should have called you Miss Dean, but I wasn't right on top of my form at the time. You *are* Gloria Dean, aren't you? Of course you are."

"Was," said Polly, "but . . ."

"Oh you're married?" Was there a hint of disappointment in his voice? A faintly yellow tinge of jealousy around the edges of his words? "Naturally, you would be."

"No, I'm not married. Gloria Dean was my stage name for a while, but I've left show business now. My real name isn't half so romantic. Polly Fenner."

"Polly Fenner." He rolled the words around his tongue. "Polly. It's a lovely name. It's only that I've always thought of you as 'Gloria' since I saw you in 'C'mon, Gang!' Remember it?"

"Do I! Ran for seven months, and had 'em rolling in the aisles at every performance. Remember Rino and Bettina, the Italian dancing act? They made enough to start a small café, out of 'C'mon, Gang!', and went back home."

"Back to Italy?"

"Italy? They came from Bootle. Harry and Betty Maggs. And how about Jack Flash, the magician? He's the famous Prestini, now. Oh, they were good old days!"

Threep sighed. "Yes, it's certainly more years ago than I care to . . ."

"Not so long as all that, surely?" Polly eyed him a trifle coldly. He was overstressing the silver threads among the gold theme. Threep saw his mistake.

"Well, not really. Just seems a long time. What would you say it was – seven years?"

She laughed suddenly. "Well, perhaps a little longer than

that. Now, you take this drop of medicine and pop off to sleep. We'll have a nice long talk in the morning."

She ladled the medicine into a compliant throat, then placed a thermometer between his lips. A thought struck him.

"Eye doo ont leez iss clace?" he asked, curiously.

"A fair question," said Polly, deftly removing the obstruction. "Now, what did you say?"

"I asked why you wanted to leave this place. Too quiet for you here, I suppose?"

"*I* don't want to leave. Mrs Bollanger wants me to. I could stay for ever. I love it here."

Threep pondered this. Really, Hester was the limit! How long was she going to be allowed to get away with this bull-dozing policy, just shoving people aside for her own convenience? And telling him that Polly wanted to leave, too!

"Tell me," he asked, "just to gratify a sick man's whim, who was the man who was here with you, the day before yesterday? Miss Kettle saw him, and didn't recognize him. Feels a bit frustrated about it. She told Mrs Bollanger, though, and *she'll* find out, even if she has to engage a dowser to do it."

Polly looked at him a moment. Why not tell him? Anyone could see that he could be trusted. She made up her mind.

"George Loder," she said, simply.

Had she said the U.S. President, or even David Livingstone, she couldn't have created a greater impression. Polly, who'd always had an eye on public reaction, felt a certain satisfaction. Threep was surprised, and made no attempt to hide it. His jaw dropped like a mechanical scoop.

"L-Loder?" he mouthed. "Helen's – er —?"

"Yes. Helen's er. Why not? We met purely – and 'purely' is the operative word – by accident, and hadn't seen each other for years. He couldn't have been expected to meet Mrs Bollanger in that state. . . ."

"What state?"

"All over mud."

"Mud? Dammit – er, pardon – it wasn't raining that day, was it? It wasn't raining at The Leas, anyway," he pointed out, in the interests of meteorological accuracy.

"No, but he'd just been in Mercer's pond . . ."

"Good Lord! Eccentric, isn't he?"

Polly paused. She couldn't help feeling that perhaps she wasn't telling this properly. That Threep wasn't with her was fairly obvious, though nobody could criticize him as a listener. Shades of astonishment passed and re-passed over his face, like a man watching a rapid succession of card tricks. Polly tried again, starting at the beginning to see if that helped.

"He arrived here on an earlier train, before he was expected" – this certainly rang true, to Threep – "and decided to walk up to The Leas. I met him just after he'd pulled a little boy out of the pond. He came here with me for a wash and brush-up."

"I see. Nothing indiscreet in that, surely?"

"Nothing at all, except that Mrs Watt happened to be out, and Mrs Bollanger called on me while George was in here – er – changing."

"My word! You do live, don't you? What happened?"

"He hid under the bed until Mrs Bollanger had gone, then went back to the station and pretended he'd just arrived on the four-thirty."

Threep chewed this over. Young Loder'd certainly carried it off well. And fancy his knowing Glo – Polly. Must have a chat about it, some time. Meanwhile . . .

"I see," he said, thoughtfully. "That explains a lot. If

Hester ever finds out that it was Loder whom Miss Kettle saw, there'll be no wedding-bells for him. And Helen'd have you out of here so quick that you'd be dizzy."

"Anyway," said Polly, "don't you worry about it. You should be sleeping, now, not concerning yourself with my problems."

"You're very kind to me. I hope I'm not being too much of a nuisance."

"Not at all. I'd do it for anyone. Especially you," she added. "After all, we *are* old friends, really, aren't we?"

"We are. And listen" – his voice became almost fierce – "you're *not* going to leave this cottage. Is that understood? You're staying here, or I'll know the reason why!"

And Polly felt that he meant it.

Mrs Bollanger put down her empty milk-glass like someone trumping an ace.

"Where did you say Mr Loder's gone?" she asked.

Helen avoided her eye.

"He said he was going for a walk. He should . . ."

"A walk? At this time of the night? More likely gone back to that public house again! The man's never happy unless what passes for his brain is swimming in alcohol!"

Helen thought this a trifle unfair, but said nothing. Where did it get you? Better let the steam-roller go straight over one, than have it stop half-way.

"Well," Mrs Bollanger issued her ukase, "I'm going to lock up as usual. If he's sober when he returns he'll ring the bell. If not, he'll probably spend the night out, sleeping it off in some outhouse or other. I know that type too well."

"I dare say, Mother," answered Helen, unthinkingly.

Her mother aimed a suspicious glance at her, but said

nothing. She rose, locked the front door, then came back and paused significantly in the lounge doorway. Helen obediently went up to bed, Mrs Bollanger snapping off the lights after her as she went.

If Mr Loder *did* ring the door-bell, he'd have her to face. And if he showed the slightest sign of liquor —!

George sat on the garden-roller, nursing his aching shin. What weisenheimer had played this trick on him? And what was the point of it? He stood up to hammer on the locked door, then thought better of it. Nearly eleven o'clock. The first person aroused would be Mrs Bollanger. He just knew it. Then he'd have to explain. Blast Mercer's pond! And Mercer with it. May his pegs never fatten!

His eyes became more used to the gloom, and he was able to inspect his cell. The moon's rays, filtering through the dusty window-panes, showed him the door; not very solid, but strong enough to make an unholy row if he tried to break it down.

He looked at it more closely. Ah! The two iron hinges were each fixed by three screws into the wooden cross-pieces. He cast around for a screwdriver, or something in lieu. Never again, he vowed, would he come out without a screwdriver, a jemmy, torch and battering-ram. Here in the country, a man couldn't call himself dressed without them. Apparently his luck wasn't completely out; he found a small, sharp-pointed trowel on the bench. George commenced Operation Break-out.

Half an hour later, he stood outside the shed, free but perplexed. The case was gone. Why? Covered in mud and weeds, it had certainly been no *objet d'art*; nor could it have been easily seen in the shadow down by the door. It suddenly dawned on George that somebody'd seen him put the case there – had probably followed him from the pond for the purpose of getting it.

Who? Ar Ron's man in blue? But, according to Ron, the man was very rich; at any rate, he'd gotter big car. If so, then the thing smacked of being a Political Crime. And he, George, was in it! Right up to the uvula! Cloak and dagger stuff!

He walked thoughtfully up to the front door, automatically turned the handle, and tried to step in. He nearly broke his nose as the door proved adamant. Locked? But surely everyone knew that he was out? And he daren't rouse the house, in this mess.

He crept stealthily around the building, cautiously trying windows and doors in the hope that one might have been left undone. There were none; the place might have been a feudal castle, prepared for one of King John's week-end visits.

He felt a bitter sense of injustice that he, an honest man, should find the place barricaded as if for a siege, while the thief of the other night had apparently walked in with a civic welcome. One law for the rich. . . .

He could ring the door-bell, of course. Nothing to stop him. And Mrs Bollanger would open the door. And she'd look at him. And he'd say – he'd say – he'd — Well, don't just stand there. Find a way in.

Then he saw the window, gaping invitingly open on the first floor at the side of the house. If he remembered rightly, that window gave on to the narrow stairway which ran from the kitchen to the top of the house; it was a kind of servants' stairway-cum-fire-exit. Once inside, he could go up to the attics, down one flight of the main staircase, then – ho! – for a bath and a bed. He'd have to forgo the drink for which his thirsty soul craved, but you can't have everything. Blessing the scatter-brained spirit that had left the window open he went for the ladder at the side of the garage. . . .

George crept as quietly as possible up the narrow, un-carpeted stair. Each step creaked in agony as he carefully placed his weight on it. He couldn't have felt more obvious if he'd been playing bagpipes. Up, ever up. At this rate, he'd soon be needing an oxygen supply. His heart bled for the unknown servants who had to use this treadmill daily, wearing out tissues and becoming old before their time, like . . .

A door! Closed, but unlocked, praise be! Excelsior! This must be the top. He stepped through on to a carpeted landing, dark and silent.

He went quietly down the main stairway, footsteps muffled by the thick carpet, the stairs creaking gently to his tread. Here was the door, just at the turn of the banister. It was like reaching port after a particularly rough Channel crossing.

The door-handle gave an almighty squeak as he turned it. He skipped quickly into the room, and was feeling his way forward to switch on the bedside-lamp when it was obligingly done for him. He gasped like a fish that's suddenly found itself on top of a flagpole as —

"Good evening, Mr Loder," said Mrs Bollanger, sitting up in bed.

For a moment or so, George's sense of propriety was shocked at the sight of Mrs Bollanger making herself at home in his bed. Then it dawned on him that the room felt un-familiar; it wasn't his. It *could* be Mrs Bollanger's.

He also remembered that her room was directly below his own. Somehow, he must have miscalculated the flights of stairs – probably when he was climbing the back stairway. Whatever he'd done, he'd certainly done it completely.

"I – I'm sorry," he said, inadequately. "I'm afraid I'm in the wrong room."

"I'm afraid you are. Whose room did you want?" It was just a quarter to twelve.

"Nobody's. I mean, my own. I went out for a walk, and I . . ."

"Fishing, no doubt?" Mrs Bollanger held a handkerchief delicately to her nose and looked pointedly at George's trousers.

"I happened to stumble into Mercer's pond. I'm a bit muddy, I'm afraid."

"You've a gift for understatement, Mr Loder. This happened on your way home, I presume?"

"Yes." Then he saw the point. "I hadn't had a drink, if that's what you mean."

"Of course not. You just happened to fall into a wired-off pond on a bright moonlight night. Then you found it a little difficult to remember which floor your room is on. It could happen to anyone. It *would* happen to you."

"Look here . . ." began George, warmly.

"I *am* looking, Mr Loder. And I think you'd better go and have a bath and do something about that mud. We'll discuss this in the morning, when you're more hygienic. Do you need a guide to show you to your room? No? Then I'll wish you good night."

George slouched away, little white-hot fires leaping up in his breast. What a woman! What a day! If this was a sample of the drowsy peace of the country, he preferred the quiet backwater of London. The pace was too fast for this simple city boy.

10

George awoke next morning with a sense of frustration hanging over him. He lit a cigarette and lay in bed, summing up events. The total wasn't a strikingly happy one.

To begin with, his wedding had been postponed for about seventy-three years, and, after last night's affair, there didn't seem to be any chance of its acceleration.

Then there was Polly's impending eviction. He'd have liked to have been able to plead her cause with Mrs Bollanger, if all had gone well. But, as matters stood, if he raised his voice in Polly's defence she'd be out quicker than a match in a gale.

At the same time, he was being hag-ridden by Myrtle Kettle. As soon as she realized that he was the man she'd seen going into Rose Cottage, she'd make the welkin ring until it cracked. And, he suspected, her triumph would be all the greater because it would allow her to score off Mrs Bollanger.

And what about Threep? Just when the missing case had been in his, George's hands, he'd let it go through sheer carelessness. What was Threep going to say? Probably have a relapse, or a brainstorm or whatever it is that people who've just had concussion have. Especially when he heard that there was an organized attempt to steal the case. No, it wasn't the kind of information to put an invalid on the high road to recovery.

He glanced at the clock. Six-thirty. Gwyneth wouldn't be around with the tea for nearly an hour. Through the open window the sun beckoned and a blackbird called. The curtains waved just perceptibly, and a smell of morning came into the room. George, who in London would have considered this almost dead of night, levered himself up and out of bed.

A few minutes later, in flannels and sweater, he was strolling around the sunken garden, digging in to his share of the morning. The stillness was accentuated by the birds' song; dew-spangled cobwebs, like bridal veils, were hung out to dry on the lavender bushes whose perfume drenched the air.

Sparrows braced their legs and heaved manfully at reluctant worms who were resolving never to be early again if they ever got out of this mess. Caterpillars moved purposefully along their chosen twigs and, having reached the end, pretended they'd been meaning to go back, anyway. It was an English summer morning, the kind the old folk used to have under Gladstone.

In the ornamental pond, sleek well-fed goldfish tooled nonchalantly to and fro. George leaned over to watch one red monster whose favourite exercise was obviously swimming, which it did well. Large goggle eyes glared sideways at George, probably remarking how gracefully these bifurcated beings got about on land.

It was a small, nondescript sort of fish that showed the brief-case to George. It nuzzled it, hovered over it, tried to read the initials on the flap, then swam in and around the handle. The next moment, its fishy world split apart as George jumped in and grabbed the case from under its surprised gills.

Yes, this was it, all right! George hastily opened it up, heedless of the water which splashed over him. Except for a handful of mud, and a bewildered minnow, the case was empty. Not that he'd expected anything else. But – and here was the pertinent question – why had the thief come here to search and discard the case? Why hadn't he legged it straight for the open country after he'd grabbed it, last night? George mulled the matter over as he rinsed the case in clear water and wandered off in search of a bath and bacon and eggs.

His spirits rose slightly, over breakfast. Mrs Bollanger had not appeared, and George and Helen had the meal on their own. It felt cosy and domestic, helping each other to sugar-bowl and toast-rack. His mind dwelt longingly on a future stretching into thousands of breakfasts together; a golden age of bacon and eggs.

"The Vicar've called to see 'oo, Miss. Says 'e's sorry to trouble 'oo, but claims it's urgent." Gwyneth stood demurely in the doorway.

"Show him in here please, Gwyneth."

The Reverend Honeydew came heartily amongst them with the offensive smugness of a man who's breakfasted hours ago. He radiated goodwill and after-shave lotion.

"Good morning, Helen. Good morning, Mr Loder. A wonderful morning, what?" He'd obviously had a hand in its creation, somewhere. "I do hope you'll forgive this intrusion, but . . ."

"Not at all, Vicar." Helen made welcoming noises. "You know we love to see you at any time. Will you have some coffee? Tea?"

"Thank you, no. I'm really on my way to see Miss Kettle. She seems to be having trouble with her chincherinchees" – George avoided Helen's eyes – "She doesn't take enough care of them, of course." George felt inclined to agree.

"I've had a card from the Sede library," continued the Vicar, "and they tell me that they have that other biography of Colonel Cobberleigh. I wonder . . ."

"Of course," Helen broke in, "I'll go along right after breakfast. I can hardly wait." She turned to George. "The

114

Vicar and I are doing a little research on Colonel Cobberleigh; he was one of the notables around here, about a hundred years ago."

"Helen has been a wonderful help, sir," chimed in the Vicar, enthusiastically, "I'm writing a book dealing with the local history, and she's been looking up facts for me in the archives. I shall be eternally in her debts."

"And why does Colonel Cobberleigh claim immortality?" George wanted to know.

"He was an eccentric old gentleman who lived at the old Manor, outside Bilton. Had a habit of shooting at the railway trains – a new invention, then – as they went past his house. But Helen is the authority on the Colonel. She'll tell you more than I can."

"I think he was rather sweet, really," said Helen. "He was always working to raise the standard of living of the local peasantry. Used to try to teach them all sorts of crafts, to bring money into the district. He's supposed to have made a wonderful wine from local herbs. Something like mead, only more potent. The recipe has been lost, I'm afraid, but there's no doubt that the wine was very popular. 'Luno', it was called."

The Vicar rose.

"Well, I must leave you, then. Do let me know if you find anything startling. After all, the new book may contain the recipe, what? I suppose that would be too much to ask!" His laugh echoed through the hall as Helen showed him out.

She came back into the room. "George, dear, I really must go into the library, now that the book is there. I'm sorry to leave you on your own, but I'd like you to be here in case Uncle Milton wants driving back from Rose Cottage this morning. I'll be back by eleven, easily. Do you mind?"

"Not at all; I was going to see Threep, anyway. I suppose you'll call in on your way to Sede?"

"Yes. I *do* hope he's better. He seemed very much improved, last evening. I've never seen him so cheerful since Mother went to Nice," she added, naïvely.

After Helen had gone, George took Threep's car and drove to the post office. He must try and find out more about the mysterious rich man from ar Ron. Ron's descriptions were apt to be a trifle vague, of course, but he might get a clue to finding the man in blue.

He found Ron idly swinging on a gate near the post office. If ever a boy was fed up with *dolce far niente*, that boy was Ron. He brightened up as George, a potential five bob, drove up and switched off the engine.

"'Lo, Mister. Didger find it?"

"Hallo, Ron. Yes, I found it all right. I suppose I owe you five shillings, even if I didn't get what I wanted. We Loders remain indebted to no man."

"Di'n't get it? I fought you said you found it?"

"I did, but it was empty by the time I looked inside."

"I know. I emptied it."

"You?" George shot seven and a half inches into the air. "Don't say *you* locked me in that shed?" His head swam a little, trying to pin down facts.

"Shed? No, 'twan't me. Honest." The idea struck him as a good one, but it wasn't his. "I said I emptied ve bag. Vere was a lot of ole papers in it, all tied up wiv red string. I tookem out before I used ve case to stand on, in ve mud."

"And what did you do with the papers?"

"'Id 'em in ve 'oller tree, by Mercer's pond. In a nundred years time, someone'll find 'um, and vey'll be a clue to ve treasure."

"What treasure?"

"I dunno; but people allus 'ides papers in 'oller trees, so I done it, too. Julie read me a story about it ve ovver night. 'Red Jasper's Secret', it was called."

"Would you like a ride in the car, and show me where you hid it?" George tried not to bubble over. "Then you can have the five shillings," he added, enticingly.

Ron slid off the gate as if it had just become red-hot and climbed into the car.

"Vere you are," he said, as they stood by the tree, a few minutes later. "In vat 'ole. Put your 'and in. I won't put mine in, 'case vere's a dragon guardin' ve papers."

George, whose courage in the matter of dragons had never been called into question, did as he was bid. He felt a thrill of hope as his hand contacted a wodge of papers lodged cross-wise in the hollow trunk. He withdrew the bundle, still tied with red tape and intact as far as he could tell. This would make Threep's day, no doubt about that. He pushed the package down into his inside pocket and handed Ron his reward.

"Now, Ron, what was this man in blue like – the one who asked you about the case?"

"Rich bloke," affirmed Ron. "'E'd gotter big car."

"Yes, but what did he look like? Was he short or tall?"

"Tall," said Ron, to whom all men were giants. "'Bout twelve foot," he added, for accuracy's sake.

George doubted this. "Bigger than I am?" he queried.

"Oh, no." Ron was sure about this. Silly question. Hadn't he just said that the bloke was only about twelve foot? A sudden thought struck him. "One fing, 'e likes newts."

"Likes newts?" A foreigner, perhaps? George had tried snails, once, in Rheims, but wasn't keen on them.

"Yes. 'E pinched mine."

"When?"

"Yestiddy. If you see a bloke wiv a jar of newts, vat's 'im."

George gave it up. Ron was only doing his best, of course, but it was doubtful if there'd be any percentage in looking for a twelve-foot man carrying a jar of newts. He could see that the newt episode rankled in Ron's mind.

Anyway, here were the papers and he'd pass on what information he thought likely to Threep. A man who's just had a slight concussion might find Ron's unexpurgated statements a trifle bewildering. He bade Ron a warm farewell and drove light-heartedly to Rose Cottage.

Threep was up, washed and dressed when Polly let George into the cottage.

"And how are we this morning?" asked George in that offensively patronizing tone the healthy adopt towards the sick.

"Fine, thanks," answered Threep. "Miss Fenner has been goodness itself."

"Take no notice of him," denied Polly. "It's entirely due to himself. He's been a perfectly patient; it's been a pleasure to have him."

"Ah, but *you* were the ministering angel," asserted Threep. "I doubt if you had a wink of sleep all night."

George felt *de trop*.

"Well, when you've finished each other's build-up, I've some news for you. I've found you-know-what," he said, meaningly. "Intact, too." He tapped his bulging inner pocket.

Threep's face glowed like a camera flash-bulb.

"Oh, well done! You must tell me all about it on the way back. Meanwhile," he turned to Polly, "I'll thank you once again and say *au revoir*. I wonder if you'd mind my calling, some time?" he asked, diffidently.

"Of course not. You'll always be welcome. I shall want to know how my patient is getting on, shan't I?" laughed Polly.

"I promise I shan't hide under the bed if Hester turns up," said Threep slyly, with a side-glance at George.

"So you've been talking, eh?" he accused Polly. He turned to Threep. "Now you know why I hid in the hall chest, that evening. I daren't let Miss Kettle recognize me at The Leas, after seeing me here last Tuesday."

"I gathered as much. I knew it couldn't be just shyness." Polly bubbled. "This I must hear. What happened?"

Threep enlightened her.

"Well, that's that," she said, as he finished an accurate and well-told account. "It's just a matter of time, now, I suppose. Know any good house-agents?"

"Don't give up yet," advised Threep. "Anything can happen before . . ."

"How right you are," commented George, heartily. "Life in Winthringham is one long saga. We live dangerously, we Moonrakers."

"Moonrakers?" queried Polly.

"Yes, Wiltshiremen are Moonrakers, I'm told. We try to rake the moon out of ponds, but we're not daft enough to try and do it with the wrong kind of rake. Amos Flower told Oi."

Threep patted Polly's hand in as fatherly a way as possible.

"Now, don't you worry, Miss Fenner. We'll not let anything happen to you. I'd better come along tomorrow," he added, cunningly, "just to let you know how things are going."

"Thank you. Please do," said Polly.

She waved to them as George drove off, Threep craning his head like a giraffe until they were out of sight. George put two and two together, but said nothing. Threep may have suffered a temporary head injury, but the heart trouble was going to be more permanent.

At The Leas, George ushered the invalid into the lounge.

"There. I'd take it easy for a while, if I were you. Shall I draw the blinds?"

"Draw the —? Dammit, I'm not dead. Fit as a fiddle except for a bit of a headache. Where's Hester?"

"I don't know. Probably with Cook. She doesn't expect you yet. And Helen's at the Sede library."

"Oh. Look, Loder, whatever you do, I want you to say nothing about the loss of those papers. After all, all's well that ends well. I may as well tell you – but keep it to yourself – that I'm expecting a Security man down here any day, now. Nothing to do with the papers, but if he found out how careless I've been there'd be the dickens to pay."

"Security man?" This was the stuff! George was wallowing in International Intrigue, now. He glanced cautiously around the room. "What's he coming for?" he asked, in a half-whisper.

"Oh, just a routine visit," answered Threep, evasively.

George felt that he was being put off. His imagination soared skywards. A Security man! You could almost call him a Secret Agent! A voracious reader of thrillers, George knew what a secret agent would look like. Eyes, mere slits, cold as steel. A scar across the forehead, souvenir of some wild chase across Albania. The mouth, thin-lipped and tight as a trap. And, of course, a sinister bulge in the hip-pocket.

He could hear the agent's voice now. Hard, metallic, full of urgency:

"Loder, I've got to trust you with this mission! There's nobody else, and I'll never live to make it. Take this package to Strumpfstrasse 17, Hamburg . . ."

"17?"

"No, 17. Tell them – aah! The swine have got me! – tell them – tell . . ."

He fell lifeless at George's feet, an arrow dripping with curare protruding from his back. George knew what he must do. He must . . .

He saw Threep looking at him curiously, and came back to earth.

"What's the matter?" asked Threep. "Headache?"

"Just thinking," said George.

Stefan sat on the running-board of Threep's car, lost in thought. The empty brief-case, last night, had been a bitter disappointment. Who'd have thought that Loder would have taken the papers out so quickly? Must have had them on his person when he'd gone into the shed. Well, it was too late to do anything, now. Loder'd be on his guard.

And now the SNABU were getting impatient for results. Didn't they realize that it took time and patience to enter an underground stronghold, protected by troops, and probe one of England's most closely-guarded secrets?

Yet, according to their latest communication, they weren't satisfied. They were sending down one of the top men, a hard ruthlessly efficient agent, who'd kill without the slightest compunction. Stefan had never met him, but knew all about him.

Anyway, he was due to arrive at any time, and would lose no time in getting in touch with Stefan, who wasn't really looking forward to it. Still, he'd be able to warn the man about Loder. Or should he? Why not let him find out for himself, thought Stefan, loyally.

It would be something, though, if Loder could be removed before the man arrived. They'd see, then, that Stefan hadn't been wasting his time. A half-formed plan began to take definite shape in his mind.

The gas fire in Loder's bedroom was the only effective answer. It would mean hiding in the room until Loder was asleep. A slight risk, there, perhaps, but one worth taking. Then, after turning the gas on, slip out quietly. They'd find Loder in the morning, a victim of another of those regrettable accidents. Stefan smiled grimly as he started to polish the car.

11

Farrer pushed a meditative broom across the platform. The problem of the house and furnishings was, like the world, too much with him. Another two hundred pounds, he felt, and there'd be no problem. Just two hundred pounds. Not much to ask, surely?

He leaned his broom against the railing as the 3.10 Down gave its warning shriek. The platform was empty, save for Mrs Long, Julie and Ron, waiting for the 3.25 Up. Mrs Long had the reprieved look of a woman who isn't going with the children.

The 3.10 clanked in, and Farrer moved to the spot where experience told him the guard's van would come to rest. "Bilton Parva! Change for Sede and Barnsby," he called, mechanically. Not, he reflected, that any traveller would be agog for the information. He was paid to shout it, so he did.

It was some surprise, therefore, that he saw a carriage door open and a tall man step out, then turn and drag out two suitcases. Farrer moved purposefully in the potential bob's direction.

"Wurr wuz 'ee fur, zur?" he asked.

The passenger looked at him askance. Alexi Karanov had an excellent English accent, but his knowledge of dialect was sketchy. Farrer patiently repeated his question. He was quite used to people outside Wiltshire not being able to speak English.

"Wurr be goin' to?" he asked, slowly and distinctly, raising his voice a little as one must do for foreigners.

"Oh. I'm going to The Moon hotel, here. Is it far? Is there a taxi?"

There was. Amos Flower's taxi stood dozing in the sun-soaked station yard, dreaming, no doubt, of the days when it was young – when its pistons beat strongly and the petrol leaped joyously through its fuel system. When taxis *were* taxis, and the country rejoiced in George the Fifth's accession.

Protruding from the front door were the soles of a large-ish pair of boots, reasonable proof that Amos was on call, if not actually alert.

"'Ang on a minnit, zur," said Farrer. "Oi'll jest see if there's anything in the van, then Oi'll come an' put 'ee roight." He went away to the less paying but more important business of removing a small crate from the guard's van.

Ron and Julie stared up at the stranger in frank and undis-guised interest, as he waited for Farrer. Ron's fascination was such that he gave no more than a perfunctory lick at the tired-looking toffee clamped in one sticky fist.

Eyes, mere slits, cold as steel, looked down at him. A scar across the sunburned forehead stood out whitely. The mouth, tight as a trap, made Ron wonder whether the man had any lips.

Julie edged away uncomfortably.

"Kerm orn, ar Ron," she ordered. "Auntie sez the London train goes from the other side."

Reluctantly, Ron allowed himself to be led away, crab-wise, in the wake of his sister.

"I gotter pitcher of 'im at 'ome," he told Julie, in a con-fidential shout, "in me *'Orror Comic.* I din't know 'e wuz real."

Farrer returned, picked up the cases, and led the way to the taxi. He opened the door quietly, bestowed the passenger and luggage, then went back and collected the broom. Taking a good two-seventy degree swing, he brought the handle down smartly on the size eleven soles. Amos grunted and struggled upright. Farrer listened in silent admiration to the strange sounds expressive of surprise and indignation which crowded the older man's lips.

"You've 'ad a bad dream, Amos," Farrer said, soothingly. "Ge'mman wants to go to The Moon. All roight?"

Still muttering something that may have been "bastinado", or maybe wasn't, Amos climbed out and wound up his engine. It afforded him some compensation to see that Farrer's labours had netted him no more than a modest three-pence. Mentally adding half a crown in excess of his normal excess, he set off.

His passenger leaned forward.

"Tell me, where is – ah, Stony Lane, I believe it's called?"

"Stony Lane?" Amos shouted above the rattle and roar of a protesting engine. "You'm just comin' to the Bilton end of 'n. See?" He slowed down to let the man see the tree-framed entrance, heavily strung with barbed wire. "'Tother end comes out at Winthrin'm, 'bout 'arf a moile along."

"Ah, Winthringham. And how do I get there? The lane is closed, I see."

"Down back wurr we just come from, turn roight at the pond, an' up the Sede road. 'Tis a powerful long ways; Oi could take 'ee there," said Amos, hopefully.

Karanov leaned back. So. Better get along first thing in the morning and contact Forty-seven. This evening he'd just stroll around, get his bearings, and hear what there was to hear about "The Colonel". Whatever happened, he must have all the information by next Wednesday, the deadline for the Three-Power talks.

From all reports, there wasn't much point in placing any

reliance in Forty-seven. Described by the SNABU as a broken reed, Forty-seven had an unenviable future. If any.

The taxi stopped, coughed, sighed, and a great silence descended on the countryside.

"Yurr's The Moon, zur." Amos opened the door and carried the suitcases into the cool hall. Karanov followed him in. "That'll be eight-an'-six," continued Amos, hopefully, breathing deeply and wiping non-existent beads of perspiration from a brow to which sweat came as rarely as snowdrops to the Sahara.

The man dropped a half-crown and a two-shilling piece into the extended palm, and turned to the reception desk.

"'Ere, woss this?" demanded Amos, indignantly. The correct fare, and not even a tanner tip? Was this the brave new world them ruddy politicians boasted about?

Karanov turned and looked at him, wordlessly, his eyes cutting through Amos like a cheese-wire.

"Thank 'ee, zur. 'Dartnoon, zur," said Amos hurriedly, and backed out of the door.

Karanov smiled grimly as he heard the engine wheeze into life. The door slammed indignantly and the taxi rumbled away bearing a bemused and gently-simmering Amos.

The late afternoon shadows were lengthening as the Reverend Honeydew sat typing under the shade of his solitary beech tree. Except for a literary-minded fly or so, nothing disturbed him as his plump forefingers poised over the keys, swooping on the unsuspecting letters like kingfishers on his beloved Avon.

He extracted the quarto sheet from the typewriter and leaned back. His typing, besides being slow, hadn't the professional typist's stamp of accuracy; any similarity between

the typed word and the intended, in fact, was purely coinci-
dental. He read the page carefully, pen alert for errors and
omissions:

"There aRe tsill signs of COlonel cObberleigh's activities
in BIlton and sirrounding district£ One old basket" – (here
he inserted the word 'maker') – "who lives at Hoale can
trace his craft directly to the cOlonel's influence. The reciøpt
for the wine 'Luno' is – alas! – lost, though a book in the
Sede library mentions the wine as being most potent and very
popular with the villagagers."

He looked up as a shoe crunched on the gravel path.

"Ah, Mr Threep!" he exclaimed, a welcoming beam on
his face. "How nice to see you on your feet again! Do sit
down. How are you?"

"Quite fit, thank you, Vicar." Threep took the proffered
chair. "I was just passing, and Helen asked me to tell you that
she spent an hour or so in the Sede reference library, this
morning. Apparently she's unearthed a few more interesting
facts about Colonel Cobberleigh."

"Excellent! Excellent!" enthused the Vicar, as if he'd just
been presented with a brand-new transept. "No reference to
'Luno', I suppose?" he asked hopefully.

"Luno?"

"Yes, a local wine. It could be important, if we started
making it again, but the recipe's been lost."

"She didn't mention it. She says she'll let you have the full
write-up as soon as she's typed her notes; probably this
evening."

"Please tell her that I'm most grateful, most grateful. Indeed, I'd never have got as far as this without her help. You
know," he informed Threep impressively, "she may not
realize it, but she knows more about the Colonel than anyone
else alive."

Threep absorbed this information without envy or interest. All right, so Helen was the greatest living authority on a dead colonel who'd made wine and took pot-shots at railway trains. So what? He suppressed a yawn.

"How interesting," he said, politely. His thoughts wandered off as the Vicar talked of his forthcoming book. That phone call, this afternoon, thought Threep, had come as a pleasant surprise. It was nice to know that the Security man's visit had been cancelled. Security people worried him – made him nervous and jumpy.

"Yes," he said, interestedly, as the Vicar paused for a well-earned breath.

Should he have reported that attempt on his brief-case, though? Who was this mysterious man in blue? Was he still in the vicinity?

"Yes," he said, mechanically, filling in another hiatus in the Vicar's monologue.

"Do you really think so?" persisted the Vicar, a trifle coldly.

"Er, pardon?" Threep joined him.

"I asked whether you thought that a book on local history would be considered unimportant."

"Sorry. I thought you said 'important'," lied Threep. "Of course it's important. Really needed. Bilton is crying out for it. Please let me know if there's anything I can do to help, won't you?"

The Vicar, soothed, remounted his hobby-horse and carried Threep along with him.

Scientists, one way or another, can usually be depended upon to make news. What were once backroom boys are nowadays showroom specimens. One newspaper will confidenly shout, "British Scientists Among Best," while another, disgruntled no doubt by the failure of its editor's refrigerator will come out with, "What Are Britain's Scientists Doing?" They click for publicity either way.

Very occasionally one comes across the backroom type, unhonoured and unsung, though still presumably Among Best, content to remain undisturbed among his retorts, crucibles and catalysts.

Whilst the Vicar was holding Milton Threep enthralled with the doings of Colonel Cobberleigh, two such self-effacing characters were discussing their present experiments and the meagre success attached thereto. The conversation took the usual form – an omega here, a delta there, and a few Bessel functions to give it body. The more interesting point about the discussion was that it was taking place seven feet below the cobbles of Stony Lane.

Doctors Ungel and Schnille, whose work on the pinitron had put their mother country, Britain, so far ahead of foreign scientists, were worried.

Small wonder. On their sole efforts depended the success of "The Colonel", a weapon which it was hoped would make war too dangerous to be popular even with politicians. By a flick of a switch, and a little elementary range-finding, "The Colonel" was destined to wipe out whole populations before one could say "*pi rho gamma*".

But it wasn't doing it. Not that they'd actually tried it out on whole populations yet – public opinion being what it is – but they'd gone about it in a small way, using an unsuspecting frog, an unwilling hare, and Sheilagh, the cow with explora-tory instincts. Also, a tree or so had been destroyed, with the peculiar effects described by Amos Flower – like pansy petals, smelling of 'ops.

"But it won't repeat, Ungel," wailed Schnille. "You never know what's going to happen next!"

"Poor frequency-control, of course. And we've seen how the directional properties change with drift. The reflector efficiency must deteriorate as its distance differs appreciably from the lambda-relationship but . . ."

"Obviously. And what will happen when the power of one oscillator exceeds the other, just as the directional efficiency fails? Complete disintegration of everything and everyone within a few wavelengths of the aerials. Whom do you think is going to operate it under those conditions?"

"Exactly. The day of the thin red hero is over. Have you written any of this up, yet?"

"No. I'm hoping to have some results by the time Souder arrives on Wednesday. So far, our reports have added nothing to what is generally known, but . . ."

"You realize, then, that if anything happens to us 'The Colonel' would be lost to – er – civilization?"

"I do. But it won't. And by Wednesday morning I'll have the complete report, as far as we've gone, even if I have to write all Tuesday night."

"Well, if you haven't got it before Souder turns up, I'd advise you to turn 'The Colonel' on yourself. Or turn it on him, and do us both a favour."

George and Threep sat on the bench outside the Angry Hen. It was almost dark, and they'd stopped for a drink on their way back from the Vicarage after having delivered Helen's notes to a delighted Reverend Honeydew.

They hadn't noticed Alexi Karanov, standing quietly at the bar, or seen his fleeting look of interest as Jno. Murk had called a polite "Good evening, Mr Threep". Nor were they aware that he'd moved across to the window-seat where he'd be able to hear every word of their conversation as they talked outside.

"I'd like to know more about the Colonel," he heard George say. Karanov's ears twitched a good inch.

"Not my subject, I'm afraid," answered Threep. "Helen's the real authority, of course. She's done all the study and research. Got masses of typescript on the subject."

"I'd never have believed it," mused George. "But then, there're a lot of things I wouldn't have believed, around here. That case of yours, now . . ."

"Sh-sh," interrupted Threep, nervously, and looked over his shoulder through the open window. Karanov stared back at him, his expression as transparently innocent as a car-salesman's smile. Threep changed the subject.

Karanov considered what he'd just heard. So this – who was it? Helen – was the real authority. Well, that made matters simpler. It was doubtful whether the woman would be guarded – the English were fools in that respect. He, Karanov, would soon devise a way of getting hold of the woman, or her information. He wasn't called "The Fox" for nothing! Tomorrow, Forty-seven would tell him who Helen was; then "The Fox" would take over!

"Bob," Gwyneth leaned back against the door-post, preparatory for their "Good-night" chat, "why don't we put the two 'undred down on a house, and buy the furniture on the never-never?"

Farrer didn't reply for a moment. The idea of hire-purchase had also occurred to him, but he'd refused to entertain it. It sounded all right, of course, but so did belladonna.

"O's furnicher'd it be? Theirs or ours? Oi'd be scared to put me feet up on a chair, or spill a drop o' gravy on the table, 'case they ever wanted 'n back."

Gwyneth bridled.

"I should think so! Put yewer big feet on my chairs, boyo, or spray gravy about and I'll be be'ind you!"

"Oi didn't mean that, loike." Farrer didn't want to give the impression that he was haphazard feeder. "It's just that 'twouldn't seem to be ours."

Silence fell. All evening they'd been discussing ways and means. Farrer's two hundred pounds only seemed to make things worse; if they'd no money at all, there'd only be one problem. As matters stood, they needed another two hundred, and wondered what to do with the two hundred they already had. Two problems.

Gwyneth sighed. "Wouldn't it be lovely if you was to win a reward for something?"

"Fer what?" Farrer only needed the inspiration.

"Oh, I don't know. Catchin' a railway thief on the London mail, say. You'd be in all the papers, and on the B.B.C. 'Gallant Porter's Desperate Fight,' they'd say, and send reporters to the 'ospital for an interview."

"Woss mean, 'ospital?" Farrer needed money, but wasn't that desperate. "Anyway, Oi don't travel on the London train. They wouldn't give me two 'undred, neither. Oi tell 'ee what, though," he continued, as a bright thought struck him, "Oi've got a chanst 'o winnin' a bit, nex' week."

"'Ave you, Bob?" Gwyneth turned hopeful eyes up to his. Farrer gulped, then looked away. A man can stand just so much. He could have drowned himself in either of those brown pools.

"Yes. Oi'm entering fer the 'ome-made woine contest, at the feet. Two-pun-ten, the proize is." He looked at her proudly, like a Great Dane waiting for a pat.

"Two-pound-ten! Oh, Bob, what good's that? Two 'undred we want! What wine is it?" she asked, her curiosity getting the better of her indignation at the offer of this chicken-feed.

"'Tis an old receep we've 'ad in the 'ouse since 'fore Oi were born. Gran' made some, once, an' Granpop liked 'n so much 'e drank a 'ole pint."

"Didn't it make 'im drunk?"

"Oi dunno. 'E was sober enough when they revived 'n, two days after."

Gwyneth pondered this.

"'Ow long've you 'ad it?"

"Oi made 'n last year, but 'twere too late fer the feet, so Oi put 'n in fer this year. Ten boddles, Oi got. 'Tis clear as a dew-pond. Make they judges sit up, Oi'll warrant!"

"Well, I 'ope you win, boyo. Mrs Bollanger's one of the judges, though."

"If she 'as a good sip, she'll do cartwheels, Oi rackon."

"She'll make *me* do cartwheels if I don't get in. It's gone eleven, and I'll bet she's listenin' for me." She turned her face up to his. "Good night, Bob."

As Gwyneth and Farrer were saying their fourth "Good night", George sat on the side of his bed, removing a pensive tie.

How much longer could he dodge this Kettle woman? Even if he kept out of her sight for a day or so, they'd be bound to meet at the fête. Wouldn't it be as well to make a clean breast of the matter to Helen? After all, what harm had he done? Just because he'd been in Polly's bedroom, surely . . .?

"But," Helen would say, "why did you have to hide from Mother?" Well, why did he? How could he explain that terribly vulnerable feeling which comes to a man clad only in a coloured bedspread, when his future mother-in-law approaches? Like a nudist in an apiary. Sweet and loving as Helen was, she'd never understand.

He shied a shoe at an uninvited moth which was exploring the corner-cupboard door. He missed. The moth sneered and started flirting with the electric-light bulb.

Inside the cupboard, Stefan jumped. The shoe had sounded like a thunderclap. Stefan didn't like it. In fact, there wasn't much about the whole project that Stefan did like. He'd had o lock himself in the cupboard three hours ago, to be on the safe side, and although the cupboard was roomy as cupboards go, it had no pretensions to all mod. cons. or even single accom. for gent. Stefan felt like a displaced chrysalis.

Added to this, various unidentified insects had explored him, and many had evidently decided to stay. Sweat was running down between his shoulder-blades, and fluff tickled his nostrils. And now this damn' Loder was throwing grenades at the cupboard door. Life wasn't being easy for an honest spy.

Through a chink in the door he could see the light, but nothing else. He'd planned to wait for an hour after the light was extinguished, come out of his lair, turn on the gas-fire, and leave quietly. An unambitious programme which had looked like pie in the safety of his bedroom.

Here, in the cupboard, it was more realistic. Just suppose he couldn't get out? Suppose the house caught fire while he was locked in? Suppose Loder stayed awake all night? He put these and other gloomy possibilities from his mind.

The french window had presented a minor problem, but not for long; he would close and lock it before he left the room, and leave the key on the floor near by. That way, people would think that Loder had probably mislaid the key and hadn't bothered to look for it, leaving the window closed. The plan wasn't watertight, but there was no reason for suspecting anyone of foul play, least of all the chauffeur. Stefan waited.

It was nearly one o'clock when at last he stepped on to the landing, carefully closing George's door behind him. A little olive oil previously applied to the hinges had ensured a noiseless exit. He tiptoed to the servants' staircase with the warm, comfortable feeling of a job well carried out in the face of difficulties. Something attempted, something done. . . .

In the bedroom he'd just left, the faint hiss of gas formed a background for George's gentle snores. It had been a long day. . . .

12

Milton Threep lay on his back and stared into the darkness of his bedroom, turning over the events of the past few days. The more he considered George's story about his last night's adventure, the more worried he became. That there'd been a definite attempt to steal his brief-case was obvious. And if the thief – or thieves – knew of the brief-case, what did they know of "The Colonel"?

He sat up as a single note from Bilton church reverberated across the fields. Half past twelve, one o'clock, or half past one. Not that it mattered; he wouldn't get to sleep for hours yet. He got out of bed, wondering whether George was awake. Perhaps they could go over the whole thing again, and see if there might be some small but important point they'd overlooked.

He put on his dressing-gown, then paused. Mightn't Loder be a trifle irritated at being called in the small hours, just for a chummy talk? Better leave it until the morning, perhaps. He sat on the side of the bed, brooding.

But it *was* vitally important. How were they to be sure that another attempt wouldn't be made tonight? Even at this very minute? He looked nervously in the direction of the door. Not that the thief would find the case in a hurry; he'd taken good care of that! Why should Loder want to sleep like a – a sloth, wasn't it? – just when he was needed? Downright selfishness, especially as he, Threep, couldn't sleep.

He decided on the time-honoured political refuge, a compromise. He'd just go down to Loder's room, knock on the door, and if there was no answer he'd let sleeping logs lie. He went softly from the room, along the landing.

His tentative tap on George's door brought no response. Asleep, of course. Better leave it until morning and . . .

Curious. Strong smell of gas. Seemed to come from this door, too. Surely Loder wouldn't have a fire on, in this weather? Even so, it shouldn't smell like an inefficient gas-works. He rapped louder and went in.

The almost overpowering reek of gas made him cough as he switched on the light and turned off the gas-tap. George lay still, breathing like a leaky steam-valve, his face an interesting shade of shot-silk. Threep gave him a preliminary shake, then went to the window.

Closed and locked! Had Loder . . .? He saw the key, where Stefan had left it, and opened the window as far as it would go. He turned back to George and shook him.

"Loder! Loder!" he hissed, straining manfully at the limp body. George grunted and opened a reluctant eye.

"Uh? What . . .? Eh?" He tried to lift his head. "Oh, my confounded head! What on earth . . .?

"There's been a slight accident," Threep told him. "Better come to the window for a minute. You'll soon be all right. You left your gas-fire turned on, by the look of things."

"*I* left . . .?" George staggered to the window and gulped in the night air like a demonstration-model suction cleaner. It tasted sweeter than anything he'd ever known.

"That's better," encouraged Threep, as George withdrew his head into the room. "Purple didn't suit you. How do you feel now?"

"Like a gasometer that's going to be sick," answered George, who liked to be accurate. "What on earth happened?"

"That's what I'd like to know. I came down to talk to you

and found the gas turned fully on. Did you do it? Felt you couldn't face things, perhaps?" Threep knew the form from his Sunday papers.

"Couldn't face what? That, if you'll pardon my mentioning it, is the most damn-fool piece of deduction I've heard. Why should I bother about facing anything, now I've met Mrs Bollanger? Someone turned that gas on after I went to sleep. And my guess is that it was the same parishioner who locked me in the garden-shed."

"But why? How far does that advance him? Does anyone want to get rid of you?"

"This bloke does, apparently. And yet, with all due respect, I'd have thought that *you* were a better bet for bumping off. Or has the chap got us mixed up?"

"Either way, he seems pretty ruthless. I'd better report it to the police. No; this isn't a normal crime like larceny or housebreaking; I'll report it direct to the Department. They mayn't want to give the thing too much publicity. Do you mind?" he asked George. "After all, you're the injured party."

"Do as you think best. If it hadn't been for you, I'd be in the past tense by now. I'd like to thank you for that."

"Don't mention it." Threep gave the impression that the odd spot of life-saving was all in the night's work to him. "What I'd like to know is how the man got in and out of the room without being seen. We've made a point of locking up securely since we had our unknown visitor, the other night. I wonder if it was the same chap?"

"Could it be one of the staff? Who is there, altogether?"

"There's cook, Gwyneth, Lamb the gardener, Stefan, and the daily woman who comes in to 'do' for Hester, as she puts it."

"Mightn't she have tried to do for me?"

"I doubt it. She scarcely does for us."

"What about cook?"

"It wouldn't be cook. She's a strong Nonconformist."

"Nonconformists don't gas people, you find?"

"Rarely. Religious scruples. Passing from cook, there's Gwyneth."

"Not Gwyneth. She 'oodn't do it, look you. Too beautiful."

"So was Borgia. Still, I think you're right. What about Lamb, the gardener?"

"I wouldn't know. We haven't met socially, though I've seen him once or twice. As he's been bending over his flower-beds, each time, the only lasting memory I have is of well-filled corduroys."

"No, I'd give Lamb a clean bill. Gentle as his namesake, unless you've trodden on his herbaceous borders. You haven't, have you?"

"Not guilty. And surely the gas-chamber's a little drastic? Un-English, wouldn't you say? No, we discount Lamb. Now, what about Stefan?"

"He's an unknown quantity, of course. Doesn't speak enough English to know what's going on. Refugee, you know. Arrived here with nothing and was only too glad to get the job and the suit that went with it. We —"

"A big car and a blue suit!" George brought his hands together with a slap that sent Threep a couple of feet into the air. "Of course! What's the betting that he isn't ar Ron's mystery man? After all, anyone can pretend not to speak English; look at the train-announcers on the railway stations."

"I wonder." Threep thought a moment. "If we describe him to that boy of yours, we may get something a little more explicit. But why does he want to get rid of you? Come to that, I'm not convinced that my crash was accidental."

Threep didn't see why George should have all the attention. "Why should the steering suddenly crack up on a chauffeur-maintained car?"

"Too late to find out, now. As you know, Stefan was on the spot immediately after the crash. He'd have had ample opportunity to rectify any sabotage. And, if you remember, Stefan brought the car around for *me*, that afternoon." George's wits were breaking all records, now. "You decided to drive it at the last moment."

"Well, we may be right. But it still doesn't tell us why Stefan is so bitterly anti-Loder. If he'd tried to erase me from the list of probable starters, I could understand it," said Threep modestly. "Whatever happens, we'll watch Stefan for a day or so."

"This week's understatement. I'll haunt him," said George, purposefully. "I want to live out a reasonable span, narrow and uninteresting as my life may be. At the moment, I'm all I've got."

Threep went to the door.

"We'll go into this matter in the morning; go straight down and see this Ron. Meanwhile, I'd lock that window, if I were you; the ivy is quite strong enough to bear a man's weight. You might as well bolt the door, too," he advised. "Still, that's up to you," he said, with the easy nonchalance of one whose life isn't threatened. "I'll see you at breakfast, then." He paused, and put his head back round the door.

"I hope," he added, kindly.

Alexi Karanov walked slowly up the road towards The Leas. Somehow, he must get in touch with the chauffeur, otherwise known as Forty-seven. The morning, as wonderful a morning as one of our leading morning-producing counties can serve up, was wasted on him. To Karanov, weather was just something one walked about in, or dressed against. It might easily as well been a wet Monday in Ealing.

He stood uncertainly in the half-hidden drive entrance when the Mottram swung out in front of him. His spirits rose as he saw the blue-uniformed figure behind the wheel of the otherwise empty car. Luck was with him. He raised a hand.

Stefan stamped impatiently on the brake. What now? Somebody who wanted to know the way to some impossibly-named place, without doubt. His eyes narrowed as he saw the medallion the man was fingering unostentatiously. He produced his own.

"Forty-seven," he announced himself, respectfully. "You are ..."

"Number Three," replied Karanov from his lofty height up the numerical ladder. "Can we talk here? Be quick."

"Get in," answered Stefan. "I am going to Bilton. We can talk on the way."

"First," asked Karanov, as they rolled smoothly down the road, "according to your last report, you have discovered no more about 'The Colonel'. Is that still so?"

"Well ..."

"HAVE YOU?"

"No."

"Are you aware of the existence of any documents regard- the progress of the experiments?"

"I suppose there are ..."

"ARE YOU?"

"No."

"Tell me, then, who is Helen?"

The question came as a surprise to Stefan.

"Helen?"

"Yes. HELEN. Dolt! Who is she?"

"Oh, Helen. That would be Helen Bollanger, the daughter of my employer. She is not important. I . . ."

"Not important? Fool! Imbecile! She is the key-woman, the greatest authority on 'The Colonel'! Are you quite blind and deaf?"

"But I thought Loder . . ." began Stefan, miserably. He'd gone wrong somewhere, but couldn't see where.

"Loder? Who is this Loder?"

"A young fellow engaged to the girl. I killed him last night," said Stefan simply.

"I know the man. He was nobody." Karanov implied that Stefan had been wasting his time. "Now, we must act quickly. This Helen: she has all the papers we want, probably in her room. *I* found that out, within an hour or so of my arrival. When can you get them? I must have them before Wednesday."

Stefan reflected.

"The best time will be on Monday. They're holding a garden fête and everyone will be there, servants and all. The Bollangers are more or less running it, so I'll have the house to myself. It should be fairly simple."

"It will need to be simple if we are to depend on you. All right; I'll see that the girl is kept out of the way in case she returns while you are searching her room. Is there somewhere where I can hide her, where a scream or so won't be noticed?"

"Yes. There's an empty cottage, belonging to that oaf Flower, about a mile up the Sede road. You can't miss it. it has a ' To Let' board outside. . . ."

"Right. Leave that part to me; we'll meet there after you've found the papers. Now," he continued, "tell me what this Helen looks like."

"Blonde," said Stefan, to whom women meant little.

He'd have described Cleopatra as a darkish female. "Her eyes are blue," he suddenly remembered.

"Very well." Karanov was satisfied. There would hardly be more than one blonde, blue-eyed young woman at The Leas. "We are getting near the village; I'd better leave you now. Stop here."

He got out and a worried Stefan drove on to Bilton. Life got complicated. The good old days were gone, when a man could take an honest machine-gun, and clean up his employers quickly and neatly. The world was getting soft.

Polly walked briskly up the road to The Leas, a determined tilt to her chin. In the patch pocket of her blue dress reposed a note addressed to Helen; a note which asked Helen whether she could give any good reason why she, Polly, should not be allowed to extend her tenancy of Rose Cottage. Polly knew that there would be no point in trying to see Helen – Mrs Bollanger would soon head her off. Which was why she intended to put her note in the letter-box of The Leas before the house was properly awake.

How could she give up all this, she asked herself, savouring the morning, as Wiltshire, smiling sleepily, prepared for another perfect day. Skylarks soared over the dewy fields, while blackbirds trilled proudly above the chatter of the feathered riff-raff of the hedgerows. A cuckoo, sounding just like someone imitating a cuckoo, practised throwing his voice from opposite corners of a near-by wood.

She moved hastily nearer the hedge as Stefan rocketed the Mottram up the road, returning to The Leas from the village after his *tête-à-tête* with Number Three.

Polly paused at the wired-off entrance to Stony Lane, with its small forest of notice-boards. "W.D. Property. Keep Out," snapped one, tersely. "Danger. Unexploded Bombs," lied another. "Trespassers Will Be Prosecuted," warned a third, weakly falling back on the law. She turned her attention to the khaki-clad sentry near by.

Private Waller peered nervously at the dark shape under the blackberry bush, from whence came faint scuffling sounds. To the soldier's city-bred mind the noise could mean anything. A snake, perhaps, or a flippin' fox. Or a wild-cat. Wild-cats were dangerous, weren't they? Liable to fly at a bloke and scratch his adjectival eyes out.

The question was, did his duties as sentry cover strange noises under bushes? He poked a tentative bayonet at the shadow, wishing his rifle was three times longer. The shadow moved and Private Waller skipped back hastily. He skipped again as a soft voice behind him said, "What have you got there?"

He turned and saw Polly, whose curiosity had proved stronger than the barbed wire, looking interestedly over his shoulder at the bush. Glad of another human being's company – especially one shaped like this one – the soldier explained.

"Su'thin's movin' abaht under this 'ere bush. I gotter keep patrollin' by 'ere, an' I don't want nothin' jumpin' aht at me. I just tickled it up a bit with me bay'nit."

Polly bent and prodded under the bush with a piece of dead wood.

"Why, it's only a hedgehog," she exclaimed. "He won't hurt you. Just ignore him; he's doing no harm."

The sentry looked at the ball of spines with a keen interest.

"Blimey! That's the fust one I seen alive. Like a bleedin' pin-cushion, ennit?"

Polly admitted that there was, perhaps, a certain similarity to a bleedin' pin-cushion. "They're awfully good to eat," she informed him. "I believe the gipsies bake them in clay, or boil them in milk. I've forgotten which."

"Can't say I'd go a bundle on 'em meself. All them flippin' squills."

"Squills?"

"Yes : them spikes all over it."

"Oh, quills. Well, you don't eat them, you know. After all, you could say that a chicken is unappetising because of its feathers."

"People don't eat chicken's fevvers," pointed out the epicure.

"Exactly. Nor do they eat squi – quills."

"I s'pose you're right. I'd still sooner 'ave a bit o' rabbit, or a nice jugged 'are. Me Ma's a dab at jugged 'are."

"Well, *chacun à son goût*, I suppose."

"Goo?" The unexplained change in the conversation made Private Waller suddenly realize that all wasn't as it should be. Duty had been neglected.

"'Ere, wotchoo doin' 'ere?"

"Doing? I was explaining to you about hedgehogs. Remember?"

"Yes, but wotcher *doin'* 'ere? Nobody can't come up this 'ere lane wivaht not 'avin' permishun."

Polly sorted it out. "Why can't they?"

"'Cos we stops 'em."

"Why?"

"I dunno. I didn't ask the sergeant. Orders, I s'pose."

"Well, you must obey your orders, mustn't you?" Polly was quite willing to see the official point of view, as long as it didn't affect her personally. She smiled and the soldier's sense of duty fell without firing a shot.

Polly looked at the tiny wrist-watch on a proportionately tiny wrist.

"Heavens! Eight o'clock, and I've had no breakfast yet! Just hold these wires apart for me, will you?"

145

"'Arf a tick." The sentry leaned his rifle against a handy notice-board. "'Ere y'are," he said, separating two strands of wire. He looked virtuously heavenwards as Polly climbed through.

"I gotter go, nah," he said, reluctantly, as Polly stood at the other side of the fence. "If they misses yer fer 'arf a second they 'as 'arf the perishin' Army aht after yer. You knows 'ow it is."

Polly could guess how it was, though she'd never had half the perishin' Army after her, she thought, not without a pang of regret. She waved him a friendly good-bye, and turned away towards The Leas.

Across the road, Karanov, who'd walked back to study the topography of the Winthringham end of the lane, saw Polly leave. Blonde, eh? She passed him and walked up the drive to deliver her letter. Blue eyes, too.

So that was the mysterious Helen. The "greatest authority". No wonder the sentry had helped her through the wires of the forbidden Stony Lane. He walked on, deep in thought.

13

The morning was warm and well-aired by the time George and Threep made their way down to the post office.

"How's the head now?" asked Threep.

"Not too bad, except that someone seems to be trying to scoop it out, and my tongue feels like a used gas-tube. Still, I suppose I'm lucky to be here at all."

"I think Hester suspected something at breakfast. We were both late down, of course, and I for one found it difficult to keep off the subject of gas."

"One must admit that the small-talk did sound a bit small. I kept wanting to talk about Stefan."

"If this – this, Ron, is it? – recognizes Stefan from our description, I think we'll be able to take more positive steps. Otherwise, we haven't any real proof, you know. Stefan *could* be innocent."

"So could Svengali." George was willing to give the benefit of the doubt. "Still, as far as I am concerned, Stefan dun it. Why, he even looks like a murderer."

"If we went around accusing everyone who looks like a murderer, ninety per cent of the Opposition would have to defend themselves," said Threep, reasonably. "However, here we are. We'll ask Mrs Long if we can have a word with Ron."

The shop, empty of customers, smelled of boiled sweets, carbolic soap, new bread and furniture polish. It was a clean wholesome smell, and gave George the almost irrepressible feeling that he should be standing on tiptoes at the counter with a hoarded penny. Mrs Long appeared, like a Sybil, from the back room.

"Good morning. What can I get you?"

"Ah, good morning, Mrs Long." Threep took the lead. "I wonder if we could have a word with your nephew? Ronald, isn't it?"

A wary look came over Mrs Long's face. What'd the young Tartar been up to, this time? When people spoke of him as "Ronald", it usually meant trouble. Surely Mr Lamb hadn't reported that trivial matter of the cockerel? If only Ron's mother hadn't sent that Indian head-dress . . .

"What was it about, Mr Threep? I'm sure Ron . . ."

"Oh, there's nothing wrong." Relief, not unmixed with surprise, swept over Mrs Long's countenance. "We'd like a little information from him about a gentleman who spoke to him the other day."

"Well, I'm afraid you'll have to wait 'til Monday. Ron an' Julie've gone to London to their Ma for a day or so. Is there anything I can ask 'n? I'm writing today."

"Conf—. No, I don't think so, thank you. It's not really important; I'll see him when he comes back. Monday, you say?"

"Yes, 'e pertickler wants to be back for the feet, an' 'is father's boat sails on Monday. Stuart, 'e is."

"A Scot?"

"No, a stuart on a ship; same's a waiter. The children don't see much of 'n. I'm not sure they're any worse off for that." Plainly, Mrs Long thought stuarts no better than they should be, gadding about the oceans like that. "That's why the kids spend so much time with me. Their mother . . ."

Threep stemmed the spate. "Well, there's no point in waiting, then. We'll look in on Monday, unless we see the lad at the fête Good morning, Mrs Long."

"So that's that," remarked George as they stood outside the shop. "We'll have to wait for our principal witness. Meanwhile, I'm not giving Stefan an inch. I'll feel happier when your cloak-and-dagger man turns up."

"I'd rather you forgot about the 'cloak-and-dagger' man, as you call him," said Threep. "In fact, it would be better if you didn't mention it again, even between our two selves. I shouldn't have told you in the first place, I suppose. Anyway, he's not coming now."

"As you please." George spoke a trifle distantly. He didn't believe it. This was the first time anyone had doubted his ability to keep a still tongue about murder and international intrigue. "Are you coming back to the house?" he asked, as Threep stood gazing into the shop window. George couldn't feel that Threep was interested in Giant Gob-stoppers, even at the give-away price of three for fourpence, as advertised.

"I – er – that is, I thought of calling on Miss Fenner." Threep tried to look as if the idea had just struck him. "I find I've left my cigarette-case there," he said, absent-mindedly taking a cigarette from the case. "I'll follow later."

"I see." And George did. "I'll mention it to Mrs Bollanger, shall I?" he asked, helpfully.

"Don't bother. Just say I've gone. What are you grinning at?"

"Nothing," said George. "I'll see you at lunch."

Polly was cutting roses as Threep paused shyly at the gate of the cottage. She looked cool and crisp in a simple blue dress, and a hat that would have sheltered a moderately-sized circus. The white background of the cottage showed her to her best advantage. As she well knew. She turned as the latch lifted.

"Good morning, Mr Threep. And how is my ex-patient this morning?"

"Quite fit, thanks to you. No need to ask how you are – you shame the roses." This was pretty good for Threep.

"Oh!" She gave a cry of alarm. "Is my face as red as that?"

Threep made hasty amendments.

"No, no. I simply meant you're blooming."

"My blooming what?"

He gave up the unequal struggle.

"Nothing," he said, miserably.

Polly relented. Poor dear, he wasn't equipped for verbal fencing. Just a simple-minded M.P.

"Do come in. I was just going to have some coffee. Will you join me?"

Threep's spirits rose as they went into the cottage. As if a lamp had been rubbed, Mrs Watt appeared with a tray of coffee and biscuits. Polly drew up a pouffe.

"You take the armchair – you'll find it more comfortable. I'll sit here." She arranged herself on the pouffe, gracefully as a ballerina. "Give me a cigarette, please."

Light as a butterfly, thought Threep, wondering idly how much she weighed. Polly could have told him: seven pounds too much for her peace of mind.

"You know," he said, as he held a light for her cigarette, "I don't see how Hester can possibly turn you out of here without Helen's consent."

"Nor could she. But Helen will consent. She's as much freedom of speech as a ventriloquist's dummy. I've spoken to her once or twice about renewing the lease, and she's been evasive, to say the least of it. You could almost see her looking over her shoulder in case Mrs Bollanger was within tongue-shot. Anyway, I've just written her another note about it. Not that it'll do much good. But I'll try almost anything."

"There's one way we can get over it," said Threep, thoughtfully, sipping his coffee.

"No." Polly was firm. "I draw the line at murder. And I see no other way."

"Hester wants the cottage for me. Suppose I take it, making sure that there's a sub-letting clause in the agreement. I could then let it to you and nobody could do a thing about it."

He paused, aghast, that he should have thought of such a thing, let alone utter it. To his surprise, the ceiling remained *in situ.*

Polly's eyes widened.

"And would you really do that for me? You realize that you'd be exiled from The Leas for evermore, spurned by your kith and kin, every man's hand against you . . ."

"That wouldn't matter," said Threep, stoutly. That look on Polly's face would have sent him to the stake humming gay airs. "You'd be safe, and that's the main thing."

Polly took a deep breath.

"Well, I think you're very sweet." Threep's soul peeped into Heaven. "But I couldn't let you do a thing like that for me. We'll just have to wait and see what happens. After all, something turned up for Mr Micawber, didn't it?"

"Maybe, but Micawber's isn't the case under review at the moment."

"Well, Helen *may* suddenly reassert herself. Perhaps you could feed her surreptitious slices of raw beef, or something. But I'll never forget your offer." She laid a soft hand upon his, and his soul, whose big morning it was, turned somersaults in the Elysian fields. "It's very comforting to know that there's someone out there rooting for me."

Threep covered the hand with his other one.

151

"As long as I live you'll have someone rooting for you," he said, shakily.

"George," Helen came out on to the lawn where George sat on his shoulder-blades in a deck-chair, "what really happened last night?"

"Happened?" He tried to sit up.

"Yes; something happened. I could tell by the way you and Uncle Milton behaved, at breakfast."

"Behaved?"

"Yes, Sir Echo. You both came down late, you especially looking like a deep-frozen cod; then you both talked the most obvious trivialities, like a pair of cross-talk comedians. Come on, out with it."

"You're imagining things. What could have happened? True, I was a little tired this morning, but that was because Threep came down to my room during the night, to talk about the accident. Kept me gassing for a couple of hours." He wished he'd used a different idiom.

Helen looked at him dubiously. The story had a ring of truth but wasn't completely convincing. She dog-eared the subject, ready to bring up some time when he was off his guard.

"Talking of gas, did you notice the strong smell upstairs, this morning? Mother's phoned the plumber to come and search for the leak. Seems to be coming from your landing, too."

"Gas? I can't really say I noticed it. Faint smell of geraniums, perhaps. Not gas."

"Gas, George. Not geraniums. If you think that geraniums smell like that, have a walk around the greenhouses."

"I did, yesterday. Nearly gassed myself. It was the geraniums, I think. Almost overpowering. We'll have none at our wedding. If there *is* a wedding," he added, pessimistically.

"You're not changing your mind, are you, George?"

"How could I change my mind? I was never any good at accepting second best. No, my dear; I may hobble to the altar, bent and gnarled, but I'll hobble with you or nobody."

"You do say nice things sometimes, George, when you're not thinking." Helen bent and kissed him on the forehead. "I don't think we'll have to wait that long, though; Mother'll relent soon. Can't you do something to win her approval?"

"You mean like saving her life, or something? Perhaps if you pushed her into the fishpond, I could . . ."

"George! No, I mean do something she'd think a lot of."

"Suicide, maybe?"

"You're being very dense, aren't you, dear? Look, she's very fond of Wordsworth. Couldn't you lead the conversation around to poetry, and quote some Wordsworth?"

"I don't know any Wordsworth, except bits of 'Ode to A Grecian Urn', and that's only because I had to stay in after school once and learn it."

"Keats. But don't you know *any* poetry?"

George thought. The only verse he could bring to mind was one concerning the eccentricities of a certain young lady of Gloucester, and doubted whether this would be acceptable.

"No." He decided against it.

"Well, why not look up some Wordsworth, and bring in a casual quotation? How about 'Daffodils'?"

"Daffodils?" George didn't see how the topic had gone botanical.

"Yes, dear; a poem," said Helen, patiently.

"Sorry. I thought you meant a bunch. I'll try, but isn't there anything else she has a yen for? Or anything she particularly dislikes? No, perhaps that's too broad a subject."

"I can't think of anything." It struck Helen that her mother had very few likes. She brightened. "Why don't you learn and recite a poem by Wordsworth at the fête? I'm sure Mother would jump at it, if you were to offer. Miss Bean's cancelled her poem and Miss Kettle's dying to get in."

"Me?" George looked at her in horror. Was this his betrothed – the sweet innocent girl he loved? Had she suddenly gone mad? Or was this a sadistic streak bequeathed from her mother? "Me?" To blazes with grammar; this was a crisis. "Stand on a stage in front of a lot of strangers – strangers, mark you, who have never done me an ill turn – and spout poetry I dislike written by a man I've never heard of? You can't mean it!"

"You wouldn't do a little thing like that, for me?"

"You call that a little thing? You don't know what you're asking. I've always had a horror of public appearances. The last time I was on the stage, at the impressionable age of eight, I was dragged there kicking and screaming to collect my Sunday-school prize. After that soul-searing experience I've always made sure that I do nothing to qualify me to go on the stage. Can't you think of anything simpler, like strangling a bear or something?"

"No." Helen was determined, now. The thing had become a test of George's love. "If you think anything at all of me, you'll do it."

The injustice of it all struck George.

"Well, if you thought anything of me, you'd tell your mother that we're getting married, anyway, without pillorying me in front of a lot of Moonrakers – people who'll probably heave wurzels at me as soon as I start to recite your precious 'Bluebells'. The air'll be thick . . ."

"'Daffodils.' And nobody'll throw anything at you. Of course, if you're frightened . . ."

"All right." The Loder blood was up. "I'll do it." Helen's eyes lit up. "But," George continued, "let's start this partnership on an equal shares basis. After I've done this foul thing, will you go to your mother and say, 'Mother, George and I are going to be married; go and jump in the lake.' Will you do that?"

Helen looked at him for a full half-minute. "All right, George," she announced, finally, "I'll do it. Leaving out the lake part. There!"

"There's my girl!" George kissed her fondly. Then he decided to push his luck a little further.

"Look," said the opportunist, as off-handedly as possible, "while you're about it, why not renew Miss – er – Miss Fenner's tenancy of Rose Cottage? She mentioned, yesterday, that she'd love to stay."

"Why this altruistic – if it *is* altruistic – interest in Miss Fenner's affairs?" A definite chilliness crept into Helen's voice.

"Well, it just seemed to me that she's on her own, and it . . ."

"That's not necessarily true, according to Miss Kettle. And, if it is, it won't hurt her to be on her own somewhere else. I wonder if you'd bother about the matter if it applied to Miss Kettle, and not Miss Fenner? You men are all the same when it comes to a pretty face."

"Pretty? Would you say that Miss Fenner was pretty?" George saw the danger-signals, and prepared his retreat route. "Well-preserved, perhaps. What would you say her age was – fifty or so?"

"Oh, not more than forty-five, I shouldn't think." Helen's claws retracted slightly. "Anyway, Uncle Milton wants the cottage, so she'll have to go. As a matter of fact, I had a note from her this morning, asking about an extension of the lease. There's nothing I can do. Yet, you know, I shall be sorry to turn her out. But Mother . . ." It wasn't necessary to finish the sentence. They knew who shaped their ends.

George let the matter drop. Let Threep work it out for Polly and himself. He, George, had done enough for one morning. Rather consolidate his gains than risk a complete loss.

"Of course, darling," he said, meekly.

Stefan turned off the tap and began to coil the hose he'd been using on the car. His mind was still grappling with the events of last night and this morning.

Number Three's news regarding Helen Bollanger had set him back sharply. Who'd have guessed such a thing? Not that he had the slightest doubt about it, now. If Number Three said a thing was so, then it was so. And Loder wasn't even a pawn in the game. Curious, because he'd have sworn . . .

On the subject of Loder, how did he come to be sitting on the lawn, flaunting his health in front of Stefan's very eyes? What had gone wrong with the gas plan? Not that it mattered now, of course, but it was irritating, just the same. One liked things to go smoothly, whether it was filching the odd document or gassing a man. He put on his cap and tunic and went around to the hall for the day's orders; he gave Helen and George a polite salute as he passed them.

George answered with a cold nod. Somehow, he could infuse no warmth into his feelings for Stefan. Chauffeurs who went around gassing their employers' guests, felt George, were not good chauffeurs. Curious feeling, though, watching your own would-be murderer wandering around an English country house without let or hindrance. The old feudal system had given way to this, then, this Russian Theatre atmosphere where people are murdered *ad lib*, just to fit in with the dialogue. Well, he wasn't going to be *ad libbed* for anyone. He turned to Helen.

"How's the Colonel's affair going on?" he asked. "I hear you're making great strides."

"Oh, I'm enjoying it, George. We've found one or two more facts, all adding to the general picture. I'm getting to know what the old gentleman was really like, now."

"What did he do, besides snipe at railway trains and make wine?"

"Lots of things. He built Rose Cottage, you know. It was going to be a present for his bride, but she died before their wedding day. It gets terribly fascinating, George, delving into people's pasts."

"I know. See Sunday papers. I'd be interested in finding a bottle of that wine, though. 'Luno,' you called it, I think!"

"Yes. It *would* be fun."

Mrs Bollanger arrived in their midst, complete with pruning-gloves, secateurs, basket, and a large yellow book entitled, in huge red letters, *The Gardener's Friend*. She obviously meant business. George would have hated to be a surplus twig. A snail, oozing stationarily along the path, gave a scared glance over where its shoulder should have been and galloped off to warn the others.

"Oh, Mr Loder." Mrs Bollanger looked at George as if she'd just plucked him from the underside of a cabbage leaf. "I wonder if you'd take this book along to Miss Kettle for me? She lives at The Elms, just a few minutes along the road. Do you mind?" She didn't add, "As if it mattered." George knew, and she knew that he knew.

His peaceful morning drained swiftly away without a gurgle. Miss Kettle, of all people! If ever a man was hag-ridden, he was. He'd been putting off this meeting for as long as possible – living in a fool's paradise, as it were; now the past had caught up with him. Miss Kettle would be bound to recognize him as Polly's visitor. Between the

Bollanger hammer and the Kettle anvil, he'd end up as a shapeless mass. Dumbly, he took the book.

Then he cheered up. Couldn't he just leave the thing on the doorstep, and walk away? Of course he could! He smiled happily.

"Only too pleased," he said.

Mrs Bollanger delivered her *coup de grâce*.

"Oh, and tell her that I'll send her the cuttings this evening. Please be sure to tell her; I don't want her worrying around here."

So that was that. No question of leaving the book and melting away, now. He'd have to look Miss Kettle in the face and give her the message. She'd be able to go over him with a microscope during that time.

The wildest schemes were considered and discarded as he trod the short distance to The Elms. Leave the book with a note? Shout through the letter-box, and run?

Here he was, at the garden gate. He dragged slowly up the path, brain racing. Paused at the neat front door.

This was it.

14

Myrtle Kettle straightened up from her weeding as she caught the rear view of a man walking from her gate to the front door. He'd passed without noticing her, she guessed, due to this bank of Michaelmas daisies. She opened her mouth to call to him, then stopped as the man began to behave in what she afterwards described as "a peculiar manner".

He put down the large yellow volume which Miss Kettle recognized as her *Gardener's Friend*, took a handkerchief from his breast pocket and tied it around his mouth. Another handkerchief, from a trouser pocket, then went around his cheek. Showing about a square inch of face, he picked up the book and rang the door-bell.

To George, the Great Idea had come at the last moment, born of desperation. With his face tied up like this, surely nobody could possibly recognize him? True, he was only postponing the inevitable – Miss Kettle must meet him soon, quite possibly at the fête – but it would at least give him time to think. Seeing him semi-mummified like this, she'd naturally suppose he had toothache. Had he known that she was watching his preparations with a deep and absorbing interest, he'd have felt less confident.

Miss Kettle felt herself trembling. A masked attack? She hadn't been able to catch a glimpse of the man's face – nor did she want to. Here, she felt, was her premonition being fulfilled; and the double-barrelled gun was upstairs, unloaded!

As George turned again, to put more weight on the

door-bell, she stepped quickly across the yard or so of grass that led to the side door, let herself in quietly, and went upstairs.

With shaking fingers she loaded the cartridges into the breach. The barrel gave a reassuring click as she closed it and cocked the trigger. Now, thought Miss Kettle, grimly bring on your masked men! She opened the bedroom window and leaned out, pointing the gun ostentatiously at George's Fair Isle pullover.

"What is it?" she whinnied. "What do you want?"

George stepped back and looked up. Miss Kettle's features, foreshortened by the height, looked grim and forbidding, and her hundred-horse-power steel-rimmed spectacles did nothing to soften her countenance. Even more forbidding were the two blue-black adamantine barrels pointing at him. It was, thought, George, a real old-fashioned country welcome.

"Good morning," he mumbled through the layers of handkerchief, "Mrs Bollanger asked me to give you this book." He pretended not to notice the gun.

"Oh, did she?"

"Yes. And she said she'd send the cuttings this evening."

"She did, did she?"

Apparently this elderly Annie Oakley was a woman of action rather than words. George felt that there were other things to be said, but couldn't think of any. How would it be if he inquired after her chincherinchees? Or might she think that he was trying to be familiar? Especially as he didn't know what chincherinchees were. The gun remained pointing unwaveringly in his direction.

"And who are you?" asked the voice from aloft.

"My name is Loder – George Loder," he said, frankly. "I'm staying with Mrs Bollanger for a few days. I'm sorry I'm all wrapped up, like this" – he gave an apologetic laugh – "but I've a bad toothache."

"Have you, now?"

"Yes. I must see the dentist. Mewell. L. Mewell," he added, in case she got mixed up with any other Mewell.

"Well, if you'll just put the book down on the doorstep, I'll be down later." Miss Kettle still wasn't taking any chances. "Thank Mrs Bollanger for me, please."

George put the book inside the tiny porch.

"I've put it here."

"Have you?"

"Yes. On the floor," he added, fatuously, to let her know that it wasn't suspended in mid-air.

"Have you?"

George shuffled his feet uncomfortably. The conversation was too one-sided, no friendly phrase for phrase. He turned to go.

"I'll get along, then." He didn't think she'd try and persuade him to stay. Nor did she.

"Good morning, Mr – er, Loder."

"Good morning, Miss Oakley."

"Miss who?"

"Miss Kettle. Good morning."

She watched him walk the length of the path and out of the gate, a guilty look between his shoulder-blades. He paused a few yards down the road, to transfer the handkerchiefs to his pockets. Miss Kettle shook her head and unloaded the gun.

"Funny old harpie," said George to himself. "Probably got a burglar-fixation, or something." He ambled back to The Leas, happy in the knowledge that another crisis had been postponed, if not averted. Sufficient unto the day . . .

Milton Threep walked on air from Rose Cottage towards The Leas. Polly. He turned the name over and over. Polly Fenner. A lovely name, lovely as its owner. And this was the name Hester was trying to besmirch. Not as long as he could buckle on a sword! Or, anyway, fill a fountain-pen.

He was passing the Angry Hen, and decided not to. The bar-parlour looked freshly cleaned and inviting as he consulted his watch. Ten to eleven; might as well sit quietly, with a drink, and think things over.

Threep knew that something big had happened to him, bigger than anything ever before. Since his accident, his whole outlook had changed; everything he did seemed to be dependant on Polly. For the first time in his life he wished he were younger, taller, slimmer – oh, everything he wasn't. How on earth did Polly manage to speak to him without bursting into peals of derisive laughter? Must be her stage training.

He perched himself on a stool and ordered a dry sherry. Jno. Murk offered him one of his old glasses, exquisitely cut, in which the sherry reposed, palely inviting. Threep sipped, found the sherry eminently drinkable, and abandoned himself to reverie.

How fine Polly and he looked, walking down the aisle! Polly in some silk stuff or other, with veil thrown back, looking up at him with shy pride. Himself, tall, deep-chested, slim-hipped, masterfully holding . . .

"A double Scotch."

He looked up distastefully, as a dry voice shattered his dream to fragments. The stranger who'd been sitting behind them, last night, was standing at the bar demanding sustenance. Why must he choose to come in here to swill his liquor? Threep smothered his irritation. After all, the man couldn't know that he'd just broken up a perfect marriage.

"Good morning," said Threep politely. The man could represent a potential vote. You couldn't be too careful.

"Good morning," answered Karanov. This meeting, he

felt, might be useful, if he could get this Threep into conversation. He fell back on the weather, surest topic for getting Englishmen to talk. "Lovely morning, isn't it?" he observed.

It was. Threep looked through the open door and across the counterpane of fields, green, golden, yellow, to where the sky, blue as a Dane's eye, joined the trees and meadows in the faint haze over Bilton Parva.

A kindly breeze, soft as a sigh, brought perfume from Jno.'s bee-loud lavender, mingled with the faint smell of warm tar, into the bar-parlour. Where every prospect pleaseth, thought Threep, and only Hester . . . He suddenly realized that the other man was talking.

". . . some kind of fête, here, I understand?"

"Fate? Oh, fête; yes, we're holding a fête on Monday. All the usual things, you know – flower-show, a concert, home-made wine competition, baby-show, and an excellent children's dancing act." Threep felt that a boost for Polly wouldn't come amiss.

"I must come along. Where is it to be held, exactly?"

"In the field – May's paddock, it's called – behind the big house farther up the road."

"Oh, yes; The Leas. I passed it, this morning. Beautiful building. Have you been inside it?"

"I live there. It's a . . . ." He glanced at his watch. "Good Lord! I must be getting back." There was his report to write; the attempt on George's life, and the brief-case episode, while it was still fresh in his mind. He slid off the stool, just as George came thirstily in at the door. Neither noticed the quick look of surprise on Karanov's face as he looked at the newcomer.

"Hallo," said George. "I thought you were going to Rose Cottage. Polly not at home?"

"Hallo, Loder. Yes, I've seen Miss Fenner. I'm on my way back to The Leas, now."

"It'll take you some time at this rate, won't it? Have another?"

"Thank you, no. I must go back. Is Hester in?"

"Yes, you're missing nothing. Keep me company a while." George ordered half a pint of bitter.

"No." Threep made his reluctant way to the door. "I've work to do. I'll see you at lunch, I suppose." He turned to Karanov. "Good morning."

"Good morning," answered the other, as Threep left.

George looked across at the man. Was this a friend of Threep's? If so, why hadn't Threep introduced him? One of his parliamentary buddies, perhaps?

"You know Mr Threep?" he asked.

Karanov lowered his glass.

"Mr . . . ?"

"Threep. He's just left."

"Left where?"

"Here. He's just gone out."

"Oh. No, I can't say I've met him before. Should I have?"

"Not necessarily. I just thought you might have."

"No," said Karanov, removing all doubt.

George took a thoughtful pull at his glass. He wasn't at all satisfied. Why was the chap so anxious to disclaim all knowledge of Threep? Almost as if . . .

Of course! George saw it all in a flash. This was the M.I.5 merchant! It stuck out like a sore thumb. No wonder he was keeping his association with Threep dark.

He gazed enviously at Karanov over the rim of his glass. A secret agent! George tried stretching his neck sideways to see whether there was a tell-tale bulge in the other's hip pocket, nearly capsizing his stool in attempting an impossible angle. He gave what he hoped was an enigmatic smile in response to Karanov's raised eyebrow.

Meanwhile, the spy thought furiously. This was undoubtedly the Loder who Forty-seven had said was dead. Alive, and by the look of the gymnastics on the stool, kicking. Was Forty-seven trying to double-cross the SNABU? He'd bear watching, during the next day or so.

"You're holidaying around here?" asked George. It would be interesting to hear the agent's "cover" story.

"Just for a few days. I'm rather interested in the earthworks at Barnsby. You live here?"

"No. I'm staying at The Leas – the house farther along the road. My fiancée lives there."

"Ah, I think I had the pleasure of a fleeting glimpse of her, this morning. Golden hair, blue eyes, blue dress? I congratulate you."

George reflected. Helen *was* wearing her blue dress. "Thank you. Yes, that was she." He smiled the idiotic smile of a man talking to a stranger of the girl he loves.

Karanov was satisfied. Now he was sure he could recognize the woman, he'd be able to carry out his part of the plan. It wasn't only that he didn't trust Forty-seven; he just liked to double-check everything. Karanov had come up the hard way.

George would dearly have loved to have said, quietly, "Look, I know all. I'm practically one of you. Whenever you need help, I shall be here." He decided against it. These people went their own way about things. How about if he gave a veiled hint . . .?

"Don't forget," he said, trying to infuse a double meaning into the words, "look me up if you need anything while you're here, won't you? Here's my card" – Karanov took the

165

white slip which described George as a Consulting Engineer –
"so bear it in mind, *anything* I can do will be a pleasure. You
understand?"

Karanov nodded. Chap was a bit keen, perhaps, but you
couldn't blame a man for doing a bit of advertising, on the
side. These businessmen . . . Anyway, the card might come in
useful. He put it away, carefully.

"I'll remember," he said. And George felt that he'd been
accepted.

Amos Flower took a deep draught from his tankard and
wiped a practised hand across his lips.

"First this evenin'," he observed. This was true. The Angry
Hen had opened its doors a scant three minutes previously.
"Beer ain't wot it was, though," he continued. "W'en Oi
were a young 'un, two pints o' beer at fourpence 'd knock 'ee
from 'ere to D'vizes. Now, you 'as to save up fer three weeks
to buy 'arf a pint o' coloured water. No wonder the publicans
gets fat." He looked reproachfully at Jno.

"Don't talk so wet," the landlord defended himself. "The
beer's the same. 'Tis you, gettin' 'ardened to it. You'm soaked
in it, that's wot."

"A drop o' beer, took reg'lar, never 'urt no one," said
Amos, with cold dignity. "Better'n all thishyer woine an'
muck. A chap gi' Oi some o' that Eye-talian stuff, at Sede –
'Can't I', 'e called it – an' it took three pints to wash the taste
outer me mouth arter it. Oi loikes a drop o' port, though,
when Oi can get 'n."

"Ar, without payin' for 'n." Farrer ducked through the
low doorway to the bar. "Evenin', all. 'Arf o' the usual,
please, John."

"'Allo, Bob." Amos gave a welcoming beam. "Oi ain't
seed yer much to talk to, lately, 'cept in the line o' business.

'Ave 'ee thought about the cottage, since? 'Andsome bit o' property fer a young married couple, 'sno."

Farrer took a long drink, placed his glass carefully on the counter, and wiped his lips.

"Ar, Oi *ave* thought about 'n. An' wot Oi've thought ain't nobody's business. 'Sno wot you can do wi' thy cottage?" he asked, earnestly. "You can . . ."

"Now, Bob, there's no call to be insultin'." Amos held up a restraining hand. "Oi was on'y tryin' to do 'ee a good turn. Oi've 'ad enough people ask for 'n. On'y terday that young Miss Fenner spoke about 'n."

Farrer looked his astonishment. He knew and liked Polly. "Mean ter say she's goin' ter give up Rose Cottage for thy 'eap o' rubble? 'Aven't 'ad an accident to 'er 'ead, 'ave 'er?"

"No she 'aven't. She reckernizes a good property when she sees one. Besides," naïvely, "she've gotter get outer Rose Cottage. That bloke Threep wants 'n." Amos could be trusted to have accurate details.

"Threep!" Farrer spat the word, causing a surprised Amos to spill a drop of beer down an already well-christened waistcoat. "Oi'll gi' 'n Threep! Causes more trouble 'ere than 'e does in Parlyment. Spoke to me as if Oi were a grease-box or somethin'. 'Luke heah, my man,' 'e says, 'H-wen's the next flippin' train in?' 'e says. Oi told 'n to foind out," said Farrer, sacrificing accuracy for interest-value. He mused over the injustice of things. "Fancy 'im turnin' out a nice young lady loike Miss Fenner. She's worth three of 'e."

"Ar," agreed Amos. "A clever young 'umman, Miss Fenner. She've got more brains in 'er little finger than she've got in the rest of 'er body."

"More brains . . .?" Farrer didn't get it. The compliment was well-intended, no doubt, but didn't bear analysis.

167

"She'm puttin' on a dancin' act wi' the youngsters, at the feet. Bally, 'tis called. Pretty to watch, too."

"Oo's judgin' the veg., this year? Vicar, Oi s'pose. 'E knows as much about veg. as Oi d' know about Lat'n," announced Farrer, whose classical education had been admittedly sketchy. "Just 'cos a bloke speaks lah-de-dah, they takes it for granted 'e knows everything. 'Oo judges they? Us? No, we does wot we'm told."

"Well, that's 'ow it is." Amos sighed like one who is constantly fighting a losing battle to make the world a better, purer place. "There'll always be them wot's put on, and always them wot puts. Take ole Myrtle Kettle, now. She'd cut my throat wi' a blunt sickle, given 'arf a chanst. Said Oi sold 'er 'er own tomatter plants. 'Ow could she say that," he inquired, with righteous indignation. "They coulda bin anybody's."

"They could if *you* sold 'em to 'er," remarked Farrer, sagely. He chuckled. "Oi'd gi' a quid to 'ave seen 'er face, though, when she put 'em in the green'ouse wit t'others and found they weren't there. O' course, findin' 'er own label on the lot you sold 'er didn't 'elp things along much."

"Thass wot *she* said, the lyin' ole 'aybag. Oi'll pay 'er out, if Oi gets the chanst. She's showin' woine agen, at the feet, Oi s'pose?"

"She usually does," agreed Farrer. "So'm Oi, this year. Bet mine's a bit different to 'ers, though. 'Ers is usually non-alco'olic, I believe. Mine'd start a rough-'ouse in a nunnery."

"Oh?" A thoughtful look passed over Amos's face. An idea was struggling for birth. The corners of his lips slipped back to his ears. Pay out Miss Kettle? Here was a plan dropped right into his lap. He drained his glass, and the smile remained on his face for the rest of the evening.

Amos had found a way.

15

The mellow notes of Bilton Parva's St Thomas rolled softly over the dew-laden fields, calling the faithful to prayer. That is, those of the faithful who hadn't turned over for another half an hour, contentedly realizing that it was Sunday morning. St Thomas's call was answered by Winthringham's St Peter's – more sonorously, as befitted a church that was old when St Paul's was new – and passed on to Hoale's St Cecilia's. Listening carefully, one could just discern Barnsby's Methodist, brisk and business-like, striking double time.

One by one, the bells clanged to a stop; the countryside rested in the calm stillness which descends on the Sabbath, especially when the sun is shining and the veil of ground-mist is lifting from the fields.

In May's paddock, Farrer walked slowly, head well forward until he looked like an ambulatory question-mark, gathering mushrooms for breakfast. No Caeser ever enjoyed mushrooms as Farrer did. Freshly gathered – "best from a field where 'osses 'as bin" – and with a thickish rasher of Wiltshire bacon, here was food for the gods. And if the gods were partial to a slice of fried bread with it, well, that was all right with Farrer.

Some of the more delectable mushrooms, of course, would find their way to Gwyneth's plate, making his own taste the sweeter.

Thoughts of his affianced cast gloom over an otherwise enjoyable operation. Gwyneth. A house. Two hundred pounds. Where was two hundred pounds going to come from? If the industry he served couldn't make that amount, how could he be expected to?

At Rose Cottage, Polly's stilt-like heels clicked up the path and on to the road. She was wearing a simple shark-skin costume, crowned by a ridiculous tulle-and-feather piece of foolery destined to make the leading choir-boy miss a semi-quaver or so. As she glanced back at the cottage, drowsing in the morning sun, she felt a catch in her throat. This was what she had to give up; well, it had been nice while it lasted.

Mrs Long, at the post office, cooked her solitary breakfast with the subconscious feeling that she should be telling somebody not to do something. She always felt like this whenever Ron and Julie left the house after a long visit. She told herself that she was grateful for the break – nice and quiet, and no interruptions. She glanced at the edge of the table, where Ron's nose usually appeared in his daily inquiry for bre'n'-butter with a bit of sugar on it. "Well, they'll be back from London tomorrow morning," Mrs Long told herself. And was surprisingly cheered thereby.

Myrtle Kettle, her lath-like form swathed in a red-and-white striped dress, topped by a flower-pot hat, walked up the church path, her prayer-book clutched virtuously to her side. She looked like a maypole. Her face carried the grim expression of one who intends to put the Devil in his place for another week at least. She was thinking of tomorrow's fête, and the status-lowering refreshment stall she'd been bulldozed into running. Her nose quivered as she saw Amos Flower pass the church, trying to look like a man who's not coming back from somewhere with a ferret in his pocket.

At The Leas, Mrs Bollanger was giving final orders to Gwyneth, who was deputizing for Cook. Cook claimed her right to attend what she called "early church", once a month, while Gwyneth "did" the breakfasts.

"I shall be back this afternoon, before tea," said Mrs Bollanger, taking a sunshade from the hall-stand. "Cook has her orders for luncheon, and please remind her that the Vicar will be here for late supper. Stefan will remain in Salisbury for his lunch." Her mistress was attending a Woman's Institute Rally, in Salisbury; Gwyneth felt that these rallies should be held more often.

"Yes 'M," she said, demurely. "And the longer 'oo two stays away, the better we'll like it," she added, *sotto voce*, as Mrs Bollanger descended the steps to the waiting car.

George, looking from his window, felt that life was good. He'd had a perfect early-morning cup of tea; there was a tantalizing smell of kidneys and bacon mingling with the perfume of roses and coffee; the car, Mrs Bollanger safely aboard, had just rolled down the drive. What more could one ask? All this, and Helen too, felt George, was enough to spoil a man. He whistled an air from "William Tell" as he shed his pyjama-jacket.

Lying in a tepid bath, Threep glared distastefully at his stomach, rising like a whale's back from the water. What sort of figure was that, for a man of his age? Not fifty-one, yet, dammit, and already shaped like an over-ripe pear. What had that article said, about a few minutes' exercise a day? He'd do it! He'd make himself worthy of Polly. He climbed determinedly out of his bath and started a few tentative toe-touching exercises. He'd never realized, before, that his toes were so far away. He felt as tall and supple as a telegraph-pole.

His mind wandered gloomily forward to tomorrow's fête, as he grunted up and down. Stiff collar and flannel suit, squiring Hester around the stalls at a hundred and sixty in the shade. Still, Polly'd be there. He brightened up, redoubled his efforts, struck his head against a shaving-cabinet and said an un-Parliamentary word. He decided to live with the stomach he'd got.

Helen pushed back her bedclothes and stretched luxuriously. Sunday, and Mother was off to Salisbury. She wondered why she felt so happy, and decided that it was because of George's decision to recite at the fête. She'd give him a good coaching, this morning, anyway. She patted a yawn back into place, and sat up.

As the Mottram sped over the unencumbered roads towards Salisbury's beckoning spire, Stefan considered his plans for tomorrow. No mistakes this time! Still, "The Fox" was helping now; nothing could go wrong.

Helen Bollanger was due for a rough time, of course, but as Stefan saw it, you can't have an omelet without breaking an egg or so. She deserved all she got, anyway, for her sly, underhand methods. He pressed the accelerator the last eighth of an inch to the floorboards and the Mottram gave of its best.

At The Moon, Alexi Karanov ate his simple breakfast of grape-fruit, toast and coffee, his mind running methodically over the arrangements for breaking down "The Colonel's" secret.

He'd hire Flower's taxi – buy it, if necessary – and get the girl away with as little fuss as possible. With Loder's visiting-card in his pocket, it shouldn't be difficult to devise a method of enticing the woman into the taxi. Once there, he knew several ways of keeping her quiet.

The empty cottage which he'd looked over yesterday seemed just right for the enterprise. If Forty-seven failed to find the papers – and he'd be likely to, unless the girl had their hiding-place well sign-posted – the cottage's lonely situation would allow him to get information out of her without her screams attracting embarrassing attention. Yes, he'd thought of everything.

Clara Watt leaned on the gate of old Mrs Ammidge's cottage, describing to P.C. Ammidge the lines upon which the annual fête was usually run.

"Starts 'bout ten o'clock, and carries on all day," she said. "Everyone goes. The vegetable show 'as entries from as far away as Barnsby." No mere parochial affair, this, evidently.

"Anything else, besides a veg. show?" Ammidge yawned.

"Anything else? How about children's sports, concert, try-your-luck stalls, baby-show – oh, all sorts!" Mrs Watt gave a vague wave of her hand to indicate the scope of an International Exhibition.

"No gamblin', I 'opes," cautioned P.C. Ammidge.

"Gamblin'? Wot dos't think we are? We'm not like they Monty Carlo lot; no, nor D'vizes, neither!"

"I'm glad to 'ear it, I'm sure. I'll 'ave a walk round, though. 'Twouldn't surprise me to find that Amos Flower runnin' a Crown 'n Anchor board, or rooletty."

"They don't let Amos run anything since 'e organized the pound-note raffle. Thirty-nine tickets 'e sold, at sixpence each; then 'is son-in-law won it. So 'e said."

"Coulda bin true, couldn't it?"

"'Is son-in-law was serving in Singapore, at the time." Mrs Watt made no accusations, just presented the unsavoury facts as known. "Funny thing," she added, reminiscently, "we counted at least fifty people 'oo said they'd bought tickets."

Helen and George sat in the lounge, two glasses of sherry in front of them. On George's face was the concentrated expression of a man who's found a bone in his mouthful of fish.

"For oft when on my couch I lie," he said, unconvincingly, "In vacant or in pensive mood, My something something something eye, Which is . . . Oh, what's next?" He reached for his glass.

173

"No you don't," Helen interposed a hand. "No more until you've learned the verse. It's the last one, George," she cajoled. "Come on, you managed the others *so* quickly. Have another glance at the book, and try again."

George groaned and picked up the book.

"Ah, that's it. They flash upon the inward eye, Which is the gift of solitude. Look, darling, what's the good? I'll learn this, today, but it will go again by tomorrow. The moment I stand in front of that audience – Bingo! – the words will vanish like smoke from a schoolboy's cigarette."

"Of course they won't! Just tell yourself that you've got to do it, and you will."

"I'm afraid I haven't that much authority. If I tell myself to do something, I usually refuse to do it. No discipline. I just don't seem to care a rap for my orders. Recalcitrant type."

"You're not trying, George."

"Your mother thinks I am – very."

"Very well, but remember that it's your fault if we have to wait years for the wedding."

"Give me that book. I'll learn this poem and spout it at those poor, unsuspecting souls tomorrow if it's the last thing I do. And it probably will be."

"There's a good boy!"

And George, who had as much poetry in his soul as a mentally-retarded Vandal, shut his eyes and memorized afresh.

St Peter's church, squat and moth-eaten, lies but a short pilgrimage from the Vicarage. From the outside no one – not even an American tourist – would have given the place a second glance. This bothered nobody, least of all the Vicar, for the church wasn't intended to catch the passing trade. It held the monopoly of souls for Winthringham, and was content with that.

Inside, however, the building was as beautiful as multi-coloured windows, mellowed grey stones, and the artistic hands of the Women's Institute could make it.

Red, gold and blue pools danced on its well-worn flagged floor as the evening sun, syncopated by the swaying branches outside, poured in through the stained-glass windows. The wine-coloured carpet, down the aisle, looked warm and rich; the polished crucifixes shimmered and glittered, their jewels glowing with deep fires.

From the pulpit, the Vicar's voice boomed forth, giving the wicked hell. For this Sunday evening sermon he'd chosen as his text, "Nevertheless, being crafty, I caught you with guile," and it was going over big. His one sorrow was that Amos Flower wasn't there to hear it.

He gave an inquiring glance, now and then, at the portly stranger who'd taken an unobtrusive position near the west door. The roundest man the Vicar had ever seen, he carried an aura of wealth around him, from his shiny red face to his brown-and-white buckskin shoes. Even the cunningly-cut alpaca jacket failed to hide the rotundity beneath, and the expensive lightweight trousers tightened over thighs like a couple of bolsters.

Marcus Rogers *was* rich. Hard work, and a bright idea, had taken him from farm-boy to super-tax. Every time a bottle of Roger's Apple Champagne is drunk – and a bottle is opened approximately every five minutes, somewhere – a little more profit flows into Marcus's well-lined pockets.

Nearly forty years, he mused, since he'd shaken the loam of Winthringham from his feet and opened up on his own, in a rented Bristol shop. Semi-starvation, insufficient sleep, impending bankruptcy – all had been faced and had their sting removed before Roger's Apple Champagne had finally caught on and swept the country.

He'd always wanted to come back, just to see if the old place looked the same, and now he'd done it. And he wasn't disappointed. The old place *did* look the same, and probably would until the Last Trump. Except for that barbed wire across Stony Lane; that had annoyed him.

He'd have a look around at the fête, tomorrow, before moving on to London on Tuesday. Doubtful if there'd be anyone he'd know, of course. Forty years was a long time. Who'd there be? Let's see: old Hatchard – Lord! he'd be about a hundred and four, now! Probably lain outside this little church for many a long year. Amos Flower? He'd be getting on, too, if he were still alive. And, if he knew Amos, he'd still be alive, all right!

Myrtle Kettle sat in the third pew from the front. To the silent delight of the choir, she was again wearing the flower-pot hat. Where, she wondered, was the mysterious masked man who'd claimed he was staying at The Leas? He was certainly not with Mrs Bollanger's party, at present.

They sat, Mrs Bollanger, Helen and Threep, smack under the pulpit. Mrs Bollanger, white-swathed and immobile, stared hard at the choir to detect any surreptitious whispering or caramel-sucking. The choir, well aware of her scrutiny, maintained looks of ethereal innocence.

Helen, at her side, was breath-taking in a dark frock, white shoes and white filmy hat. The organist had adjusted his mirror to take full advantage of this.

Milton Threep sat thinking of Polly. Somehow, between them, they must overcome Hester's antipathy; or, failing that, Helen must be made to extend the lease whether Hester liked it or not. He admitted to himself that he hadn't much faith in either proposition.

Farther back, nearer the door, Mrs Long sat quietly content. She looked forward to these Sunday evenings when she could relax in the peace and beauty of the church, un-worried and unhurried by the demanding "Ping!" of the shop door-bell. It was pleasant, too, to be on the customers' side of the counter. One got so tired of knowing only the top halves of people.

On the other side of the aisle, Polly tried to keep her mind off Mrs Bollanger and concentrate on the sermon. This was the life for her, she knew. Surely it wasn't too much to ask, to be allowed to stay? She decided to slip in a quiet prayer about it. It wouldn't carry the same weight as the Vicar's professional pleas, of course – he having the correct format – but it was worth trying.

Meanwhile, she cast an occasional motherly glance at Milton Threep. He looked just like a little boy, she thought, dragged to church in his Sunday best. She wondered where George was.

George was at The Leas, reciting "Daffodils" for the third time, unprompted. At last, he was word-perfect. Now, all he had to do was to offer his services for tomorrow. Bring the matter up at supper, tonight, perhaps?

He felt that he'd better do something quickly. When he'd declined Mrs Bollanger's invitation to church, she'd looked at him much as the Grand Inquisitor would have regarded a devil-worshipper. His excuse that he'd several letters to write before the morning mail, had been accepted with a certain amount of reserve. His stock with Mrs Bollanger had never been lower; perhaps this poetry caper would restore matters.

Voices from the hall warned him that the family had re-turned, the Vicar with them. He stood up as they came into the lounge with the smug look of people who've been to church and feel all the better for it.

Supper was an almost cheerful meal. Beside an excellent

Russian salad, and a technically perfect pêche Melba, a carefully-chilled Liebfraumilch helped to loosen tongues.

"Do you know who the stranger was, in church, Vicar?" asked Helen. Description was unnecessary. The smallest change in the pattern of the congregation was noticed by all.

"No." The Vicar helped himself to galantine of chicken.

"I didn't manage to get a word with him. I'd have liked to; there was a five-pound note in the collection which I suspect came from him." Such generosity, the Vicar felt, should be nurtured and encouraged.

"Perhaps we'll see him at the fête, tomorrow," said Threep. "His face seemed somehow familiar."

"Ah, the fête." The Vicar smiled at Mrs Bollanger. "I suppose you'll be glad to see it safely launched. I don't think you'll have to worry about the weather, anyway." He spoke as though he'd arranged for the dry spell to continue for a day or so longer.

"I think it will be successful." Mrs Bollanger knew it would. Or else. "There's only that tiresome gap in the concert programme. You remember Miss Bean has had to cancel her poem?"

"How about asking Miss Kettle to step in?" asked the Vicar, thinking he was being helpful.

"A little awkward for her, I think. She's looking after the refreshments, you know. We mustn't flog the willing horse."

George mentally complimented her on her choice of phrase. He caught the appealing look in Helen's eyes and realized that this was his Big Chance.

"Might I help, do you think?" he asked, diffidently.

Mrs Bollanger started as if a slug had offered to do a bit of weeding.

"You? Help?" she asked, unflatteringly. "What do you do? It's a Church fête, you know," she added, meaningly. Three-card tricks, Find The Lady, or risqué stories would not be acceptable.

"I can't do much, certainly," said George, humbly, "but perhaps they'd appreciate it if I spou – recited a short poem? Or maybe they mightn't be keen on Wordsworth? I'm afraid I get rather carried away on the subject of William Wordsworth b. 1770, d. 1850," he added.

"Do you?" He couldn't fail to notice the softening of Mrs Bollanger's tone. There was, she tacitly informed him, a little good in the blackest of men. "Which poem had you in mind?"

"Which ever you please," gambled George. "How about 'Daffodils'? That should do, I think," he suggested, as if he'd searched through a huge repertoire.

"Have you considered 'Lucy'?" The Vicar had his favourites, too.

"Not really. Does she want to recite?" George didn't mind standing down.

"He means the poem, 'Lucy', interposed Helen, quickly.

"Of course. Do you think it would be suitable?"

"No. Perhaps you're right," decided Mrs Bollanger. "Though 'England' mightn't be inappropriate." She assumed the face of a woman who is going to recite, and declaimed:

"Milton, thou shouldst be living at this hour . . ."

"Eh? Pardon?" Milton Threep's mind returned from Rose Cottage. Mrs Bollanger looked at him, and he curled back into his wine-glass.

"Very well, then, Mr Loder. If you will go on between Miss Gibb's song, and Miss Fenner's ballet, that will be most satisfactory." She conjured an unaccustomed smile to her lips, and George felt that he'd moved on a little. Whether he could hold his gains when Miss Kettle recognized him, tomorrow, was a different matter.

But tomorrow, as someone once rather cleverly pointed out, was another day.

16

Milton Threep exhaled powerfully, like a London Tube door closing, and ran an easing finger around the inside of his collar.

"It's going to be another scorcher today. I can hardly remember what rain feels like." He spoke wistfully, as a man who knows that a steady fall of earth-reviving rain would have saved him donning a flannel suit and neckwear which was beginning to feel like an enthusiastically-applied tourniquet.

George, standing at the hall door, agreed with the forecast. Even at this early hour, with the distaff side yet to breakfast, the dew had already gone; the sun gleamed coppery, like a tarnished warming-pan, and the air had the consistency of dusty felt.

All Nature lay in a brooding uneasy stillness. Birds, who'd sung merrily enough yesterday, now mooned about in silent contemplation of the baked earth, under which worms wriggled with impunity. Sammy, the kitchen cat, ambled listlessly past a sparrow that couldn't have cared less.

In the fields, cows stood oblong and immobile, too languid to lift a tufted tail to the myriad flies who knew when they were on to a good thing. The brook running from May's paddock through to Stony Lane and its forbidden ground, was a mere trickle – no more than a streak of damp earth in the aridness surrounding it. The morning waited, breathlessly, for the curtain to go up on the day's drama.

There were sounds of activity from May's paddock,

though, as Lamb the gardener, Stefan, and one or two volunteers put the finishing touches to the marquee, tents and stalls for the fête.

It was noticed with some surprise and much conjecture, that Amos Flower was among those present. That Amos should be abroad at this early hour was enough to excite comment; that he should also be working, with no prospect of remuneration, was news of the man-bites-dog order.

True, he seemed to be spending a lot of time in the vicinity of the home-made wine exhibits – rows of bottles on a snowy cloth, under a canvas awning – but he'd also given some help and much advice. As Lamb said, "'Tidn't many as've seed Amos workin'. To see 'n workin' fer nothin's danged near mirac'lus."

Already, lady helpers, dressed in their best to show that they were not just ordinary stall-holders, were laying out the stalls and calling Heaven to witness that they'd never seen such haphazard organization. It was bad enough last year, but . . . Had *they* been on the Committee, now, they'd . . . The talk, in fact, followed the same pattern as in all previous years.

There was the refreshment stall, with its neatly-stacked glasses, cups and saucers, and modestly-covered cake-trays. At one end was a tea-urn – cold, as yet – and two large glass bowls containing what appeared to be heavy swamp-water in which floated sad-looking bits of orange- and lemon-peel. Crates, under the trestle-table, held dozens of bottles of fizzy drinks, already at the tepidity required for fêtes and treats.

Next to this cooling fount was the vegetable stand, already bearing bloated-looking specimens of the earth's bounty. Complacent marrows; sinuous runner-beans and honest earthy potatoes. There's be much argument and many accusations regarding this stall, later on in the evening, in the **Angry Hen**.

The First-Aid centre, Committee, and arena for the Bonny Baby Competition were housed in the large marquee at one end of the paddock; at the other end was a raised dais, about three feet above the ground, where speeches, concert, and prize-giving would be held. George, now walking around with Threep, eyed it much as an aristocrat might have watched the guillotine being erected.

There were other sundry small stalls; hoop-la, dart-throwing, a White Elephant stall (the title of this raised the children's hopes until they saw it for what it was) an Aunt Sally and a coconut-shy whose coconuts lay smugly impregnable on their stands.

Committeemen, awed by their own importance, rushed in and out of the marquee giving and cancelling final instructions. Their resigned looks showed clearly that they were perforce dealing with stone-deaf morons, but were coping due to sheer initiative and energy.

It was, of course, no different from a hundred other fêtes taking place all over England at that very minute.

Towards half past ten, the preparations died down and the public began to arrive with that vague let-loose-in-a-field look which is part and parcel of the English fête-attender's make-up. Gaily-coloured dresses, grey flannels, sober blacks and eye-searing shirts mingled and intermingled with kaleidoscopic confusion.

Bilton, Winthringham and district was not a thickly-populated area, but could put on a brave show for a fête. Everyone had turned out, including old Joe Penny, who'd come because he'd got the impression that it was an Old Age Pensioners' treat. Joe thought that all outdoor functions were O.A.P. treats and always turned up, optimistically hoping that the current one wouldn't be as disappointing as the last.

A stir of activity from the direction of the dais turned the crowd towards it. A dozen chairs had been set out, seated upon which were the Committee, the Vicar, Mrs Bollanger, Helen and Threep. A self-conscious, humid-looking Threep who'd have to say "a few words" to open the fête officially.

The Vicar rose and walked to the edge of the dais.

"Dearly belove..." he began, "that is, ladies and gentlemen, if you'll just gather around for a moment, I'll ask our distinguished honorary Chairman to open the fête. After that, I want you all to enjoy yourselves." ("But go easy on the lemonade," thought George) "Have a go at all the stalls, and spend lots of money." He leaned forward, waggishly, as if he were going to tell them a risqué parable. "It's your money we're after, you know, and it's all for a good cause. Now, I'm sure you've heard me often enough, so I'll call on Milton Threep, M.P., to open the fête." He stepped back heavily on to Threep's toe, and clapped his hands encouragingly as his victim limped forward.

"Ladies and gentlemen," Threep began, concealing the agony of a throbbing corn (after all, the show must go on) "I know you've all had a look around and seen some of the treats prepared for you, and I think you'll all agree that this year's fête bids fair to outdo all others. I'd like to take this opportunity of thanking the Committee" – he half-turned, and the Committee simpered shyly as if this was the last thing they'd expected – "for the amount of work they've put into this – er – function.

"Remember that your money will be spent in a good cause" – what *was* the cause? he wondered – "so spend freely for the cause, because the cause, of course, will cause – er – because the money will be well spent." He waited a moment to let this great thought sink in.

Joe Penny, whose hearing had gradually deteriorated over

the few years since his eightieth birthday, leaned over to his neighbour.

"Wodd 'er say?" he asked, piercingly. "I voted for 'n laast 'Lection an' 'er didden' do nothin' fer Oi. W'en's the free tea?"

There was a titter, and Threep hurried on.

"Now, it gives me great pleasure to declare this fête open." He sat down to a patter of self-conscious applause.

Mrs Bollanger stood up.

"There has had to be a slight change in the advertised programme," she announced. "Due to the extra large number of entries for the Home-made Wine Competition, the wine-judging will commence at two o'clock, while the concert is still running. I would also like to remind you that there are adequate waste-paper facilities around the grounds. Thank you."

The multitude, duly chastened, broke up for its orgy of pleasure, gambling and squandering. Winthringham and district was officially *en fête*.

George managed to capture Helen and they walked around the ground, pausing at the various stalls.

"You *do* look warm, George." Helen looked at him critically. "Why don't you have a lemonade, or an ice-cream? I think I'll have one, too."

"Good idea." George received the suggestion with enthusiasm. "Where's the stall?"

"Over there. Look, Miss Kettle's in charge of it."

Miss Kettle! George halted as if he'd been lassoed.

"I don't think I'll bother, now," he muttered. "Waste of money, anyway."

Helen gave him a cold glance. This parsimony in George was a little unexpected.

"I have a little money, if you don't want to break into a shilling. Come on."

"It isn't that." He thought quickly. "It's just that I wanted you to hear me say my poem before we become separated again."

It had the effect he'd expected.

"Oh, please do, George. And don't forget to put some expression into it."

He recited the poem with self-conscious accuracy, gradually heading her away from the Kettle sphere of influence. The words had all the force and expression of a nervous budgerigar reciting "Il Penseroso" but Helen realized that she couldn't afford to be critical at this stage.

"Word perfect, dear. But you're sure you won't go and dry up, when you're announced?"

"Absolutely. Nothing can stop me, now. Irving could have picked up tips from me."

(The gods sat up. Rash mortal! Didn't he know better than to boast under an open sky? Zeus called the Muses to him, whispered in their ears, and they tripped away, giggling. Well, the man had asked for it!)

Helen's eyes shone.

"I'm so glad, dear. Mother seems to be liking you more already."

"Yes. Did you notice that she handed me my coffee instead of pouring it over my head, last night? A definite move in the right direction, that. We'll be singing 'Dear Old Pals' by this evening."

"Come on, now," a hearty female voice cut in, "how about a shot at the coconuts? Four balls for sixpence; ladies halfway."

George, *pour encourager les autres*, had sixpennyworth. No sooner had he picked up the balls, which seemed to be a composition of thin celluloid and feathers, than the coconuts moved away towards the horizon. He succeeded in hitting two, but they just yawned and settled down more comfortably in their beds of sawdust.

Spurred on by Helen's presence, he patronized stall after stall, avoiding the refreshment-stand as if it were a fever-ridden swamp. Finally, he was rewarded with a bag of giant mints at the hoop-la booth. Honour satisfied, they contented themselves by watching other sweating, self-conscious seekers after fame and fortune.

The Vicar, Mrs Bollanger and Milton Threep walked around sprinkling their official blessing upon all. A hush would descend upon each knot of sportsmen they visited, the active competitor foozling his shots badly as he felt the Olympian eye upon him.

As each minute passed, Threep could feel his collar being twisted more tightly about his neck; the soles of his shoes began to smoulder and his mouth became full of warm lint. His mind dwelt longingly on The Leas, half-drawn blinds, and a refrigerator liberally stocked with tall frosted bottles. He skilfully detached himself from the royal party and wandered over to Helen and George.

"Seems to be going quite well, don't you think?" he remarked.

George, though more comfortably attired in blazer and flannels, was beginning to feel the strain.

"I suppose you could say that. Personally, I'd prefer straight boiling oil. Merrie England! If this is the kind of thing O. Cromwell tried to suppress, Olly'd have my vote every time."

"How'd you feel about coming over to the house for something cold, Loder? There's some lager on the ice, I happen to know." He'd also happened to put it there.

"An idea, yes. We'll give it full consideration. How about you, Helen?"

187

"I think I'll go back to Mother before she starts calling for you, Uncle Milton. You two run off and have your drink, but I'd make it a quick one, if I were you. See you later."

She made her way across to Mrs Bollanger, and the two men ambled out of the paddock. George stopped as a pair of small figures approached.

"Hallo, young Ron and Julie," he hailed. "Did you have a nice trip?"

"'S. Me Dad brung me a water-pistol. Look." Ron exhibited a lethal-looking water-pistol, sending a stream of water expertly at a near-by gate-post. "Better'n frew yer teef. An' a scooter," he remembered. "I got it at Auntie Norah's."

"Ron," Threep came straight down to business. "Who was the gentleman in the car who asked you about the case?"

"Wot case?"

"You know, the one you had in the pond. A gentleman in blue asked after it."

"Oh, 'im. I tole yer wot 'e looks like."

"I know," said George. "Big car, blue suit, likes newts and is twelve feet tall. But can you tell me anything about him that'd make him stand out in a crowd?"

"Don't think so." Ron's gaze wandered longingly towards the paddock, happy hunting-ground for lemonade, candy-floss, coconuts and warm canvassy smells. His eyes suddenly lit up.

"Vere 'e is. Bloke over by ve big tent." He pointed excitedly.

Stefan, the bloke over by ve big tent, looked up just in time to see the quartet and the eager, pointing finger. So. This was where Forty-seven made his exit; it was fairly obvious why he was being singled out by the boy. Well, they'd do nothing for an hour or so, anyway; by then, his task would be completed. It wasn't the first time he'd cut it fine.

Meanwhile, George pressed largess and giant mints into Ron's eager hand, contributing to future stomach-aches.

"Well, what are you going to do?" he asked Threep, as the two children sped off towards their fête.

"I think I'll ring the Ministry at once. Some of them are almost sure to have started work – it's nearly twelve o'clock. I've asked Ammidge to turn up, later, and he'll keep an eye on Stefan, too. There's no hurry."

"I suppose you're right. There isn't much Stefan can do while we're all out here. Your brief-case is safe enough, isn't it?"

"At the moment, it's safer than a Scot's saxpence. Come on, let's have that drink." And Threep set the pace for The Leas.

Stefan followed a few minutes later, deep in thought. He'd have to finish this business directly after lunch, when the servants, as well as the family, would all be at the fête. He didn't want to risk Gwyneth or the daily woman disturbing him; bodies hampered one so.

He made a rapid mental check of the arrangements. First, change into outdoor clothes and pack his few belongings. Then, a thorough search of the room, and pick up the papers. Take the Mottram down to the empty cottage and collect Number Three; a quick dash to Airstrip Nineteen, just over the Dorset border, and the job was complete. What *could* go wrong?

He went up to his bedroom to complete the first phase of the plan. A small phial, in a leather container, went into the breast pocket of his neat grey suit. An automatic pistol and a bunch of curiously-shaped keys were also apparently indispensable to his well-being. He was now officially free for the day; all that was required was that he should be seen at the fête. He strolled back to May's paddock.

Amos Flower walked around the side-shows with the contented feeling of one whose plans are nearing fruition. Fortune had smiled on Amos from the first; he'd simply intended to exchange the labels on Miss Kettle's and Farrer's entries for the home-made wine competition. But the Flower luck had pushed him even further.

Miss Kettle, he'd found, had put an extra bottle of her own innoccuous brew into a bucket of cold water, under her refreshment-stall, to provide herself with a cooling drink during the heat of the day. It had been easy for Amos to substitute this bottle for Farrer's entry, and make the necessary adjustment with the labels. Even the two bottles were identical; proof, of course, that the Devil looks after his own.

"That'll teach Bob Farrer to bash Oi wi' a broom-'andle," chuckled Amos, "an' Oi 'opes 'is woine's as good as 'e sez, fer ole Myrtle Kettles sake!"

He mentally rubbed his hands and wandered over to the White Elephant stall to see whether an honest penny could be turned, now that the paddock was rapidly emptying for the midday meal. All was grist, to Amos's mill. . . .

Polly Fenner carefully adjusted her cartwheel straw hat to a suitably careless angle and called to Mrs Watt who was washing the luncheon dishes in the tiny kitchen. Polly had lunched early, in preparation for the afternoon's work at the fête.

"I'm just going down to the Vicarage, Mrs Watt, to make sure they've sent the piano to May's paddock. Shall you be here when I come back?"

"I don't think so. It's arpars twelve, an' I wants to go 'ome an' change for the feet. I'll look in on me way back to the paddock. You'll be gettin' yer own bit o' tea, won't 'ee? I shan't be back yurr 'til mornin'."

"That's right. I'll see you at the fête, then."

Polly walked down the road, wishing for a breeze to cool the laundry-like atmosphere. The walk to the Vicarage seemed like a desert trek, each pace a separate effort. She hoped it would be cooler in May's paddock, where the sun wouldn't reflect as strongly as it did off the hard, dusty road.

Karanov, driving Amos's hired care back to Bilton, gave a start as he passed Polly on the road. Helen Bollanger, and by herself! This was luck. He stopped and called to her.

"Good morning. I wonder whether you can help me? I'm looking for a Mr Loder" – he waved George's card ostentatiously before Polly's eyes – "staying near here, I believe. Do you happen . . .?"

"George? Why, yes. He's staying at The Leas. You're coming away from it. Straight up the road, and it's the first big house on the left. You can't miss it."

"Thank you. I'll call after lunch. Can I give you a lift anywhere?"

"Well, just as far as the Vicarage, please. It's no distance, really," said Polly as she climbed in, and the car started off, "but I hate walking any farther than to my garden-hammock, this weather. Are you staying in Bilton, Mr . . .?"

"Norton. Just for a day or so."

Not without protest, the old car sped along the sun-baked road. They'd passed the lane leading to the Vicarage before Polly was fully aware of it.

"Here it is. You've passed it. Stop, please. I say, stop!" Polly grew alarmed. Her alarm turned to panic as she saw the man's grim expression, like a cat who's just had a mouse inquire for a night's lodgings. "If you don't stop, I'll scream!"

"Do that," answered Karanov, coolly, "the road is deserted, and likely to remain so. On the other hand, screaming annoys me, and I might be tempted to use this."

"This" was a small bottle which he'd dexterously uncorked and was holding in his free hand. Polly's eyes popped towards it – she'd read her share of thrillers.

"What – what is it?" she whispered.

"A little preparation of my own. This carries on where vitriol leaves off. One spot on that rather nice skin of yours . . ."

Polly shuddered. She liked her skin, and took a lot of trouble over it. She gazed, fascinated, at the bottle, like a rabbit watching a cobra doing rope tricks. She felt a queasy feeling around her midriff.

"What do you want?" she asked, hoping her guess was wrong. After all, would a man go to these lengths, just for company?

"Just do as you're told and answer a few questions, and no harm will come to you. Otherwise . . ." He gave the bottle a meaning look. Polly tried to squeeze into the glove-pocket.

The car pulled up outside a tired-looking cottage, half hidden from the road by its high privet hedge. A board, hanging drunkenly from a post, informed those interested that the cottage was to let, furnished. Further details were freely available, it seemed, from A. Flower.

"This will do," announced Karanov. "Get out, please."

As she put a trembling hand to the door-handle:

"You won't forget that I have the bottle here, will you?" he mentioned, casually.

Polly went resignedly up to the cottage door.

17

Luncheon at The Leas was a semi-picnic affair, which, under normal conditions, George would have enjoyed. Mrs Bollanger was almost polite to him, and Helen's expression was one in which love, pride and encouragement were nicely intermingled. If ever a man should have been basking in kindly feeling, George should. But he wasn't.

Overshadowing all his thoughts and actions was the knowledge that soon he must stand up and recite in public. And not only in public, but in front of Miss Kettle. A sense of foreboding pressed down upon him like a ton of cotton-wool.

Why on earth had he let himself be talked into this madness? Not for a minute did he consider whether the end justified the means – Helen was worth any sacrifice. He just wished he'd had more choice of sacrifices, that was all.

Mrs Bollanger rose from the table.

"Make sure you're there in plenty of time, won't you, Mr Loder? The audience gets so out of hand if there's any gap in the programme."

George assented, wondering whether they'd get more out of hand when they heard the gap's alternative. Mrs Bollanger went out to whip in the Committee.

"Cheer up, George." Helen read his thoughts. "It will be all over in an hour or so. You'll think nothing of it, then."

"I don't think much of it now. I'm in – if you'll excuse the indelicacy – a lather of perspiration which isn't solely due to the weather. I've changed my collar twice today, already."

"It is close." Threep dabbed a handkerchief on a pate-encroaching forehead. "I shouldn't be surprised if we had a storm."

George lifted his head, eager as a castaway who's sighted a sail. Good old Threep! This was the first practical bit of cheer he'd had today. Rain! Heaven's benison to a parched earth! It supported life, made crops flourish, filled reservoirs, and broke up Church fêtes. He looked out of the window at the brassy sky.

"Do you really think so?" he asked, pathetically hopeful.

"Oh, we won't get it before this evening," answered Threep, cruelly. George's spirits crash-dived again.

"I must go." Helen pushed her chair back. "I promised the Vicar I'd help with the vegetable-judging. Don't be late, will you, George?"

In the grounds there seemed even less air than inside the house. Everything drooped – leaves, grass, flowers, Helen. She looked forward to the end of the day, a bath and a lazy hour on the lawn in the cool of the evening. It might be disloyal to think of it, but she could imagine nothing better than a heavy shower of rain at this very moment.

From his window above the garage, Stefan watched her go. That left Threep, Loder and Gwyneth in the house, Cook and the daily woman having already gone. Not long now.

Ten minutes later, the two men left, followed shortly afterwards by Gwyneth. Even the hardened Stefan had to admit that Gwyneth enhanced the scenery. She knew well what went with black-lacquer hair and peach-bloom skin. A lemon dress, wide black shiny belt, and black patent shoes. Undoubtedly what the furniture-dealers would describe as a "classy Welsh dresser".

Stefan went down to the kitchen, up the staff stairway, and

into Helen's room. Now, the most obvious places first; there wasn't much Stefan didn't know about searching.

Fifteen minutes later, the room looked as if it had been used as a last-ditch battleground, and Stefan sat on the side of the bed, angry and perplexed.

Surely the papers must be here? If Number Three said so, then it was so. But where? He'd found reams of typescript dealing with local history, but nothing else, The local history couldn't be a code, he decided; the mathematical formulae alone would preclude that. He turned his attention once more to the chimney.

"Something I can get for you, Stefan?"

Helen's cool voice from behind him made the chauffeur spin around like a dervish. He uttered an exclamation that would have shocked and interested Helen, had she been able to understand it.

She looked angrily around the room. Really, it was a bit much when one couldn't attend a simple village fête without having millions of chauffeurs crawling all over one's bedroom! And she'd never have known who'd ransacked the room, if she hadn't happened to come back for that bottle of witch-hazel.

Stefan hung his head in the attitude of one who is in the wrong and is bitterly sorry. He edged towards her.

"I looking for pepper," he said, shamefacedly.

"Pepper?" The soft answer turneth away wrath, and this was the softest answer Helen had heard. It also put her off her guard. "What do you mean – pepper?"

"Pepper with writing on. Printed pepper," amplified Stefan, playing for time. He was almost within reach, now.

"Oh. And what was on this paper? And why should it be in my bedroom?"

Helen could never really describe what happened next.

She remembered Stefan taking a handkerchief from his pocket, ostensibly to mop a bedewed brow. The next moment, a sinewy arm had encircled her, pinning both arms to her sides. In a twinkling, Stefan had crushed a small phial into the handkerchief and clamped the sickly-sweet smelling cloth over her nose and mouth.

She struggled for breath, panic-stricken, as the room swung around in ever-increasing circles. Then she plunged down a dark tunnel into nothingness. Stefan, head well averted, slowly relaxed his grip.

Hoisting the limp form across one shoulder, he carried her down to the kitchen and out into the garage. Number Three had obviously slipped up, somewhere, but he, Stefan, had retrieved the situation, he thought, complacently.

Karanov stepped back from his task of securing Polly to a large wooden chair in Amos Flower's cottage. There was something here he didn't quite understand; and Number Three hated things he didn't understand.

Either this girl was a consummate actress, or she really knew nothing about "The Colonel". And why this stubborn insistence that she wasn't Helen Bollanger? One thing Karanov couldn't stand was dishonesty in others. How far did she expect it to get her? Well, he'd have to try persuasion. He took the phial from his pocket.

Polly gulped. That was life. Nearly forty years without a threat of acid, and here it was, twice in one day. If she ever got out of this, she assured herself, she'd never buy another acid-drop.

"Now, Miss Bollanger; I think we've had enough of this foolishness. Tell me . . ."

A car drew up outside. To Polly's relief, Karanov pocketed the phial and lifted the curtain an inch or so.

Ah, Forty-seven! Now let the woman deny her identity! He dropped the curtain and went to the front door as he heard Stefan's footsteps coming up the path.

Stefan's look of surprise matched his own as he opened the door.

"Who is that?" he asked, as Stefan carried Helen's disinterested form into the room.

"Helen Bollanger," answered Stefan. "But when did you get here? And what is *she* doing?" He looked at Polly who was beginning to wonder how many women could be expected to turn up. If this was going to be a hen party . . .

"Helen Bollanger?" Karanov's eyebrows raised. "Then who have I got here?" he asked, with the natural curiosity of a man who's found that he's kidnapped the wrong woman.

"That? Miss Fenner. Nobody in particular." Stefan saw no percentage in ex-actresses.

Polly bristled.

"Sez you! I could show you Press notices that . . ."

"Quiet, woman!" snapped Karanov. Polly curled up. Helen stirred, then opened her eyes.

Karanov turned to Stefan, and for a minute or so they spoke rapidly in a language which sounded to Polly like mutilated shorthand.

Karanov crossed over to Helen who was now sitting up and taking an interest in current affairs.

"Tell me," he asked, "where are the papers which you are keeping? Answer me!" he barked, as Helen passed a hand over her forehead.

"Don't shout at me!" she rebuked, sharply. She gave Polly an encouraging smile.

Polly quaked. It was all very well Helen showing her spirit, but in Polly's opinion there was a time and a place for everything; and this was neither. No point in antagonizing these two potential acid-sprayers. Helen, she supposed, was the stuff from which the old Frontier housewives were made – a woman who'd load flintlocks for "her man", nonchalantly pulling burning Sioux arrows from the thatch at the same time. Just my luck, she thought, to get kidnapped with a woman like that.

"Stubborn, eh?" grated Karanov. He took the phial from his pocket again, and Polly sighed. This man had a one-track mind. Her eyes widened as he came across to her chair. "I'll give you just ten seconds, Miss Bollanger. If you haven't started talking by then, Miss Fenner here will try the effects of a few drops of acid. I'll leave enough for you, of course," he mocked.

Polly stiffened. She hoped Helen wasn't going to be too brave. It was all very well for these heroines, but she herself was an actress, not a heroine. Given the choice between death or a fate worse than death, Polly'd have plumped for the latter. Every woman to her bent, and Polly was bent on staying alive and uncorroded.

"Listen." Polly breathed again as she heard Helen's cool voice. "I don't know what you want, and I'm sure nothing I can tell you is important enough to warrant this – this melodramatic treatment. Now, what is it all about?"

"You know very well. Where are the papers concerning 'The Colonel'? They should be in your room . . ."

Three short lines ridged themselves between Helen's eyes.

"Why, so they are. But why go to all this trouble? You can read all you want to know about Colonel Cobberleigh in the Sede library."

"Colonel Cobberleigh? Do you mean . . . ?"

Realization dawned on Stefan as he remembered the typescript he'd skimmed through in Helen's room. He turned eagerly to Karanov and they broke into crackling volubility incomprehensible to their captives. Finally, Karanov spoke to Helen.

"So. There might have been a misunderstanding."

"Oh, don't apologize. Could have happened to anyone," interposed Polly, trying to show she bore no ill-will.

"Be quiet. We shall leave you here – no doubt someone will be along during the next day or so. By then we shall be far away." He turned to Stefan. "Tie Miss Bollanger up with the other one, and gag them both. We'll use your car – I've left Flower's wreck in the next field."

He watched as Stefan brought his old Boy Scout's training into use, tying Helen efficiently into the other chair.

"You know," he continued, as Stefan finished off with an artistic bow in the tape he'd brought along, "I think we should have gone for the brief-case after all. Well, it's not too late. Come."

"But . . .", protested Stefan.

Karanov swung around, eyes frosted.

"There are no buts. We do not leave without the case. Come!"

They left the cottage. A moment later, the two captives heard the Mottram purr smoothly up the road. Polly rolled her eyes at Helen, who nodded; words were unnecessary.

No humdrum life, theirs.

"And now," announced the Vicar, who was sharing with Mrs Bollanger the task of Master of Ceremonies, "I have much pleasure in introducing Mr Farrer who will recite 'The Farmer's Daughter'. Mr Farrer."

May's paddock rippled with applause as Farrer stalked on to the stage. He'd discarded his tight blue uniform for a tight blue suit, and doubtless felt glad of the change. He waited, serenely, until the handclapping and encouraging shouts of "Good ole Bob!" had died down.

"Ladies an' gennlemen. You've all yurd the song called 'The Farmer's Boy'. Well, this pome's about a farmer's gurl." He closed his eyes, put his hands behind his back, thrust one knee forward, and launched into his opus:

> "A farmer 'ad a daughter fair,
> 'E called 'er Liddle Nellie;
> 'Er mother came
> An' 'ad 'er name
> Tattooed upon 'er ankle."

Mrs Bollanger stiffened, and little steel darts shot from her eyes. Grimly, she made her way from her chair to the dais.

"When Nell a sojer came to woo," continued the bard,

> "A Sergeant of the Lancers,
> 'E didn't make
> A single break
> 'Cos Nell knew all the answers."

"Thank you, Farrer." Mrs Bollanger walked on to the stage, clapping her hands as a signal to applaud a completed "turn". Farrer opened his eyes and turned a surprised face towards her.

"Oi 'aven't finished 'n yet," he assured her. "Oi got another se'mteen verses."

He turned to his public, who were now hanging on to his words in respectful and delighted silence, shut his eyes again, and declaimed:

> "'E took 'er for a walk one day . . ."

"Farrer!" hissed Mrs Bollanger. The audience hugged itself.

> "'E said it was quite lawful . . ."

"Leave the stage at once! You must NOT go on ..."

"'Is breath was sweet,
But oh! 'is feet,

"WILL YOU STOP?" Mrs Bollanger seethed.

"Was summat flippin' awful," persisted Farrer,
doggedly.

The Vicar, with the tact of a man who's had to deal with
Mothers' Union arguments, approached.

"The wine-judging's about to start, Farrer. I'm sure you
want to be present for that, don't you? We'll have to forgo
the rest of your poem, I'm afraid."

Regretfully, Farrer desisted. He'd got high hopes for his
wine entry, and wanted to be there to see the judging. Amid a
roar of applause he went, beaming, from the limelight.

George wiped his eyes.

"Take me home, now; I've seen everything. And to think
that people pay good money for television sets! Come on,
Threep; let's go to Bacchus's fount. If Farrer's entered a wine
I've a pretty shrewd idea that it won't stand much of a chance
with Mrs Bollanger!"

The incident wasn't over, however. George wandered off,
leaving Threep to listen. Farrer stood in front of Mrs Bollanger, in sulky silence, while she gave him her full and considered opinion of his "pome". Though he towered above her
by almost a couple of feet, it seemed to all that Mrs Bollanger
looked down at him as her tongue lashed.

". . . And do not offer your – ah – services at any other
function I happen to be connected with! I intend to speak very
strongly to Mr Chillebotham about this!" Mr Chillebotham
was the Stationmaster, a disciplinarian who made Attila
sound like an old softy.

Farrer felt a rounded arm thrust into his.

"You said it beautiful, Bob, bach," enthused Gwyneth. "It made everyone laugh, anyway. Do 'em good."

Mrs Bollanger's hackles rose higher.

"Your opinion is neither critical nor interesting, Gwyneth. Go back to the house at once!"

In Gwyneth rose the spirit that had cocked a snoot at the English back in the days when the Welsh marches had been risky ones.

"I'm off dooty 'til tea, 'M, and I'll soot meself. I'm staying by yere."

"Gwyneth! Are you being impertinent, or just foolish? Go . . ."

"Be'st calling moi gurl foolish?" Farrer took up the cudgels. "If you d' think Oi'll stand fer that, then you're a bigger bl . . ."

"Now, Bob! No language, please! Remember there's one lady yere, anyway." Turning to Mrs Bollanger, Gwyneth brought her main armament to bear. "You can take a week's notice, 'M. And," she added, bitingly, "I 'opes your next parlourmaid won't want to do what she wants. That'll just soot you. Come on, Bob."

They marched away, another peasants' revolt successfully accomplished. Gwyneth rather spoiled the full effect by giggling.

"Oh, Bob! You shouldn't 'ave done it, but it *was* funny!"

"Mebbe. But now you've got no job an' nowhere to go. Will 'ee go back 'ome 'til we're wed?"

"I s'pose I'll 'ave to. Nobody else around 'ere wants a parlourmaid; unless I can get something in Devizes."

"Well, we'll jump that ditch when we reach 'n. But Oi *did* love 'ee, the way you stood up to she."

"Did you, boyo? Then I'm glad it 'appened." She chuckled reminiscently. "'Ow did that verse go, again, about 'is feet . . .?"

George, hovering near the home-made wine stall, smiled as they passed by, little realizing the repercussions the affair was to have. He peered around in search of Helen.

Queer that she should have disappeared like this. Or was it so queer? Anyone who remained in this sticky, noise-laden atmosphere when they weren't obliged to, thought George, needed a searching head-examination. Helen had probably done a shrewdie and slipped off to the house for half an hour's peace. Might as well go and see.

Back at The Leas, in the lounge, Karanov and Stefan were beginning to accept the fact that the house was bereft of brief-cases.

"Are you sure he hasn't taken it to the bank?" asked Karanov.

"Quite sure. He hasn't been out of my sight for more than half an hour at a time. If he . . ."

"Look," Karanov interrupted, nodding towards the window. "That's Loder coming up the drive, isn't it? Get him out of the way. No, don't," he smiled slowly, and Stefan replaced his knife. "I think I see the way. Stay here, but keep out of sight." He went out into the hall as George came up the steps.

"Good afternoon, Mr Loder." Karanov gave a welcoming smile, which reminded George, somehow, of a thirsty fox. "You have come at an opportune moment."

George's spirits rose. He'd been wondering what this M.I.5 merchant had been doing, the last day or so. Working under cover, of course. Tightening the net around Stefan, hounding the man down like . . . He realized that he was being asked something.

". . . And it is vital that I see Mr Threep, here in private, immediately. I wonder if you'd be so good as to . . .?"

George saw it all. Naturally, the man didn't want to be seen talking to Threep; and now that matters were rapidly coming to a head, he'd no doubt want to make his report.

"Of course. He's at the fête. I'll go straight back and tell him. By the way, you haven't seen Miss Bollanger come in? My fiancée, you remember?"

"I've been waiting here some time, and nobody's come in or gone out," answered Karanov, informatively. "Please forgive my seeming impatience, but this matter with Mr Threep is most urgent, and I have delayed . . ."

"Yes, I understand." George glanced at his watch. "I must run, too. I'm due on the stage in a few minutes."

Thoughts of Helen receded a little, swamped by his minor role in Threep's spy drama; also, his forthcoming recitation was beginning to lean on him a little more heavily.

"If you'll sit down, I dare say he'll be here in a few minutes. I'll tell him right away." And he hurried off to May's paddock.

18

Marcus Rogers idled in front of the wine-stall, reading the labels on the bottles. Wine of any kind – especially the home-made varieties – never failed to draw him. He wondered whether he'd get a chance to taste any of these.

Mrs Bollanger and the Vicar stood, irresolutely, at the end of the table.

"Most annoying!" Mrs Bollanger declared. Something usually was. "Mr Ford knew that he was helping to judge the wines. He shouldn't have accepted the office if he wasn't intending to come."

At that moment, Mr Ford, the Schoolmaster, was selfishly sleeping in a Devizes hospital bed, having just lost an unnecessary but painful appendix. Mr Ford had helped to judge the home-made wines ever since his trip to France, in 1933. This made him the accepted wine expert, which pleased him. It also pleased Mrs Bollanger, whose opinions the expert had endorsed with the fidelity of an echo. This year, however, someone else must pick up the torch.

Marcus Rogers raised a five-guinea panama.

"Perhaps I could help?" His voice still carried a trace of Wiltshire clover-fields. "My name's Rogers, Marcus Rogers. I don't know whether that conveys anything to you, but I do know a little about wines."

The Vicar held out an enthusiastic hand.

"My dear sir! We should be most grateful! Mrs Bollanger, you've heard of Mr Rogers, surely? Soft drinks, isn't it?"

Rogers winced. "A Winthringham man, too, I believe? This is most fortunate, most fortunate!"

Mrs Bollanger permitted herself to smile.

"We'll be glad of your help, Mr – ah – Rogers. Had we known that Mr Ford was so unreliable we shouldn't have asked him. We are late already. Shall we make a start now?"

The crowd grew larger as the exhibits were tasted and graded. To Farrer's disgust, his entry was hardly remarked upon. Word had gone around that this new bloke was a wine expert, and Farrer had been modestly confident. Well, that's how it went. He looked across at Amos, who shook his head commiseratingly.

The Vicar mounted the dais and held up his hand for silence. He looked like a non-practising Fascist.

"Ladies and gentlemen. As usual, this has been a very close competition. Very close indeed. I should like, first of all, to thank Mr Marcus Rogers for stepping into the breach at the last moment and helping to judge for us.

"Now, after much thought and deliberation, we have decided to award the first prize to Mrs Smedley . . ."

"Hear hear!" The applause was led by a Mr Smedley.

". . . the second prize goes to Miss Gibbs . . ." a mild handclap, here, ". . . and the third prize to Mr Murk" – a vociferous cheer for the landlord of the Angry Hen – "who have all entered excellent wines.

"It just remains for me to thank all who have submitted entries and made this competition the success it has been. Now," he continued, "if you will return to your seats, the next item on the concert programme will commence without further delay."

George, who had just delivered his message to a perplexed Threep, moved reluctantly towards the gallows. D minus 1!

A song from Miss Gibbs, of vintner fame, then he must prepare his neck. He felt suddenly cold.

Miss Gibb's performance was accepted by the audience without comment. They felt that they'd gone into this thing with their eyes open and had only themselves to blame.

Miss Gibbs bowed, simpered, and fluttered off. The stage was all George's. He only wished that someone would come and take it off his hands.

"And now," announced Mrs Bollanger, as though this was the long-awaited star turn, "we have a recitation from a visitor to Winthringham." Her face softened almost imperceptibly as George shuffled forward.

"Ladies and gentlemen, Mr Loder!"

Milton Threep turned a bewildered face from Karanov to Stefan, then back again, like a spectator at the Centre Court. Things were happening at a speed which left Threep standing. To a politician whose favourite phrase is "I must have notice of that question", Karanov's rapid-fire examination meant little.

Threep had perspired gently back to The Leas in response to George's muttered "Someone you know wants to see you. He's waiting at the house. This is urgent!" If ever a man had been Carrying A Message, that man was George. Threep could almost have sworn that George had said "Hist!"

Then, as soon as Threep had stepped into the lounge, this hatchet-faced horror and Stefan had held him up at the point of a professionally-levelled revolver and begun questioning him.

That they knew something of "The Colonel" was fairly obvious. Threep, the sharp edge of his intellect dulled by years of Parliamentary sittings, was in no position to outwit the two spies.

"Where is your brief-case?" asked Karanov, finally.

Threep tried to draw himself up haughtily, but had little to draw on.

"Where you will never find it," he answered, a Newboltian ring in his voice.

"Oh?" The muzzle of the revolver lowered towards Threep's stomach, and he saw the hammer begin to rise.

"In Rose Cottage," he said hastily. He'd have been braver, if only they hadn't aimed at his stomach. Indigestion was bad enough, but . . .

"Are 'The Colonel's' papers in the case?" asked Karanov.

Threep hesitated a moment. Surely help must come soon. Dare he risk it? The muzzle lowered again.

"Yes," he said.

"And where is this cottage?" asked Karanov.

Stefan told him.

"Very well. We will take this man with us, and find out whether he is bluffing. If you are . . ." he added, menacingly.

Threep earnestly assured him that he wasn't.

"Make one sound, or try to attract attention on the way there, and your body will be found in a ditch. Understand?"

Threep did. He could almost see the headlines in the London papers. "Diplomat Dumped in Ditch." "Prominent Politician Plugged." "By-Election in Wilts." No, it mustn't be. Publicity was a good thing, but it had to be publicity of the right kind. He went quietly.

Rose Cottage, to his relief, was empty; which was as he'd expected. He didn't want Polly mixed up in this sorry business. She was safe, anyway, he thought, with martyr-like complacency. The revolver prodded his well-covered ribs.

"Well, where is the brief-case?" The cheerful neatness of the room cut no ice with Karanov. Even if it had been stuffed with Sheraton furniture or Adam fireplaces, it would still have left him cold.

Threep walked over to the radiogram and opened the record-cupboard door. The brief-case peered out, self-consciously. Stefan darted forward.

"Are the papers there?" Karanov tried to keep his voice level.

Stefan opened the flap, exposing a wad of typescript, blue-prints, and photographs. Karanov turned to Threep, cocking the revolver as he did so.

"Good. Then we have no more need of you."

Threep felt his knees giving. Sweat ran down his neck, despite the chill in his stomach. The muzzle of the revolver looked like the entrance to the Severn Tunnel. He could almost feel the bullet, a ton of rushing metal, tearing into his heart, when Stefan raised a warning hand.

"Sh-sh!" he said. "There's a policeman outside!"

The reprieve hit Threep harder than the bullet could have done. He sighed and slumped to the floor without any fuss or bother.

Outside, Ammidge and Clara Watt inspected the Mottram, standing at the gate. Ammidge, uniformed and on duty, perspired profusely. Clara, however, had gone home and changed into her "blue spotted", as she described it. Years ago, no doubt, the blue spotted had been cool and comfortable; now, it held her ample form in thrall, accentuating her every curve and fold until she resembled a motor-tyre advertisement.

"Looks like Mrs Bollanger've come visitin'," guessed Clara. "She won't find Miss Fenner in, anyway. I s'pose I'd better go in an' find out wot she d' want." A thought struck her. "If you've a minute to spare, Mr Ammidge, p'raps you'd like a cupper tea before we goes on to the feet? No 'urry, is there?"

Ammidge considered. Mr Threep had asked him to look in, some time, so there couldn't be any real hurry. Meanwhile, the day was hot, and the road dusty . . .

"That'd be very acceptable, Mrs Watt. I never says no to me cupper tea."

They walked up the short flagged path, around the side of the cottage, and in at the back door. Ammidge took off his helmet and remained in the tiny kitchen, while Clara went in to the sitting-room.

Clara's scream and the slamming of the car door smote his startled ears at the same time. Waiting only long enough to readjust his helmet – Ammidge always observed the formalities – he dashed in to the sitting-room and found Clara standing, back against the wall, horror-stricken eyes glued to a man's body lying on the floor. He hardly noticed the noise of the car moving off.

The words "No trace of a weapon", and "A well-nourished corpse", sprang into his mind as he went down on one knee. The body was still warm, anyway. Clara gave another scream as the body sat up and looked around.

"Why, it's Mr Threep! I thought you was dead!"

"So did I," answered Threep. "Quick! Where are the two men who were here? Stefan and a stranger? The car . . ."

Ammidge opened the door on to a deserted road.

"Too late, sir. The car's gone. What 'appened, please?" He pulled out a notebook.

"Better leave the details, now. The first thing to do is to try and stop the car. They aren't ordinary thieves." He gave the car number and a somewhat biased description of Karanov and Stefan, while Clara put on a timely kettle.

"Well, 'oo'd 'ave thought we was going to walk into a catastastrofe like this," she quivered. "Aren't you goin' to wait for the cupper tea, Mr Ammidge?" she asked, as the constable opened the door.

"There's some things as can't wait for tea," he answered, stern Duty gleaming from his eyes. He spoke to Threep. "I'll get on to this right away, sir. If I were you I'd sit quiet for a bit."

There was nothing that Threep wanted to do more, and the strong cup of tea which Clara brought him, muted his jangling nerves.

But, curiously enough, he didn't seem greatly worried.

George stood uncertainly in front of the sea of upturned faces in May's paddock. How the crowd had grown during that last minute, as he'd climbed on to the stage! Must be fifty thousand, at least. Nasty critical expressions most of them had, too.

Just as well he was word-perfect. Never mind the histrionics – get the words out and done with! He cleared his throat; the fierce, rasping sound made him jump.

"Dandelions," he said, simply.

The silence, coupled with the super-charged atmosphere, drowned his words. He waited for a caterpillar to stop its frenzied stamping about on a near-by twig. Then he tried again.

"Crocuses," he remarked.

The audience gazed up at him in dumb wonder. One of them clever chaps, they supposed, spouting something they should understand but didn't.

George felt a peculiar weakness spreading from his knees upwards, and a partial paralysis attacked his larynx. He heard, as from a great distance, a feeble croak, which he realized must have come from his own throat.

"Buttercups," he mouthed, again. The words died a short three inches from his lips.

A faint rumble came from above. It could have been approaching thunder, though it might also have been Zeus and The Muses, rocking with laughter. The audience barely noticed it, so intent were they on hearing what this strange chap'd say next.

He said "Bluebells".

Sweat oozed from George's temples. What *was* the name of the blasted flower? If he could only remember the title, he felt, he'd be able to romp through the poem. Still, there it was; he'd always been weak on horticulture. He wouldn't know the difference between a dahlia and a daffo . . . That's it!

"Daffodils!" he shouted. The audience swayed back, startled. A little girl in the front set up a frightened howl, and had to be led away.

A tug at George's sleeve made him turn around to find Miss Kettle's face hovering within a few inches of his own. What the blazes was she doing here? Surely she hadn't come up to denounce him in public?

But this was a new, masterful Miss Kettle, whose flowerpot hat sat jauntily back on her head; whose hair, instead of being drawn back with its usual scalp-tingling tightness, now rested in comfortable folds on her forehead. And there was a go-to-hell look in her eye that even the huge lenses couldn't dim. Almost as if she'd . . . No! Not Miss Kettle! Not alcohol . . . !

Myrtle Kettle gave George's sleeve another tug and jerked her head Down Left.

"No good. Hic. Pardon. No good at all. Rotten song. You might as well" – she searched for the *mot propre* – "scram. I'll sing 'em a song. Leave it to an old trouper." She put up a hand to adjust her hat to a more impossible and rakish angle.

George stared at her dumbly. By now, Wordsworth and

all his works had melted like the desert dew. Instead, his thoughts flew back to Rose Cottage and his first meeting with this old trouper (about a hundred years ago, wasn't it?) in Polly's company. He wondered whether Polly was down there, sympathizing, an insignificant blob in that counterpane of faces.

"G'wan," urged Miss Kettle, loudly. "I've got a song here that'll knock 'em cold. Hic," she added, parenthetically but forcefully.

The truth suddenly hit George like a guided missile. Miss Kettle had taken drink. Topped up to the tonsils. No wonder she hadn't recognized him – in her present state she'd have had difficulty in recognizing her own reflection. Why was her head weaving slowly around like a bemused ostrich? And why this new, racy dialogue? George, who was as quick on the uptake as the next man, summed it up in two words – blotto perfecto.

He was surprised that Mrs Bollanger hadn't arrived to retrieve the situation. It wasn't like her to let things get out of hand to this extent. He searched around the human sea below until he was eventually able to bring his eyes into focus. For the first time he noticed the roll of approaching thunder.

Then he saw the reason for Mrs Bollanger's delay. At the far edge of the crowd, Farrer was threatening her with a bottle, giving the audience a powerful counter-attraction to the legitimate entertainment on the stage. George's heart warmed to the porter; then he saw that the bottle wasn't being used as a weapon, but more in the nature of Exhibit A.

He strained his ears to get in on the Farrer incident, which seemed to hold promise. Due to the crowd's delighted buzzing – this had been a great day, as well they knew – and Miss Kettle, who had now started her song that was going to knock 'em cold, he found it difficult to get the whole story.

"Not my ruddy woine at all," seethed Farrer. "Some'un's swapped me boddle!"

"Ay stood there i-hin wondah
And could not for-hor-bear . . ."

trilled Miss Kettle.

"Are you making an accusation?" demanded Mrs Bollanger.

"Thishyer's sweetened dill-water . . ."

"With ra-hap-ture to gaze
On her de-heh-licate air . . ."

"The label shows the wine to be yours . . ."

"Ar, an' it says 'Gents' on the tent outside, but that don't say there's any . . ."

". . . deh-heh-heh-heh-licate air-hair,
With rahpture to g-a-a-aze . . ."

"Will somebody stop that woman?" hissed Mrs Bollanger.

The Vicar hurried up to the dais, and Farrer turned to Marcus Rogers.

"See, Mister? 'Ere's the receep fer me woine. Would it taste loike this stuff?" He held up the spurious bottle contemptuously.

Rogers glanced at the recipe, then stiffened as his eyes took in the list of herbs and quantities. There'd been a master-hand, here!

"Where did you get this?"

"'Ome. Me Gran' give it me Ma. We've allus made 'n but this is the first toime Oi've entered 'n fer the contest. And now some bar . . ."

"Yes. Quite. Can you let me taste some of your own?"

"Well, not just now." Farrer could put two and two

together; his eyes rested on Miss Kettle, one arm matily around the vicar's neck. "Oi rackon Oi knows 'oo's ad 'n, though. Not that she've 'ad much," he hastened to add in defence of his potion, "otherwise she wouldn't be standin' up there. Nor anywhere else."

"Look, I'm interested in this recipe, and I'd like a taste of the wine. Could you manage that for me?"

"Ar. Oi got a few more boddles at me Ma's. Will 'ee wait 'ere, or come along o' Oi?"

Mrs Bollanger felt that the situation had slipped sideways.

"Well, I'll leave you to make your own arrangements, Mr Rogers. Thank you for your help. Good-bye." She hurried away to where she felt her presence was most needed.

George and the Vicar, meanwhile, had managed to entice a buoyant Miss Kettle from the stage. She bowed modestly as a louder peal of thunder echoed across the heavens. Mrs Long hurried to the rescue.

"If ye'd like to give a nand, sir, just to get 'er 'ome, I'll see to 'er. I'll get 'er feet up on the settee, an' she'll be as right as rain." The thunder rolled again as George, Miss Kettle and Mrs Long weaved out of the paddock.

People glanced upwards, weighing the chances of the rain holding off. Joe Penny, Amos Flower and Mr Lamb wasted no time in useless speculation, but went their respective ways.

They knew.

19

Ar Ron wandered dejectedly around May's paddock. It was always the same. You arrived at these affairs with high hopes and full purses; purses and hopes dwindled together after that first riotous, unbridled hour. All you were left with was a stickiness about the mouth, a stomach which could best be described as toffee-blasé, and a general feeling of dissatisfaction. People became bad-tempered when you climbed on to marquee roofs, and threatening when you dipped your water-pistol into the lemonade-bowl. The fête, *qua* fête, Ron felt, was played out.

What to do? There was the new scooter, that red-and-yellow triumph of engineering, eating its head off in Aunt Norah's shed. He'd planned to scoot around the world, tomorrow, but why wait? The afternoon was young – plenty of time for an energetic boy to get as far as India and back, say, before bedtime. Ron moved purposefully out of the paddock and trotted off towards the post office.

A few minutes later, he was wheeling the scooter on to the road, the world before him. A thought struck him, and he went back for a slice of cake and a few apples. He wasn't really hungry, but he reckoned he'd need a snack, somewhere around Italy. The apples were purely to prevent scurvy, a disease which Ron knew attacked travellers' scalps.

He paused a moment to wave a nonchalant hand to the frenziedly-excited crowd who'd come to see him off. The Lord Mayor was holding the medal and sack of toffee which had been promised, along with the title of "Sir Ron" against his successful return. Mummy and Auntie Norah were crying, and wishing they hadn't been so stingy with the fruit cake on various occasions he could name. He choked down the lump in his throat and set off determinedly along the Sede road.

His left leg was just beginning to tire as he saw the cottage and its inviting board outside. Ar Ron couldn't read, but he knew what a board hanging outside a house meant, as well as the next man. It meant that that particular house was in a heavenly untenanted state, offering hours of thrills for a boy who could climb through an incompletely-closed window.

You had to be careful, of course. Sometimes they left a bloke in charge of these houses – usually an irritable character, fleet of foot and deadly of belt. Ron had had many a thrilling race, in Camden Town, spurred on by stinging flicks from leather straps applied to tight, inadequately-moving trousers. He put his scooter just inside the gate and tiptoed up the path.

A furtive glance through the letter-box revealed a short hall, empty and invitingly mysterious. Ron moved through the long grass to the window, and peeped through a chink at the side of the curtain.

Coo! Just like the pitchers! Two ladies, tied up in chairs. And gagged! This was real adventure, better than any old feet.

He retraced his steps to the door and tried the handle. To his surprise, the door opened and he stood, not completely unafraid, in the dusty hall. Grasping an imaginary pistol, he moved stealthily into the room where Helen and Polly sat counting the minutes.

Ron wasted no time in idle conjecture; he had a feeling that these ladies wanted to be untied, and he was the man to do it. What a glorious opportunity for using the two-bladed knife his father had given him, and which Aunt Norah had said he mustn't carry! He put the pistol between his teeth, whipped out the knife, and started in on the tapes.

Outside, the sky darkened and the thunder began to mutter almost continuously, punctuated by flashes of lightning like a stage storm. To Polly, anxiously watching Helen's emancipation, it all seemed unreal – like attending an allegorical play.

"Thank goodness for that!" sighed Helen, as they both stood, a few minutes later, gently exercising aching limbs. "I had an awful feeling that we were going to be left here for a day or so, and offered amongst the mod. cons. And who are you?" she asked, turning to the fairy prince.

"Let me introduce you," said Polly. "I'm surprised you haven't met. This is ar Ron, the whitest man I know. Under the dust, sweat and toffee-stains beats a stout heart. Would you mind if I kissed you, Ron? All right, I only put it forward as a suggestion," she added, as he backed defensively into a corner.

"Perhaps Ron would prefer a ride into Sede or Devizes, tomorrow, and choose the best present he can see. Would you like that, Ron?" Helen was more practical.

"Fenks," answered Ron, who'd believe it when he saw it. "Will you be all right, nah?" he asked. "I gotter get back to me tea." Might as well cancel the idea of the world trip; he'd never make up for all this delay. Still, it wouldn't have been the done thing to have gone and left women completely unprotected.

The cottage trembled as a gargantuan peal of thunder rolled across the heavens. There was a sound as though someone was throwing handfuls of gravel against the window-panes, and the storm got nicely into its spate.

"I think perhaps you'd better wait until this is over, Ron," advised Polly, pulling aside the curtain. It was like looking into an aquarium. "There's not enough rain available for it to keep up long at this rate."

"I do wish it would hurry up and finish," fretted Helen. "There's so much I want to know. What happened to Stefan and that awful man? Have people started looking for us? How did George's recitation go off – oh, a hundred things!" She turned to Ron. "Were you at the fête, Ron?"

"'S."

"Did a gentleman stand up and say a poem? A tall gentleman in a blue blazer and grey flannels?"

"'S. I knows 'im." He nodded towards Polly. "'Er 'usband."

"Her what?" Helen gave Polly an amused glance.

"'Er 'usband. You know," he turned to Polly for support. "Ve bloke wot was under your bed w'en ve ole girl come. 'E couldn't come aht 'cos 'e 'ad no trahsis." To Ron's puritanical mind nothing less than wedlock could excuse this situation.

"The old girl?" Helen gave Polly a long, calculating look. "Perhaps you'd explain, Miss Fenner? *Is* there an explanation?"

"Yes," answered Polly, calmly. "I think you're entitled to that."

Back in May's paddock, alarm and consternation began to set in. The thunder was almost continuous, now, and the sky black as a witch's heart. It didn't need a rheumatic fisherman to forecast the storm. People ran for the shelter of tents which became overcrowded; they made for trees, telling each other not to stand under that one, as everyone knew that that kind attracted lightning.

The first drops came, large as plovers' eggs, making no impression on the iron-hard ground, but disintegrating, on impact, like dusty tiaras. Then, gradually, they became absorbed. Grass took on a new life. Leaves bent gleefully to the downpour, throwing off their weeks'-old coat of dust, and appearing fresh and shining like a chimney-sweep on Sunday. Rivulets and pools began to pattern what had seemed to be level ground. Spiders gave pessimistic glances at newly-spun webs, and reconsidered the possibility of switching to nylon, or something more weather-proof.

The rain now dropped in solid sheets. It poured on tent-tops, into stalls, and danced contemptuously on such summer hats as had found no shelter. Noah, from his reasonably dry eminence, smiled reminiscently and called Shem to come and have a look.

In addition to the teeming rain, a strong wind had found its way into the paddock, whipping off stall-covers and razing tents.

A small square of canvas, about as large as a table-top, suddenly gave up the unequal struggle and parted company with the coconut-shy. It sank sadly back into the stream which had swollen out of recognition from the feeble trickle it had been that morning.

Exiguous as it was, the canvas was destined to have a definite bearing on England's future armament policy. As it rolled and flapped in the water, the current twitched and tugged at it, coercing, persuading, dragging it steadily along.

It floated, half-submerged, downstream; through the culvert and into Stony Lane where the flow, joined by a hundred tributaries, became strong and powerful.

The flood gushed down a miniature rapid, where it divided, part going down a channel in the direction of the safety-fences. The channel could easily cope with a normal downpour, but this was monsoon stuff. It might even have managed then, but the canvas lodged itself neatly across the main stream, diverting nearly all the flood towards the safety-fences.

It was fortunate for their peace of mind that Doctors Ungel and Schnille couldn't see the result. Had they been in the transmitting-room, "The Colonel's" nerve-centre, they'd have seen the steady trickle down the underground concrete walls; or heard the occasional sizzle as a spot or so of water found its way across circuits which had been left running for temperature tests.

But those fine old English gentlemen, Ungel and Schnille, were in the other room, comfortably sound-proofed, trying to write a report with about as much available data as it takes to describe a mouse-trap.

"So there it is," finished Polly. She had presented the episode of George's trousers, and his deception of Mrs Bollanger, clearly and succinctly. Ron, on a tour of the cottage, had left them to their *tête à tête*; except for the thunder, slowly dying away, there'd been no interruptions. Polly waited for Helen's comments.

The story had gripped, that was evident. Helen's face had set harder with each damning phrase, and her toe tapped rhythmically on the worn linoleum. She had the appearance of a woman who would like to lay her hands on George and a potato-masher.

"Do you imagine you behaved wisely?" she asked, flatly.

"We behaved; that's more important."

"That I have to believe, I suppose."

"Have to? You haven't, you know. Unless you can believe it without having to, you're marrying the wrong man."

"Thank you for the advice. But he was perfectly suitable when . . ."

"Suitable. How nice. Sounds as though you advertised

for him. 'Wanted, male; suitable for husband.' Don't you see, unless you're prepared to accept George and this story, you're either going to be unhappy with him or miserable without him. You've got to start on a basis of trust."

"It's easy for you to say that. You haven't got to do the trusting."

"Oh, I've had to, in my time. Or at least, I should have done, but didn't. That's why I rent Rose Cottage by myself. Of course, I realize that there are some men whom one just can't trust . . ."

"Are you suggesting that I can't trust George?"

"I? No. You suggested it. We'll skip the implied slur on my moral character. Helen, my dear, we've enough on our hands to cope with your mother's suspicions. Be on our side, for your own sake as well as George's. I've known him for a good many years and I know he wouldn't do a thing to hurt anyone he loves. And he *does* love you, you know. You're very lucky."

Helen's face softened.

"I didn't really suspect anything, Polly. Especially now that I know you. But I *do* think he should have confided in me. Never mind . . ."

"There's just one snag," said Polly, thoughtfully. "Miss Kettle saw us going into the cottage, if you remember. If she's seen George today, and recognized him, she'll be around to your mother like Paul Revere."

"I suppose so. Well, there's one answer to that. I'll tell Mother first."

"That should help things along nicely. And how do you suppose Mrs Bollanger will dispose of George's body, after she's cut it up?"

"There'll be no cutting up. If Mother feels bitter, she'll just have to rise above it. I'm the one George is going to marry."

"For which he's no doubt thankful. When shall you tell her?"

"As soon as possible. After dinner, I think. Look, the rain is nearly over. Why not come back to The Leas with me? Our bathing arrangements are a little more lavish than Rose Cottage, and I'd love to have you stay to dinner. We could pick up what you want on the way up. Will you?"

"I'd love to. And I know your mother'd be delighted. Or could I be wrong?"

"You could. But could you stand it? Somehow, I feel that we're doing the right thing for all of us."

"I'll come. To be honest, I was rather dreading going back to Rose Cottage and having the evening by myself. By the way, I seem to recollect that awful man saying that he'd left Amos Flower's taxi here. Couldn't we . . .?"

"We could! Come on." Helen went to the door. "Ron! Come on, my gallant rescuer! We're going, now."

20

George exhaled a forbidden lungful of smoke in the lounge of The Leas. He'd just left Mrs Long helping a boisterous Myrtle Kettle into her house, and didn't see any future in returning to the fête. Judging by the unnatural darkness outside, and the almost continuous peals of thunder, it wouldn't be long before May's paddock was swilled clear. He looked up as the first raindrops clattered against the window-panes.

He was more worried about Helen. His knock on her bedroom door had produced no answer; a prowl around the house and gardens had also proved fruitless. He crossed to the fireplace and rang the bell. Perhaps Gwyneth would have returned by now.

Gwyneth came, still in her outdoor clothes.

"Tea 'on't be up for a bit, sir," she anticipated his question. "I'm going to change and get things ready, now just."

"That's all right, Gwyneth. I really wanted to ask whether you'd seen Miss Helen this afternoon? I've been looking for her since lunch."

"No, sir. I can't say as I 'ave. I saw 'er at the fête . . ." As she thought of the fête, Gwyneth gulped and a large pear-shaped tear rolled down her cheek. George became alarmed; he wasn't good at weeping women.

"Why, what's the matter?" he asked, awkwardly. He felt that he should be stroking her hand or something.

"'Tis me own fault, sir." Gulp. "I told Madam off, down at the fête, and now I've lost me job. But I just couldn't stand by an' 'ear 'er goin' for my Bob." Gulp. "Like a mad bull, she was, nostrils diluted an' all." The Celtic soul ran to poetic description, under any stress.

George knew what she meant. He, too, had seen Mrs Bollanger with her nostrils diluted.

"But surely you'll find another job?" He couldn't imagine any employer turning down a girl like this. On the other hand, the employer's wife might.

"Oh, 'tisn't that. I can get a job all right," said Gwyneth, proudly. "But I can't get a job by yere. I'll 'ave to go away and leave Bob 'til 'e's found us a place to go an' live, before we can get married."

George sorted this out, deciding that the sentence could be reconstructed to appeal more to the prudish ear.

"Suppose you were to apologize to Mrs Bollanger? Say you lost your temper. Heap coals of fire on her head, as the saying is."

"Coals of fire?"

The idea appealed to Gwyneth. Drastic, but satisfying. Regretfully, she turned it down. "No, 'twouldn't do." She gulped again, remembering something else. "And poor Bob didn't get so much as a mention for 'is wine. 'E was set on it, too."

By now her shoulders were shaking like the back seat of a vintage car. George, who disliked to see anyone suffering – let alone this supreme Welsh rarebit – found it too much.

"Don't you worry, now," he soothed. He put a friendly arm across her shoulders. "I'll go into Sede, tomorrow, and see whether there's a job going there. If not, we'll try Devizes. Leave it to me; you'll still be able to see each other every day."

She looked up, eyes shining with tears and hope.

"Will 'oo reely, sir? There's kind 'oo are! I'll see Bob and tell . . ."

"Gwyneth!!!" George's arm left the girl's shoulders as if

she'd just mentioned that she had a touch of plague. They both spun around to see Mrs Bollanger, fuming and dripping, in the doorway. She stood like a rock in the centre of a rapidly-forming pool at her feet.

"When Mr Loder has quite finished with you, bring my tea up to my room. I'm going to have a bath. As for you, Mr Loder, I'll have more to say to you, later."

"Look, I can explain . . ." George stopped. There was no point in trying to explain to an empty doorway, or a trail of rainwater. "Oh, what's the use?" he asked the fireplace, as Gwyneth, handkerchief to her eyes, shot out of the room.

Marcus Rogers took a sip from his glass, closed his eyes and let the wine trickle slowly down his throat. An ecstatic look passed over his face. He opened his eyes, sipped again, and set the glass down. Farrer and his mother watched the performance with deep interest.

"Well, Mister?" Farrer knew that the stuff was good; he just wanted to hear someone else say it.

"It's nectar – just nectar. Fit for Lucullus himself."

"'E could 'ave a boddle . . ."

"And you make this wine yourself?"

"'E allus 'ave done," interposed Farrer's mother, proudly, giving a polished table an unnecessary flick with her apron, "ever since 'e left school. Got a proper touch for 'n, 'e 'ave."

"'Ave 'e – I mean, has he? And who else has the recipe?"

"Nobody." Farrer was quite certain. "We've 'ad 'n in the family for years."

"It's remarkably potent, I must say."

"Ar. Goes to yer 'ead, too."

"Have you tried selling it?"

"'Ootoo?"

"Anyone. People would clamber for this, if it was properly advertised. Why, I can just imagine it on the hoardings, covering the length and breadth of England! On the radio, television . . ."

"'Twun't be worth it. A few boddles a week, at a couple o' bob a boddle, say . . ."

"A few? What about a thousand bottles a week, at five bob a bottle?"

Farrer's eyes spread a couple of diameters.

"A thousand? Me? 'Ow the 'ell could Oi make a thousand? Even a nundred?" Bloke must be daft. "Oh, Oi dessay Oi could make 'n," said Farrer, bitterly sarcastic. "Oi'd on'y need a factory, an' some men, an' all me toime. Railway'd run itself, Oi s'pose!" Farrer had no doubt that his continued absence would cause the decline and fall of the British railway system.

"Look." Marcus Rogers leaned forward. "See that car out there?" The porter's eyes followed the pointing finger, through the window, to where the car stood in the torrential rain outside. It was a poem in green and gold, long, wide, and low. There was an aristocratic tilt to its radiator and a contemptuous gleam in its headlamps. It represented about ten years of Farrer's entire earnings.

"That car, among other things, was bought with an idea – an idea for turning out a cheap, wholesome drink. Have you heard of Roger's Apple Champagne? I'll tell you how it started . . ."

Two hours later, Rogers had gone and Farrer sat staring fixedly into the future. Half-formed plans, man-hours, figures, raw material and bottling-capacity all simmered and bubbled inside his head, like the gallons of wine he was destined to make.

A pint, a gallon, a hundred gallons – any quantity, he

vowed, would have the same Farrer quality. He'd turn out a wine fit for anyone, let alone this bloke Lew Cullus.

And, according to Mr Rogers, he'd absolutely nothing to lose. Mr Rogers was backing him to the hilt. That was the beauty of it! More beautiful still, though, was the fact that the barriers to his marriage would be swept away on a spate of wine.

They were to go along, early this evening, and buy Amos Flower's cottage, to start their bottling factory. Buy it, just like that! Farrer began to realize the power of money.

He gazed through the tiny window, over the fresh, rain-cleansed fields. The sun, which had been hidden for the past three hours, shone bravely from a large patch of blue.

And that, felt Farrer, was an omen.

From The Leas to the Angry Hen is as pretty a walk as can be found in England. Over the stile and along a well-trodden footpath there is a wide sweep of Wiltshire to the right. A chessboard of fields, whose chessmen are the scattered red and grey roofs; a Norman church or so, solid and unchanging amid the changing pattern of the farmlands; a white scar in the green, marking the chalk-pit, over near Barnsby.

To the left is a copse, deep enough for shade, yet sparse enough to allow the sun full canvas for his light and shade, golds, russets and greens. In season, too, the ground beneath the trees is a rippling sea of bluebells, from which the copse takes its name.

At the far end of the path there is another stile, leading to the road, across which lies the Angry Hen. Of course, one could walk all the way round by road, in a wide arc. But who would?

George, wandering Hen-wards along this path, felt out of tune with life. The afternoon's rain had given everything a delicious freshness. Grass, leaves and flowers had all renewed their colours. Birds dashed about excitedly calling to each other to test the earth's glorious softness, and to drop around, some time, for a nice middle-cut of worm. All nature was rejuvenated, and gloried in it. Except, maybe, the worms. But then, it's difficult to please everyone. Did the fatted calf join whole-heartedly in the general rejoicing at the return of the Prodigal Son?

All right for nature to rejoice, thought George. Nature hadn't been caught with its arm around the parlour maid. Much cause *he* had to kick his heels in the air. His exhibition at the fête was bad enough, but . . . He wondered whether he'd plumbed the depths of Mrs Bollanger's low opinion, yet.

He crossed the stile and paused as he saw a figure, obviously bent on the same errand as himself, padding up the road. Milton Threep had just finished an exhausting hour or so, giving P.C. Ammidge "all the fax". Now, he felt, he deserved something with not too much soda in it.

"Hallo, Loder." He studied George more closely. "Why so gloomy? Didn't the recitation go too well?"

"No." George passed a weary hand across his brow as Jno. poured out two large whiskies in response to his *cri de coeur*. "No. I suppose you could say that it didn't go too well. And, just to make sure that I'm well and truly ground underfoot, Mrs Bollanger found me in – er, compromising circumstances with Gwyneth, this afternoon."

"Gwyneth?" Threep's exclamation was a nice blend of disapproval, wistfulness and envy.

"Oh, it wasn't anything at all, really. Just that Mrs Bollanger came in at the wrong time. It was . . ."

"Should there have been a wrong time?" asked Threep, with the righteousness of one who didn't get the chance.

George took a deep draught of the fortifying spirit.

"Look, don't *you* start. Just listen." And he poured out the whole sorry tale.

Threep took a thoughtful sip.

"Does Helen know, yet?"

"I doubt it. She's been missing, all afternoon, and only turned up as I was coming out. She's brought Polly along to dinner." Threep's face brightened. "Says she'll tell us all about it after they've made themselves presentable. It should be an exciting meal – Polly, Mrs Bollanger, and myself. It wouldn't surprise me, now, if Miss Kettle turned up," he mused, gloomily, little realizing that the prophet's mantle was upon him. "Two more," he added, for Jno.'s benefit.

"I haven't had what you'd call a dull afternoon, myself," announced Threep, with a certain quiet pride.

"Oh? Well, if it was anything like mine . . ."

"Not exactly. I was kidnapped, robbed, almost shot dead . . ."

"Good Lord! Stefan?"

"Stefan and his accomplice." And Threep, who knew he'd never get this fortuitous combination of circumstances again – a quiet inn, an eager audience and a hell of a story – embarked upon his saga.

It lost nothing in the telling. After it was over, he sat back and basked in the sunshine of George's admiration.

"It's a wonder Stefan didn't shoot you, after you'd punched him on the jaw like that," commented George. "And they got away with the case, after all?"

"After a struggle, yes. I nearly . . ."

"'Devenin', gents. Pint, please, John."

Farrer ducked in through the doorway, still resplendent in blue suit and silver tie. He had the expression of a man who's just come into his own – an air of confidence as apparent as a child's new shoes.

"Have that with me," invited George. "Hard luck about the home-made wine competition. Still . . ."

"'Ard luck? Oi shouldn't mind if me luck is always as 'ard as that, Mister. To begin with, 'tweren't my woine wot was in that boddle at all. We found moine in Miss Kettle's refreshment stall. She'd drunk nearly a quarter of 'n. No wonder she were tiddly." He chuckled. "Good 'ealth to 'ee." There was a sound as of a sluice-gate being opened as he slaked his thirst. He set down the half-empty glass.

"O' course, Oi ain't worryin'. This chap Rogers, me partner, as you might say, 've put me in the way o' makin' a tidy sum – *an*' a career – outer me woine. Aye, Oi done a good day's work, today."

"How's that, then?"

"We'm goin' into business, sellin' it. 'E reckons it'll go by the gallon."

"Sounds good. I'd like the opportunity of sampling it, some time."

"Taste 'n now. Oi brung a boddle along fer Miss Fenner; you can 'ave 'n, and Oi'll bring she another 'un tomorrer. 'Ere, 'ave a go at this."

Taking a pint bottle from his pocket, he filled two wine-glasses, supplied by Jno., and watched anxiously as George and Threep picked them up.

"Bung-ho," said George, sniffing the wine.

It had the bouquet of rose-petals and honey, blended with the tang of a fine liqueur whisky. It was an aroma such as one is permitted to dream about, once in a lifetime; having been dreamed about, it is never recaptured.

George sipped respectfully. A golden mist drifted down his throat – honey without its stickiness, roses without their heaviness, and liqueur as smooth as a barrow-boy's patter.

It took a second or so before the bomb went off, somewhere

231

in the region of the third shirt-button. It wasn't an unpleasant explosion – just disturbing, like winning a fortune or striking oil.

Threep's face had the rapt expression of one who is consorting with angels. He'd taken rather a large sip, and was now enjoying the novel experience of having pink-edged clouds drifting around inside his head.

Farrer preened himself. Comment was uncalled-for. He'd seen that expression on other faces that had had his wine poured into them. He knew.

George took a deep breath.

"Farrer, what is there to say? Had I the tongue of Cato, or the descriptive powers of The Bard, I might just begin to compliment you. This defies criticism. Your very good health."

"Glad you loike 'n. Take 'n on wi' thee. Oi'll send another boddle up tomorrer, when Oi sends Miss Fenner 'ers."

George and Threep returned to The Leas, to find a large, chauffeur-driven car standing outside. The house was quiet, the downstairs rooms being deserted for the pre-prandial bathing and dressing. Gwyneth delayed Threep, as George went upstairs.

"There's someone to see 'oo, sir. Bin waitin' in the lounge this long time. Must see 'oo, 'e says."

Threep entered the lounge warily. This afternoon's experience had burned deeply into his soul. Still, it was a bit much, he felt, if one had to search all one's visitors for concealed weapons before admitting them. After all, this wasn't Chicago.

"Good evening, Souder." Here was someone he knew, anyway, thank the Lord.

"Ah, Threep. Good evening. I take it that you have not yet been acquainted with all the news?"

"News? None, except that my briefcase . . ."

"Yes, the brief-case. We've followed it up pretty closely, but the thieves eluded us, I'm afraid. Your car was found abandoned near a private airfield, near Wool. The brief-case will be somewhere over central Europe by now, I suppose. But it's not really that I came to tell you about. Something much more . . . ." Souder paused and glanced around. "Are we private here?'.

"Yes; you may say what you wish."

"It's 'The Colonel'. It is finished."

"Finished? You mean that it's a success?"

"No. It is finished. Destroyed. And, mark you, there's not a scrap of written information about it! Those fools, Ungel and Schnille, were apparently more interested in their experiments than in writing them up."

"How did it happen?"

"It appears that there was an unusual spate of water from the high ground near by, and it seeped through some rather third-rate concrete. There'll be a headache for somebody over *that* contract," he mused, happy in the knowledge that it wasn't his pigeon. "Anyway, 'The Colonel' is left permanently switched on – isolated from its aerials, of course – and the water provided a shorting-link. The whole test-cell disintegrated without leaving a trace. Believe me, Threep, if we're lucky we *might* catch up to where we were yesterday, in about ten years' time. If we ever do," he qualified.

"What about the scientists?"

"Oh, the six feet of earth between the cell and their laboratory saved them." There was a hint of impatience in his voice; obviously, he felt that there was no justice in the world. "They're a bit shaken, of course, but not – ah, disintegrated. There'll be a meeting on Thursday, and we'd like you to attend. Meanwhile, we'll keep the security conditions going down here, as if nothing had happened."

He picked up his hat and gloves, glancing at his watch.

"I must hurry along, if I'm to be at Downing Street tonight. There'll be heads rolling by morning, I'll wager," he added, comfortably. His own head, presumably, would remain connected.

Threep saw him to the door, and stood gazing down the drive long after the car had disappeared.

So "The Colonel" had retired. The fruits of brains, technology, craftsmanship – all swept away in a split second. And yet, had it survived, "The Colonel" would have been less use to the community than a telephone-switchboard.

What had Souder said? "It will take us ten years to reach the point we were at yesterday. That is, if we're lucky."

But if we're really lucky, thought Threep, we never will.

21

"And so you see, George, Uncle Milton isn't the only one with a tale to tell, though he probably tells it better. When you consider that Polly and I have been chloroformed, kidnapped, threatened with acid, tied up, then released by a romantic young man, you can't say that our lives lack colour."

Helen leaned back with the blasé smile of the woman of the world returning to the old home at the vicarage, as George took her empty cocktail glass.

"Ye gods! And some fool in London told me I'd be bored to death, in Wiltshire! How do they find time to rotate their crops, or what ever it is farmers do? I don't think we'll settle here, darling. I could afford the armoured car, but the upkeep of the field-guns would be crippling. Another drink?"

"No thanks. You have one – Mother won't be down for a while, as dinner's not until eight o'clock. And don't forget that we're taking young Ron out, tomorrow afternoon. We'll use Uncle Milton's car."

"Ar Ron. Whenever anything big happens, that boy's somewhere in it. I shouldn't be surprised if he turned out to be the brains behind Stefan and his accomplice. I foresee a great future for Ron, if he . . ."

"And what have you two been doing?" Helen broke in, as Polly and Threep came in from the veranda.

"We've been swapping adventure stories," answered Polly, lightly. "You can't let these men out of your sight for a moment without someone kidnapping them. Never mind, Milton," she laid a hand on his arm, "it's all over, now."

Threep looked into her eyes, lower – thank Heaven! – than his own. His heart didn't skip a beat; it had an eight-bar rest. He made up his mind. What if he did make a fool of himself? It would take months before he could screw his courage up to this point again.

"Would – would you mind – er, marrying me?" he suggested, the casual phrasing somewhat belied by the sherry glass he was trying to stuff into his breast pocket.

"*So* romantic, my dear!" murmured an unsurprised Polly to nobody in particular.

"*What* did you say, Uncle Milton?" Helen gripped the arms of her chair as if it was just going to take off.

"I've an idea it was a private conversation, dear," answered Polly. "He was wondering how it'd be if he and I were to marry. At least, that's how I got it."

"WELL, WILL YOU?" Everyone jumped. Threep hadn't meant to shout; just to speak clearly and calmly and let that grinning ass Loder see that he wasn't the only one with sangfroid.

"Don't bully, Milton. You're not talking to the Opposition leader, now. Of course I'll marry you. That silver tongue of yours would charm the heart of any girl."

Threep took an eager step forward, tripped over the pouffe, and fell to his hands and knees at Polly's feet.

"Damn," he said, distinctly.

Polly turned to Helen.

"See what I mean? I just couldn't stand a stereotyped proposal, anyway. Other girls . . ."

Her voice became muffled as Threep rose and planted an inexpert kiss on the south-east corner of her mouth. He aimed again, improving rapidly.

After the general round of congratulations and kissing had died down:

"When shall you tell Mrs Bollanger?" asked Polly.

It was as if she'd introduced an adder into Arcady. The idiotically happy look slipped down off Threep's face.

"No point in telling her just yet, is there?" he muttered. "I think she'd like it better if . . ."

"She's not going to like it at all, whenever you serve it up. Tell her this evening, while we're all here to support you. What are you worrying about, anyway? You're a free agent, aren't you?"

"Who? Me?" The description was a novel one, to Threep. Polly felt a twinge of impatience.

"If you don't tell her tonight, Milton, I'll think you don't really want to marry me. It's up to you!"

Gloom descended upon Threep. Polly was right, of course, but it wasn't going to be easy. He'd have preferred to tell a cougar that he was taking her only cub.

Gwyneth twinkled into the lounge, eyes shining.

"Oh, Miss Helen – Mr Loder! Bob Farrer's just called in with some lovely noos! 'E's leaving the railway and startin' up a wine business with Mr Rogers, an' they've bought Amos Flower's cottage to work in, an' Bob's buyin' a new bungalow near Sede, an' we're getting married sooner than we thought, an' . . ."

"How lovely, Gwyneth!" Helen smiled. "I suppose you're very happy?"

"Speechless with happiness, perhaps?" said Polly, *sotto voce*.

"'Appy, Miss? I 'oodn't change places with the Queen! I on'y wish I didn't 'ave to leave yere, though, before the wedding."

"Why should you leave?"

237

"I gave in me notice, this afternoon, after Madam'd told Bob off. She 'oodn't let me stay now."

Helen didn't answer. She wished she could tell Gwyneth to stay as long as she liked. Whose house was it, anyway?

"We'll see what can be done, Gwyneth," she said, finally. "I might be able to find you a temporary place somewhere locally. Don't you worry."

"Well, there's someone whose problems have disappeared with a rush, right after her darkest hour," commented George, as the door closed behind Gwyneth's trim figure. "I wonder whether ours will?"

It was most unlikely. With her mother in the offing, Helen became a different woman, meek and pliable. If she couldn't be hardened, could her mother not be softened? Was there a way . . . ?

"Well, after all the excitement, my face is shining like a fog-lamp." Polly studied a small mirror. "Is there time to go up for repairs, Helen?"

"Yes, I feel the same way. Uncle Milton, you won't forget the wine, will you? We won't be long." Helen and Polly went upstairs.

"Wine! That's it!" George caught the surprised Threep excitedly by the shoulder. "What are we drinking, Threep?"

"Well, if I'd known you were that thirsty, I'd have . . ."

"It's not that. Listen; I've been trying to get Helen to stand up to her mother ever since I came here, but I know when I'm beaten. It's just struck me that if we can't harden Helen, we'll have to soften Mrs Bollanger."

"Impossible. You'd never boil her for long enough."

"Is it? You'll agree that half a glass of Farrer's wine would have turned Judge Jeffreys into a sickly sentimentalist? Surely a whole glass will scale the flint off Mrs Bollanger?"

"You mean . . . ?"

"Yes, I do. Substitute Farrer's wine for her usual tipple, then sit back and watch. As soon as she's had a glassful, wade in and tell her about your wedding. Helen will see how easy it is; she's bound to grab her chance, then. Here's the way out for all of us."

Threep looked at George admiringly.

"How do you do it, Loder? Do you build these ideas up, or do they just happen to you?"

"Oh, I don't know." George gave credit where it was due. "My parents were pretty bright, you know. Now, how about getting on with this wine caper, before people come down?"

"Loder, I'm with you in spirit, all the way. But if you think I'm going to mess about with Hester's wine . . ." He shuddered. "No," he continued, firmly. "It's your idea and you're entitled to the glory. *You* carry it out. I've put the wine in to cool; Hester's is the half-bottle of Sauternes, Helen's the Graves, and Polly you and I are having the Hock."

"All right, I'll do it. Stay here and keep people away while I go and arrange the Micky Finn."

"Do you think it's the right thing to do?"

"No; would anyone waste Farrer's liquid gold on the uneducated female palate, under normal circumstances? I'll never forgive Miss Kettle for swigging it like cold fourpenny. Still, desperate situations call for desperate remedies. Threep, our troubles cease tonight!"

Conditions at dinner, that evening, reminded George of a film he'd once seen in which several characters who, for some doubtless very good reason that he couldn't call to mind, were sitting at the bottom of a dry well, waiting for a grisly-minded type above to drop a bomb down. The grisly-minded one, however, kept dropping stones, instead, just to spin out the entertainment. The atmosphere below could only be described as tense. And that's just what it was at the dinner-table, thought George: tense.

Two pairs of male eyes were fastened on Mrs Bollanger's wine-glass, its contents, so far, inviolate. Signed the pledge, I'll bet, hazarded George: it just needed that to complete my day.

"When is Miss Fenner vacating Rose Cottage, Helen?" asked Mrs Bollanger, who'd so far refused to acknowledge that Polly was with them.

"We – we've not really discussed it, yet, Mother. There's no hurry, of course."

"No?" Mrs Bollanger raised her eyebrows. "You surprise me."

Silence swooped down, and Polly gave Threep a meaning glance.

"Er," he remarked, leaving the company no richer for his eloquence.

"You were saying, Milton?" Mrs Bollanger picked up her glass. Threep's eyes bulged painfully, and George's spirits rose.

"I've – er, some news for you," hesitated Threep.

Mrs Bollanger lowered her glass, untasted. George's spirits went down with it, and Threep mopped his brow. "You haven't drunk any wine," he said, accusingly.

"That's not news, Milton. I know I've had no wine."

"Why don't you drink your nice wine?" he urged, desperately. "It's cold, and in find cond —"

"Are you quite well, Milton? Why has my diet suddenly become of such absorbing interest?"

That's done it, thought George. She'll have the whole story out of him in fifty-five seconds flat.

Threep was saved by Gwyneth coming in, bearing news and hot chocolate sauce.

"Miss Kettle've come, 'M. Says she's sorry, but she

thought you'd've finished dinner by now, and can she 'ave a word with you, please?"

George wallowed in his slough of despond. Fate was certainly piling it on. Now, of course, Miss Kettle would denounce him, and before Mrs Bollanger had had so much as a sip of the mellowing mead. Just one of those days, he supposed.

Gwyneth refilled his and Helen's glasses and went out.

"Good evening, Miss Kettle." Mrs Bollanger gave the visitor to understand that it had been, up to present. Myrtle Kettle's spectacles swept around the dinner-table, finally resting on George who felt like an escaping prisoner caught in the searchlight's beam.

"Good evening, Mrs Bollanger. I had to come because I could not rest until you learned the truth about this afternoon's – ah, disgraceful happenings."

"We agree on their description, anyway."

"Some – some miscreant substituted an alcoholic beverage for my own bottle of refreshment, some time during the day. It had a most peculiar effect on me."

You can say that again, thought George.

"Indeed?" Mrs Bollanger didn't give an inch.

"Yes. You must accept my apologies, especially this gentleman. I hope I didn't spoil his act."

"No. I think we may safely say that you didn't spoil it. This is Mr Loder," added Mrs Bollanger, implying that no more need be said. His acts were beyond spoiling.

"Yes, we've already met." Miss Kettle was grateful for the lead. It was time the ball went over to the other court. "The first time was when he and Miss Fenner were Going Into Her Cottage. The day Mrs Watt Was Away, I think?" she reminded Polly.

"I beg your pardon?" Mrs Bollanger's gaze rested on George like two steel bars.

"Oh, didn't you know?" Myrtle Kettle's purring filled the room. She hadn't expected it to go over so big.

"Is this true?" Mrs Bollanger swung the bars around on Polly.

"I – I . . ."

"I see." Mrs Bollanger's lips set in a thin, tight line. "Well, Miss Kettle, I hardly know what to tell you. It seems that . . ."

"Why not," suggested Helen, clearly, "tell her to go and jump in the lake?"

And, having made what she considered a constructive suggestion, she took another spoonful of hot chocolate sauce and ice-cream.

22

Helen's mother touched a napkin to almost non-existent lips, staring at her daughter as if she'd just completed a backward somersault.

"*What* did you say, Helen?" Her voice sounded like a steam-roller crushing pebbles.

"I *do* wish you'd listen, Mother," said Helen, a trifle peevishly. "People go to all the trouble to try to express themselves clearly and you take not the slightest interest. If only people listened more to people when people . . . There; now you've made me forget what I was saying."

A spoonful of ice-cream restored her equanimity.

"Cook *has* done well this evening, hasn't she?" she observed.

George, Threep and Polly stared at her. If a pet rabbit had suddenly started barking, it couldn't have made a deeper impression. Mrs Bollanger's eyes narrowed until she looked like a Cyclops.

"You mightn't have noticed, but Miss Kettle has just made a most serious statement, if it happens to be true. And, after what I saw this afternoon, I've no reason to doubt it."

Miss Kettle preened herself. She was coming into her own, at last.

Helen arrested a full spoon in mid-flight.

"Of course it's true. It was the day he arrived here, wasn't it? You remember, Polly; the afternoon George wet his –

that is, when you gave him first-aid?" Helen looked brightly at Polly, inviting corroboration.

"Unk," said Polly.

Mrs Bollanger seemed to shrink very slightly. Then she rallied.

"I see. And I suppose another unfortunate combination of circumstances caused me to find Gwyneth in his arms, this afternoon?"

"Unfortunate for George, would you say? It depends on the point of view, I suppose." Helen turned to George. "You must tell me all about it, some time, dear. And do you really need to pour chocolate sauce over your cheese? Just as you wish, of course." She gave him an indulgent smile.

"Helen! Are you quite out of your mind?"

"Mother, can you truthfully say that you saw Gwyneth in George's arms?"

"Well . . ." Her mother hesitated. She'd have loved to confirm it, but . . .

"CAN YOU?" Helen's voice snapped across the table like an iceberg cracking up. Everyone jumped, including Mrs Bollanger. Threep furtively wiped chocolate sauce from his lapels.

"Well, not exactly." There was a new, almost timid, note in Mrs Bollanger's voice. "I was only in time to . . ."

"Then you must be more careful what you say, Mother, mustn't you? We know you, of course, but strangers might get the idea that you were trying to cause mischief." She spooned up the last of her sweet with evident enjoyment.

"Mischief!" Myrtle Kettle felt that she was being ignored. Her bomb was going off with a splutter instead of a bang. "I should think . . ."

"How right you are," interposed Helen. "You should think very hard before you try to stir up trouble. You must remember that I'm prepared to trust my fiancé in anyone's cottage, even if its owner is unfortunate enough to have a mind like yours."

A warm glow stole over George. He realized that he was being privileged to witness something about as commonplace as Haley's comet.

Miss Kettle tossed her head.

"I will *not* stay here to be insulted!" she neighed.

"Well, I suppose if you must go, you must," sighed Helen, regretfully. "The Angry Hen closes at ten, I know."

"I beg your pardon!"

"Granted. You must come again, some year or other. Good night, Miss Kettle," and Helen gave a bright smile around the table as the door closed on a surprised back.

Threep, who seemed to be struggling under some deep emotion, suddenly found his voice.

"Er – Hester. Polly, that is, Miss Fenner – er – Polly – has done me the honour of consenting to be my wife. We intend . . ."

"Your wife?" Mrs Bollanger seemed to swell.

Threep swallowed the tennis-ball which was causing him some difficulty in articulation.

"Yes, wy mife – my wife. We shall marry just before Christmas, as we . . ."

"And when was this arranged?"

"This evening, just before dinner." Helen gave a rippling laugh. "Uncle Milton fell over the pouffe . . ."

"Oh, I see. Intoxicated, was he?"

"No, Mrs Bollanger!" Polly's eyes flashed. "He'd just made a decision that hadn't been influenced either by you or the Chief Whip . . ."

"No wonder he fell over the pouffe. And how long has this – ah, affair been going on?"

"It hasn't been 'going on', as you put it. The first I knew about it was this evening."

Mrs Bollanger gave Polly a long look.

"If you expect me to believe that, you must think I'm a perfect fool . . ."

"Oh, none of us is perfect, Mother." Helen gave George a nut to crack. "Anyway, I don't see why Polly and Uncle Milton shouldn't marry. They're two of the nicest people I know, and I'm sure they'll be very happy. And I've just thought of something," she said, excitedly, "I'll give them Rose Cottage, as a wedding-present. Then they'll be able to stay in Winthringham. Won't it be lovely?"

"Helen, darling!" glowed Polly.

"My dear!" said Threep.

"Whacko!" said George.

"Helen! ' sizzled her mother. "What are you saying?"

"I *do* wish you'd listen, Mother," said Helen, curtly. "You can't expect everyone to say things twice, just for your benefit. You'll only make yourself unpopular, you know."

The ensuing silence was almost solid, broken only by the whirring of four brains, trying to adjust themselves to this new and self-possessed Helen.

"Have a nut?" she invited, passing the bowl to her mother.

Mrs Bollanger said pfwah.

"Oh, and I meant to tell you before," continued Helen, chattily, "George and I have decided to be married just before Christmas. My idea. We're going to Corsica for our honeymoon, aren't we, darling?" She looked fondly at the dumbfounded George.

"And what about me?" Mrs Bollanger's voice trembled ever so slightly.

"You can hardly expect to come, Mother. George has very definite views . . ."

"You know very well what I mean. Am I not to be considered?"

"But of course. I consider you've done a wonderful job, running my home. Now I'll take over; it's going to be fun."

Gwyneth stood at the door.

"I've served the coffee in the lounge, as usual, 'M. Will there be anything else?"

"No, Gwyneth, thank you," said Helen. "Oh, by the way, let's hear no more of this nonsense about leaving us in the lurch. I won't hear of it. You'll just stay here until the wedding. I want you to be married from here. And you must let me buy your gown. We'll go and choose . . ."

"Oh, Miss!" And Gwyneth's smile shone through happy tears. She turned and fled.

"Helen, I don't know what . . ." Mrs Bollanger began, in a curiously small voice. To George's surprise, he saw that her eyes were wet. Tears of self-pity, certainly, but still tears. And, somehow, he felt sorry for her. It was like watching a tiger weakening under pygmy arrows. He stood up and moved around to her side.

"Don't you worry at all," he soothed. "We shan't be able to manage without you, you know. Why, the place just wouldn't be the same. Besides, Helen and I will be in Town, most of the year, and we'll need you here." He felt safe in saying he'd need her anywhere where he wasn't. "You'll come up and see us often, won't you?"

She looked up at him, gratefully.

"Thank you, ah, George. I hope you'll both be very happy. The Leas will always be ready for your return." She rose from the table. "I think I'll retire early. The thunder seems to have given me a slight headache, and I've had a very full day. Good night to you all."

She paused at the door, looking around at the two couples at the table.

"A very full day," she repeated, and closed the door behind her.

"Helen, dear . . ."

"Helen . . ."

"Darling . . ." began three voices at once. Helen looked up, and sipped the last of her wine.

"H'm?" she inquired.

"How on earth did you do it, dear?" asked Polly. "I was trembling in my shoes!"

"Trembling? Good gracious, why?" Helen turned to George. "George, dear; I *do* feel funny. Muzzy, if you know what I mean."

"Muzzy? You're not ill, are you?" George became alarmed.

"No, not ill. Rather a nice feeling, really. Almost as though I'd had too much Sauternes. Ridilucus, of course. I only had two glasses."

"Sauternes? You had Graves, surely?"

"I did not. Mother had Graves. I never drink it. I had Sauternes, S, A, U – ternes," she finished, with a giggle.

So that was it. Not for the first time in history had the magic potion got into the wrong glass. But never, as far as George was concerned, with such gratifying results. He blessed Threep's mistake over the wine-list.

Helen giggled again.

"Did you see Miss Kettle's face when she found her news had fallen flat? Like a portrait of the artist's palette! She's no room to talk, you know," she continued, as they all went out to the lounge. "There was quite a story going the rounds about her, two or three years ago. I never say anything about a person unless it's good," she stated, primly, "and believe me, this IS good. Listen . . ."

Sunshine after storm, felt George. After their darkest hour. . . .

Stefan sat back comfortably, the roar of the aeroplane engines like music in his capacious ears. Everything had worked out for the best, after all. In less than an hour they'd be landing, and the SNABU would no doubt have some nice things to say. He smiled across at Number Three, who smiled back.

Karanov laid the brief-case upon his knees and opened up the flap. This was a great moment for both of them. Not that the contents would have much meaning for the two men – they were plain, honest spies, not scientists – but it would be satisfying just to have one peep.

Karanov drew out the wad of papers. One or two blue-prints; some pages of typescript and a few beautifully-illustrated brochures. The illustrations, to his surprise, were of humble yet indispensable apparatus. He opened up one of the blue-prints. Studied it for a moment. Then, eyes blazing, he leaped from his seat and waved the papers within an inch of the startled Stefan's nose. He spoke with a deep intensity.

For good, round, all-embracing curses, there are few languages to beat those of Central Europe.

Threep and George sat contentedly sipping a nightcap, on the veranda. Helen had gone to bed, and Threep had just returned from escorting Polly back to Rose Cottage.

The night was calm, moonlit, and had an after-rain freshness. It matched George's mood. There was just one thing disturbing his tranquility.

"Threep," he asked, "what are you going to do about that brief-case of yours?"

"Do? Nothing. It's gone; as far as I'm concerned, they deserve to get it."

So this was the masterly inactivity the Opposition talked about. George felt disappointed. Surely, by now, young men should be buckling on parachutes, or listening, grim-faced, to instructions from some quietly-spoken man with hard grey eyes, somewhere in a West End flat? Or were the books all wrong?

"But what about the papers in the case? Weren't they terribly secret?" he pursued.

"Secret? No. I didn't say they were secret. I just said that I didn't want anyone to know what I was working on, that's all," said Threep.

"Oh." George struggled with his curiosity for a moment. He gave up the struggle. "What *was* in it? Don't tell me if you don't wish to," he added, hoping the other would take no notice.

Threep stood up and yawned.

"Heigh-ho. Time for bed. We've had quite a day. You were saying? Ah, yes; the brief-case. I used it for carrying the plans for the new – ah, plumbing in The House. In a room more necessary, I'd say, than the Debating Chamber. Good night, Loder."

"Good night," answered George.

He'd never really understood politics.

23

"We can go to the agent's this afternoon then, Bob bach. There's excited I am, choosing me own bungalow!"

"Ar, 'tis a good feelin', Gwyn. We'll take a look 'round the furnicher-shops, come Thursday. Fancy," Farrer mused, "this time yestiddy we couldn't see a way out. Now 'tis crystal-clear – loike the woine wot done it all for us."

Farrer was enjoying a stolen half-hour at the back door of The Leas, sharing Gwyneth's "elevenses", before the rigours of the day really began.

"'Ave you thought of a name for the wine yet, Bob?"

"Oi 'ave. A good 'un, too. 'Ow about 'Fizzoo'?" He looked at her as though he'd just produced a ruby out of a mangold-wurzel.

"Fizzoo? But it don't fizz, does it?"

"An' a cuckoo don't cook." Farrer was a trifle nettled. It had taken him half the night to think of the name, and he was proud of it. This criticism was unexpected. "Can you think of a better 'un?"

Gwyneth laid a coral finger against her cheek.

"You want a name that describes it, but slips easy off the tongue, isn't it? The drop I 'ad was like – like – oh, I don't know – bottled moonbeams. That's it!" She caught his arm. "'Moonbeam', you should call it!"

Farrer nodded, silently. Of course it must be "Moonbeam". There just wasn't another name for it. After a full three minutes, he spoke:

"Eh, but you'm bright, Gwyn," he acknowledged, humbly. "'Ow come you be marryin' a zany like me?"

"Could it be because I *am* bright, Bob, bach?" asked Gwyneth, softly.

"So there was very little harm done, after all, Mrs Bollanger," said the Vicar, cheerfully. "The damage was much less than we'd expected; most of the stalls were ready to close when the storm broke. There should be quite a substantial sum for the Organ Fund."

"I'm pleased to hear it, Vicar." Mrs Bollanger arranged some dahlias on her writing-table. "You were saying, I believe, that this man Rogers is interested?"

"Yes, indeed. Apparently he's opening up a small bottling plant, here – nothing to spoil the amenities, he has assured me – and wants to play a part in improving the church. He expects to find employment for a number of men, too." The Vicar sighed. "Curious, but that's the very thing Colonel Cobberleigh tried to do. And he wanted to use wine as the means, too. Well, I don't suppose the 'Luno' recipe will ever be found, now."

(Away in Valhalla the gallant Colonel smiled quietly and sipped his mead-and-soda. So they'd never find it! Why worry? "Luno", "Moonbeam" – did the name matter, as long as the end was achieved?)

"By the way, Vicar, I suppose George – my future son-in-law, you know – will be seeing you soon, about the wedding. I have finally persuaded Helen to marry before Christmas. So unnecessary, putting it off, don't you think? Milton, too, has at last decided to be sensible. He and Polly Fenner will be announcing their engagement, shortly."

"Really? But this is wonderful news!"

"Yes, isn't it? I guessed, of course, that it would happen.

I've always liked Polly, as you know." Mrs Bollanger looked him straight in the eyes, daring him to deny it.

"Oh." The Vicar didn't quite understand, but realized that everything was fine. "You must be very happy, Mrs Bollanger."

"Happy, Vicar? Do you know, I really believe I am!"

"I'll get Daniells, the architect, to come here on Friday, then," said Threep to Polly, adjusting a deck-chair on Rose Cottage's postage-stamp lawn. "Whatever we do, we must preserve the outward appearance of the place."

"Yes; I wouldn't have Rose Cottage look any different." She was silent, a moment. "You don't regret anything, do you, Milton?"

"Regret? With life just starting? No, Gloria."

"Gloria?"

"It always will be, I think, dear."

Amos Flower took his first draught of beer for the day and prepared to make his considered criticism.

"Don't tell me." Jno. held up a restraining hand. "You don't like the beer. I know."

"Woi bother 'bout moi troubles?" asked Amos, equably. "Oi've only got a glass of 'n. Thees got a 'ole cellar-full."

Jno. Murk breathed deeply. There'd be some law, no doubt, prohibiting publicans from tearing their customers to pieces. A pity, but there it was.

"They tell me you've sold the cottage, then?" he remarked, more for the sake of his blood-pressure than anything else.

"Ar. Sold 'n *an'* got a job, too."

"A job?"

"Oi'm doin' the local transport side o' thishyer woine business. They needed a good man . . ."

"Wot? You'm workin' fer Bob Farrer?"

"Well, yes. Oi s'pose you could put it that way."

"Drink that an' 'ave another on the 'ouse!" directed Jno. heartily. "You'll need 'n. If Bob Farrer don't chase you from elbow to breckfuss-time, 'e don't deserve 'is luck!"

Clara Watt picked up a bulging string-bag and lingered a moment at the post office door.

"It's a dead secret, mind, Norah. Don't 'ee tell a soul. Mr Ammidge told me, in strick confidence, that Stefan was reely a spy. Disguised, o' course. 'E blew up the atom-plant, in Stony Lane, shot Mr Threep . . ."

"Shot 'n?"

"Well, as good as."

"Wot'd 'e do that for?"

"'E didn't say. Mr Ammidge, I mean. Anyway, Stefan druv off in the big car, and 'e 'aven't bin seen since."

"Well, I'm glad 'e've gone. We'm quiet folk in these parts. Let they foreigners get on wi' their spyin' and such-like. We don't . . . Good morning, Miss Kettle."

Clara left, as Myrtle Kettle edged past a small barrel of vinegar.

"Good morning. I'd like – ah . . ." The spinster decided to come out into the open. "I wonder whether you'll be seeing Mr Farrer, today?"

"I dessay. Did 'ee want something?"

"I would rather like to buy one of his bottles of wine. Not for myself, of course," she added, hastily. "It's for – for – for a friend."

"I'll ask 'n. I've yurd 'e'll be sellin' a lot of it, soon."

"Will he? Good." Miss Kettle seemed pleased to hear of Farrer's success. "You'll ask him, then? Thank you." The bell pinged her exit.

"'For a friend'!" sniffed Mrs Long disbelievingly, to a jar of Giant Gob-stoppers.

"Isn't it a marvellous morning, George?" sighed Helen, ecstatically. "Do you realize that we've been walking for over an hour?"

"Perfect, dear. What are a few old flints in the shoes, after all? Think of the early pilgrims."

He leaned against a gate and untied his shoelace.

"Funny," he mused. "Everything started just here, at Mercer's pond; then one thing led to another. If Rogers hadn't happened to be here for the fête . . ."

"Or if Stefan hadn't mistaken Colonel Cobberleigh for someone else . . ."

"Or if I hadn't come on an earlier train . . ."

"Or if Ron hadn't fallen into the pond . . ."

"There's the *fons et origo*. It always comes back to ar Ron." George replaced his shoe. "The next time I hear that Ron is in trouble, I shall head madly in the opposite direction . . ."

He felt a tug at his sleeve, and looked down at a small mud-and-sweat stained face gazing up into his own.

"Please Mister," pleaded Julie, "could yer give us a nand wiv ar Ron?"